Iron Dragoons
Terran Armor Corps Book 1

Richard Fox

PROLOGUE

Smoke and ash billowed from the volcano's crater, forming a black column that stretched upward until high winds bent the darkness across the sky over Cygnus II. Bits of lava and cooling pumice rained down from the caldera, scorching holes through the thick moss-trees clinging to the side of the volcano.

A rock the size of a trunk tumbled down the slope, knocking loose basalt shards from long-ago eruptions. The rock shattered against the jagged edge of a boulder. A moment later, the boulder heaved outward. It came loose in a tide of black and gray ash, then made its own way down the volcano.

Steaming hot air poured from the large hole left by the boulder, and a pair of soldiers clad in fifteen-foot-tall suits of armor, emerged from the extinct lava tube running deep into the burning heart of the mountain. Their metal joints squealed in protest as they worked against the invasion of ash and dust. Air wavered around them as they stepped free of the tube, their armor bleeding heat from the journey through the volcano.

The first, his armor bearing a red Templar cross on the breastplate, shook his helm free of ash and looked over the valley. To the north, stray gauss bolts and plasma blasts left lines of burning air in their wake. The thunder of distant explosions fought through the constant rumble of the growing eruption.

He pointed to a clearing at the base of the volcano where rings of barricades surrounded a cluster of buildings, each shaped like an asteroid embedded into the ground and larger than a corvette-class starship. A cable the width of a city bus ran from one of the buildings into the side of the volcano.

"There, Gideon, we've found it." The first soldier pointed down the slope.

Electricity ran up the twin vanes of the rail cannon on Gideon's back. He smacked a fist against the golden fleur-de-lis on his chest.

"Drop anchor and let's end this war with one rail cannon shot," Gideon said.

"Do that and we'll lose the planet to the Vishrakath magma coils. Colonel Martel sent us to win a final victory, not a Pyrrhic one."

"Then we find the brood mother, *brother* Tongea." Gideon's emphasis on the word almost turned it into an insult. "Will you waste time with prayer or will you keep up with me?" Gideon jumped down the slope, his massive sabatons biting into the ash carpeting the volcano, sending up a plume as he slid down.

Tongea went after him. He loaded gauss rounds into the double-barreled cannon on his right forearm from the ammo belt that ran from the weapon to an armored housing on his back. The rotary cannon on his left shoulder began spinning.

"May the Saint witness you, Dragoon," Tongea said.

"I am armor. I am fury. I will not fail. I am armor…" Gideon kept up the mantra as they reached the edge of the moss-trees line. Gideon smashed his way through a thicket almost as tall as he was, then slowed to a stop. He crouched slightly, then leaped into the air, thrusters on his legs and hips carrying him clear of the branches. He arced downward, his armor utilizing the slope to keep him airborne longer. Air whistled past his external microphones, the sound going directly to his brain through the neural cable connecting his body within the suit's armored womb.

"Activity from the Vishrakath base," Tongea said. "Plasma turrets heating up on my infrared optics."

"Surprised we got this far without being noticed." Gideon's armored feet raised up, and leg thrusters flared just before he smashed through smoldering moss-tree branches. He leaped into the air again, the thrusters on his back trailing wings of flame as they carried him higher.

A bolt of red plasma struck the mountainside, pelting him with burning branches.

Gideon zoomed in on the attacking battery and traced the power cables to a small dome near the inner ring of defenses. The Vishrakath normally buried their power cells to protect them from air attack. They'd become either lazy or complacent as the air thick with ash and smoke kept any airborne assets out of this fight. Either way, he was about to punish that mistake.

He fired his gauss cannons, and high-velocity cobalt-jacketed rounds burst from the twin barrels with a rattling snap and tore into the power cell. It exploded into white flame, pelting the surroundings with rocky shrapnel and wrecking the nearby plasma cannon emplacement. The weapon crumpled onto its side.

Vishrakath fighters scuttled away from the smoking cannon on their four-legged abdomens. Gideon unleashed a hail of bullets from his rotary cannon, ripping a line through the dirt and into a pair of aliens taking cover next to a domed building.

He landed close to the outer wall, then jumped up and slammed his armored hands into the razor wire running along the top. He vaulted over it, almost crushing an alien holding one of their spindly plasma rifles.

While the Vishrakath defied normal Earth zoological categories, Gideon considered them flesh-covered insects. They walked like an upright ant, four limbs for locomotion, two more serving as arms. A layer of gray, fatty skin covered an endoskeleton shell. The aliens adorned themselves with only functional equipment— Gideon had only ever seen them in military gear or with engineering tools. How they managed to tell each other apart was a mystery to him.

The Vishrakath soldier at Gideon's feet turned its patch of eyes to the rifle in its claws, then looked up at the Terran armor, its mandibles twitching.

Gideon backhanded the alien into the inner wall, crushing it with a crunch of black gore, then he snapped a kick into the wall and sent the partition flying into the Vishrakath base. The metal plate bounced off the dirt and landed in the remains of the power cell.

The armor charged forward, his shoulder cannon firing from side to side as his onboard trackers locked on to the confused defenders. All the alien lives were forfeit. All but one.

A string of plasma bolts struck the ground to his side, turning the dirt into glass and scorching his legs. Gideon braced his left arm in front of his body, and a kite shield unfurled from the housing. Two bolts struck the shield, hitting hard enough to strain his shoulder actuators and send him back a step.

The armor spotted a smaller Vishrakath plasma cannon as it dropped behind one of their asteroid-shaped buildings. Gideon fired his gauss shells through the top of the alien structure, blasting hunks of rock into the air and puncturing the other side. A gout of white flame burst into the air as the plasma cannon went critical.

"Should have moved after you shot at me," Gideon said.

A door slid open on a nearby alien building and three Vishrakath soldiers ran out but promptly skidded to a stop when they saw Gideon. He kicked the enemy, catching all three with one blow. The one in the middle flew back into the building as the others careened off to the side.

Gideon activated the flamethrower on his right arm and jabbed it into the open doorway. A gout of blue flame poured into the windowless building. He heard the high-pitched screams of burning Vishrakath as he withdrew his arm.

"Tongea, any sign of the brood mother?" Gideon ran toward the sound of the other armor's gauss cannons.

"They're fighting back now," Tongea sent over their suits' IR link. "Whatever rock they defend, that's where she'll be."

Gideon heard and felt a vibration in the air just before an alien grav tank swung around a dome, flames dancing across its reflective armor. The flattened teardrop of the turret swung toward Gideon. He lowered his shoulder and charged the tank.

The thrum in the air increased in pitch, and Gideon leaped to the side just before the tank fired. A compressed plasma bolt nicked his shield, ripped a corner away, and almost yanked his arm from the socket.

Regaining his footing, Gideon jumped into the air, raised a fist and drove it into the forward edge of the tank. The armor buckled beneath the impact and the rear of the tank flipped up. The tank sailed over Gideon's head and landed upside down with a crunch of metal. Gideon rammed his heel into the side, right into the crew compartment. The blow bent the tank into a V and sparks erupted from the anti-grav emitters as they went haywire.

The top of an egg-shaped building opened to the sky, and low-pitched Vishrakath words boomed through the camp.

"Intelligence said they were all at the front," Gideon said as he sent a jolt of power to his rail cannon and dug a heel into the dirt.

"Take it up with them when we get back," Tongea said before running onto the top of a nearby dome.

The Vishrakath walker rose out of its hangar like a corpse suddenly sitting up from an open coffin. Its form mimicked the Vishrakath aliens, but both arms ended in plasma cannons and it stood nearly twice as high as the Terran armor.

Gideon aimed at the walker's left elbow and opened fire. Gauss shells careened off the armor, hammering dents into the shell. Tongea added his cannon to the assault, shattering the joint and ripping the cannon clean away from the walker.

The walker twisted its other cannon arm toward

Tongea and light grew from the muzzle.

Tongea deployed his shield and ducked behind it as the plasma beam slashed through the air. It cut across the armor's shield and sent him flying backwards.

Gideon fired on the sensor nodes on the walker's head, breaking them apart with precision shots. He raised what remained of his shield as the beam cut through an alien building and traced a line straight toward Gideon.

As the beam snapped off a few feet away from him, Gideon's back foot bumped against something. He ran his heel down the object as he kept firing on the walker, and felt rock give way to the press of his sabaton—another Vishrakath building.

"Tongea, I found the brood mother. Walker won't fire on me and risk hitting where she's hiding."

"First things first." Tongea rushed toward the walker as a panel slid down from the alien armor's chest and micro-missiles swarmed out like a nest of angry wasps. Gideon's rotary cannon spun into action, unleashing a torrent of bullets that intercepted some of the missiles.

Some.

A dozen small Vishrakath missiles burst a few feet from Tongea, the explosions deforming small uranium lenses into molten lances that ripped through Tongea's limbs, piercing his shield and into his breastplate.

Tongea grunted in pain and stumbled to his knees.

The walker raised a weapon arm to strike as it advanced toward the wounded armor.

Gideon sprinted forward, his gauss cannons blazing.

As the walker twisted its torso toward him, Gideon realized his mistake. The walker could have finished Tongea off with a plasma blast. The Vishrakath pilot had baited Gideon away from the brood mother's shelter, giving the alien a clean shot.

Gideon shunted power to his thrusters and launched himself into the air. Overloading the thrusters, he shot up, higher than the walker's plasma blast that missed his feet by inches.

He smashed into the walker and grabbed its neck servos with one hand. Bracing his feet against its body, he drew his right arm back and paused a moment, waiting for the alien pilot to react. Gideon had wrecked most of his optics. If the pilot wanted to know exactly where he was…

An armor plate snapped to the side, revealing the Vishrakath behind an armored pane of glass. The alien looked straight into Gideon's helm optics, then Gideon released the yard-long blade hidden in his forearm. He stabbed the sword through the glass and impaled the alien through its chest and against the back of the cockpit.

Yanking the blade free, Gideon dropped to the ground. The walker hunched over, the muzzles of its weapon arms dragging through the dirt.

Tongea limped toward the brood mother's bunker, one arm clutched against his side.

"How bad?" Gideon asked.

"Womb…damaged. Get her. Finish this!"

Gideon sprinted past his fellow armor and saw clear fluid leaking from a hole the size of a thumbnail in Tongea's back. Gideon smashed a fist into the bunker with a shout, cracking the exterior. He beat wild blows into the rock, ripping out a hole large enough for him to go through.

The brood mother sat in a raised dais, her form nearly the size of Gideon's armor. Juvenile Vishrakath scuttled over her body and a bulging egg sac attached to her abdomen. Holo screens surrounded her, showing images of the nearby Terran-Vishrakath battle and scenes of devastation around her bunker.

Alien attendants squealed in fright and backed against the computer banks surrounding the brood mother. One charged at Gideon with a plasma rifle raised over its head. The armor stomped it into paste, then activated his flamethrower and leveled it at the brood mother.

"Surrender." His suit translated the word into squeaks and clicks she could understand.

"Kill me and this planet will be ruined," she said as she rose up, the tentacles on one hand reaching for a control panel. Gideon let off a spurt of flame and shifted his aim to the egg sac. The brood mother froze.

"Surrender. Stop the eruption, then you and the rest of your kind can leave this planet and return to Vish space," Gideon said. From the corner of his eye, he saw a map with Vishrakath units arrayed against the attacking Terran forces led by Colonel Martel at the far end of the valley. The Vishrakath lines had broken. Casualty reports were coming in fast as the Terran armor ran down their fleeing foes.

"I can accelerate the eruption in an instant," she said. "You're not fast enough to stop me. I'll kill you and that other monstrosity behind you."

"I am armor. I gave up my life a long time ago. But they still have a future." Gideon stepped toward the alien, his flamethrower trained on the egg sac. "Surrender, or you'll see them burn before you die."

"You can't have the entire galaxy, human! This was our world." The brood mother pulled her hands to her chest, and child aliens rushed over her body and into her hands for safety.

"I don't care." Gideon lowered his flamethrower slightly. "We control the void above. We have the Crucible gate. Your army is broken. You have nothing to gain in this fight but to spoil a beautiful world out of spite. Choose to live or die. Now. My patience is at an end."

The brood mother caressed her egg sac. Her mandibles clicked several times…and a tear ran from the cluster of eyes in the middle of her head.

"I submit to your…mercy," she said.

Gideon shut off his flamethrower but kept it pointed at her.

"Tongea?" he said through the linked IR. Twisting his helm around, Gideon saw the other armor had blocked the exit with his body, armed cannon raised against a crowd of Vishrakath soldiers and a pair of grav tanks.

"The Saint…" —Tongea's words came out with a struggle— "…she sees us. We are witnessed."

"It's over. Activate your med protocols now." Gideon tapped in to Tongea's armor. His right arm within the armored womb flashed red. The pain added to the neural load going through the plugs connecting him to his armor, bringing him dangerously close to redlining and frying his brain.

"*Sancti spiritus adsit nobis gratia. Kallen, ferrum*

corde..." Tongea said slowly, the beginning of a Templar prayer.

"Shutting you down." Gideon pressed his fingertips into a panel just beneath an armor plate on Tongea's back, and the damaged armor powered down, leaving only the communications and life-support systems active.

"No!" Tongea shouted. "I can't leave the battlefield..." His words were slurred with shock.

"Battle's over, brother." Gideon sent a command to Tongea's womb and it flooded the amniosis fluid inside with tranquilizers.

****

Gideon stood atop a ridgeline outside his armor, watching as the last Vishrakath transport lifted out of the valley and into the sky. The nearby volcano smoldered, but the threat of a massive eruption that would wreck Cygnus II's atmosphere was gone. He rubbed his fingers on a Toth claw hanging from his necklace, the same implement that had carved the long scars running down the side of his face.

His armor knelt behind him, the breastplate and womb open to the air. The smell of smoke and sulfur hung heavy around him and the other armor soldier on the ridge.

Colonel Martel knelt in prayer. One knee to the ground, the other bent in front of him. His armor mimed his pose and held a two-yard-long sword point-down into the thin layer of ash covering the ridge. Martel had one hand on the blade, his forehead pressed against it.

Gideon twisted a heel against the ground, hoping the colonel would finally notice that the aliens had left the planet. It was useless to speak to him while he was in prayer.

Martel crossed himself, then struggled to his feet. The man's limbs were painfully thin, a consequence of not leaving his armor since the day he set foot on Cygnus almost a year ago.

"How is Tongea?" Gideon asked.

"He lost an arm, but he can still wear his armor. Recovery will take time," Martel said. "Why didn't you kill the brood mother when you had the chance? She was the one that started this war."

"Desperate enemies fight harder. You broke them on the field of battle. If I'd killed the brood mother, they'd have had no choice but to die hard. We are armor. We know what it means to fight a last stand. I offered to let them go and the fighting stops...and we'd save this mud ball from an ecological disaster." Gideon shrugged.

"Am I redeemed in your eyes?"

"You are."

"Then I want what you promised." Gideon's face hardened. "I want my own lance."

"You'll have your lance, but you must forge it yourself."

"Back to Earth? Training?"

"Bring the Iron Dragoons back into the Corps." Martel leaned against his armor's leg and ran a hand over his bald head. "You will not fail."

"I am armor. I am fury. I will not fail." Gideon nodded. "It's been a long time since I was home."

CHAPTER 1

Sunlight filtered through the memorial hall's stained-glass ceiling. Images of angels accompanying great starships guarding Earth's skies stretched from one end of the long hallway to the other. Marble benches ran down the length, each in front of a series of semicircular alcoves that made up the walls.

Roland Shaw walked slowly, looking for an unoccupied space, passing by sitting mourners waiting for a particular nook to open up. The hallway was deathly silent despite the dozens of people. Roland had come to this memorial hall often enough to know people grieved in their own way, yet almost everyone chose to stay silent here, as if showing signs of life might scare away the spirits of the dead.

A privacy screen slid open just as Roland passed,

and a woman with a black veil hurried out of the alcove, dabbing at her eyes with a tissue. Roland stepped aside for her and looked to a Hispanic man sitting on the bench across from the new vacancy. He stared down at a statue of a skeletons wearing women's and children's clothing in his hands, a bag of fruit at his knee, lost in thought.

Roland cleared his throat ever so slightly.

The man gave him a nod and was half off his feet when he gave Roland the once-over, noticing the jet-black pants, ivory-white button-down shirt, and black coat over his arm.

"You start work soon?" the man whispered.

"Yes, sir."

"Go. The dead will wait for us. The living have much to do." He settled back down and motioned Roland into the alcove.

Roland mumbled a quick thanks and stepped over the threshold. The privacy screen swung out of the wall with a hiss and closed behind him. The alcove was a polished obsidian wall. Flowers, an open bottle of liquor and a few small pictures lined the bottom of it.

The noise-cancelling tech was so perfect Roland couldn't even hear the air conditioner blowing chill air over him, or any other sound from the rest of the memorial hall.

The designers meant for the place to be utterly private, and Roland felt a familiar swell of emotions in his chest.

"Who would you like to visit?" a computer voice asked.

"Lieutenants Thomas and Catherine Shaw, Atlantic Union Space Navy. Remains unrecovered."

There was a brief pause, then Roland's parents appeared within the obsidian wall. His mother's image was of her smiling and giving a brief wave, a video clip of her in a loop. His father was in uniform, stoic as ever. At eighteen, Roland was inching ever closer to his parents' age when they had died, both in their mid-twenties. Details of their lives and service records scrolled up next to their faces. His mother's final entry showed she died on Luna when the invading Xaros smashed the moon's defenses. His father was lost to the void, reassigned at the last second to the 8th Fleet before it went on a mission to deep space where it was lost with all hands.

"Hey, Mom, Dad, I just turned eighteen, so now I can do my term of public service. We're the Terran Union now. Colony fleets are leaving all the time, really exciting stuff...I know, Mom, that you didn't want me to ever join up after Dad died, but it's the right thing to do. You both fought to keep Earth, and me, safe from the Xaros. Those things are gone forever, but there's still plenty of bad guys out there. Yeah, I can do public service through the engineer corps or logistics, but both of you fought. I don't think I could ever face you two again if I tried to duck out of a military term. So that's my choice. I'm doing it to honor you both. Don't be mad.

"I'm busing tables for pocket money." He lifted up his coat-draped arm slightly. "Robots can do that a hell of a lot better, something my boss mentions constantly. I need some real skills, and a military stint opens up a lot more doors for me. See, Dad? I can be practical.

"They've built memorial halls in every city, on every ship and every planet. That way I know you'll be with me and I'll be with you. Ms. Gottfried at the orphanage was kind, but she was never either of you…Now I'm just rambling. I love you both."

Roland stepped back from the wall and the image of his parents faded away. The privacy screen slipped open and he hurried out, sharing a quick smile with the man on the bench before he walked down the hallway to the double doors leading outside.

A gust of hot air greeted him as he left the memorial hall. Phoenix's summers were a special kind of dry and miserable, punctuated by the occasional sandstorm. He felt sweat forming on his forehead and armpits almost immediately as he made his way to a nearby bus stop. Sunlight glinted from the surrounding skyscrapers, and lines of drones and air cars formed higher and higher tiers of pathways through the metropolis.

Home to nearly twenty-five million people and the capital of the Terran Union, Phoenix was the largest city on Earth. Roland stepped beneath the bus stop's awning and wondered—not for the first time—why the government hadn't chosen a more temperate place to put down roots.

Roland's smart watch vibrated with an incoming call. He swiped fingers over it and the face of a doughy kid his same age and in the same black-and-white uniform came up.

"Oh good, you're not dead. Yet," Jerry said.

Roland spied the drapes behind Jerry.

"Why are you at work? Our shift isn't for another hour."

"Because Smith called us all in early and I've been trying to get ahold of you forever. Some VIPs made last-minute reservations and he wants the place looking more immaculate than usual. Get over here now before he loses his mind completely. Where the heck have you been?"

Roland glanced at the bus schedule and frowned. If

he caught the next bus, and the two transfers, he'd make it to work five minutes before his normal start time.

"The memorial hall in Chandler. There's no way I can get there quick. Cover for me."

Distant yelling came over the line and Jerry winced.

"Smith just found some not-so-fresh chicken in the freezer. Take a frigging cab and get over here. I just heard Smith say the bigwig is Colonel Hale, the friggin' hero of the Ember War, and Mr. Standish, the guy that owns like every liquor store in the solar system," Jerry said. Roland's head swayed back in surprise. "It doesn't get any bigger than this. Get. Over. Here. Think of the tips."

"Hale *and* Standish? I'll take a cab." Roland snapped his forearm and his meager account balance came up. Enough for a cab to the restaurant at Euskal Tower, not enough for that and bus fare back to the orphanage.

"Jerry, don't you owe me like twenty bucks?"

"Gotta go, bye." Jerry cut the call as the yelling grew closer.

"Risk and reward." Roland drew a circle in the air over his watch and pulled up the taxi app.

****

The view of the surrounding cityscape from the fiftieth floor of Euskal Tower, one of the few buildings on Earth the Xaros hadn't annihilated, was one of his restaurant's many qualities, but Roland paid no attention to the view when he stopped in front of a window and used his reflection to help adjust his tie.

Deco's prided itself on an all-human staff, from the maître d' to the waitstaff, to all the cooks in the kitchen. Robots could do any and all the jobs faster, cheaper and with fewer mistakes, but enough of the clientele in Phoenix preferred the old-fashioned restaurant experience to warrant the choice. The manager had a soft spot for war orphans and was friends with Ms. Gottfried, hence Roland and Jerry had a shot at the much sought-after busboy positions.

In the day and age of mass automation, the opportunity for teenagers to earn any money was a rare thing indeed.

Roland opened an unmarked door and hustled down a hallway adjacent to the busy kitchen where the entire waitstaff stood against the wall, ready for the Smith's merciless inspection as he made his way down the line. Roland stopped next to Jerry and gave his own jacket a quick brush.

"I will remind you all of our VIP protocols," Smith

said. "No pictures. No chitchat and absolutely no mention of who our guests chose to dine with. Deco's has a reputation for discretion. You will keep to it or you will not work here."

The maître d' sidestepped in front of Roland and frowned. He pinched something on the busboy's lapel and removed a long blond hair that did not belong to the young man. Smith raised an eyebrow at him and Roland blushed in response.

"Tanya will handle the VIP table," Smith said, speaking of the restaurant's senior waitress. "Jerry will bus." Roland's heart sank as he realized he wouldn't get anywhere near Hale and Standish.

Smith clapped his hands together twice and the waitstaff filtered into the restaurant just as the hostess came in from the front with six guests.

Roland followed Jerry as the other busboy made his way to a curtained-off table just out of view of much of the restaurant.

"Jerry, you got to let me take this one," Roland said.

"Are you crazy? Remember the last VIP we had? That Orozco guy that does all the commercials for Standish liquors? He slipped me a hundred on his way out. Imagine how much Orozco's *boss* will give me." Jerry rubbed his hands together.

"I don't want the whole table. Just let me fill their drinks up once. These are two heroes of the Ember War and this has got to be our last chance to ever get close to somebody that famous. We're enlisting in a couple days, remember?"

"I don't know...Smith's got his stick rammed up extra high tonight."

"I'll give you my tips for the night. All of them."

"Well...when you put it that way. I'll let you tag in after they get settled, deal?"

"Deal."

Roland went to the bussers' station and readied a pitcher with water flown in from Fiji. He started toward the table of six when Smith led two men in suits and a very proper-looking woman with her hair in a tight bun to the VIP table. Smith swept the curtain aside with a flourish and bowed slightly as the three entered. Roland got a good look at the backs of their heads, and nothing else.

A waiter slipped past him and poked him with his elbow. Roland suddenly remembered his duties and went to his assigned table.

As the night progressed, he kept an eye on the VIP room, waiting as Tanya slipped in and out with drinks and appetizers. Jerry came out with a half-empty pitcher and nodded slightly to Roland.

Roland craned his neck toward the kitchen, where Smith had gone to check on the entrees. With no sign of the maître d', Roland hurried over to Jerry and took the pitcher from him.

"They're almost done with their apps," Jerry said. "Tanya's cool with this, but clear that table before Smith sees you. Got it?"

"Got it, got it. Table nine's looking low on ice tea— cover for me."

Jerry gave him a light punch on the shoulder that sent the water sloshing around the pitcher.

Roland peeked around the edge of the curtain to the VIP table. Hale looked older than the man in the news videos and *The Last Stand on Takeni*, the somewhat propagandized movie about how Hale and the strike cruiser *Breitenfeld* saved the alien Dotok from a Xaros invasion. The former Marine still had the bulk of a man who worked out regularly and the eyes of someone with iron resolve.

Roland recognized Standish from the larger-than-life-sized statues the man had in front of all his liquor stores. In person, his well-coiffed jet-black hair and oversized gold watch were in stark contrast to the mental image Roland had of him as another Marine veteran that fought beside Hale. Standish's suit shifted color slightly as he moved, adapting to the light and making him look like he was in the middle of a photo shoot dedicated to enhancing his features.

The woman who accompanied them both stood against the wall, her eyes on a data slate.

Standish drank the last of his water and set the glass down. Roland's heart beat faster as a chance presented itself. He straightened his back, cleared his throat, smiled broadly and slipped into the room.

"That's what I told her," Standish said. "I took a shower, but it still itches."

Hale chuckled and tossed back the last of his drink.

Roland refilled Standish's glass, utterly focused on not spilling a single drop on the tablecloth.

"Standish," Hale said, holding up his glass and looking at the lights through a thin sheen of amber alcohol still on the sides, "you never did tell me where you found the spirits you used to start your business."

"Trade secrets," Standish said, "but since you're about to take a colony ship to Terra Nova, I'll let you in on it. Wait—what's your name, kid?"

Roland froze.

"Me? Sir?"

"No, the mouse in your pocket."

"Roland…Shaw. I just do water and clear tables and—"

"Roland, I'm about to say something to my old commander and friend that I trust with my life. Word of this story gets out and then…" Standish pointed a finger at Roland and frowned.

"No. Never, sir! At Deco's we—"

"Remember the first time we hit Phoenix and got Ibarra out from under this building?" Standish asked Hale. "Of course you do. What a crap day that was. While you were tossing grenades at Xaros from the back of that truck I hot-wired, I noticed a rather large liquor store was still intact. Once things settled down after the Battle of Ceres, I led a raid to liberate the contents before some army dogs or squids could get their filthy hands on it."

"Then you opened the black market for liquor across the fleet," Hale said.

"I found a market niche in need of my services," Standish said with a twinkle in his eye as he took a sip of whiskey.

"Gentlemen, if you're done with your appetizers, I'll take your plates," Roland said.

"How old are you, son?" Hale asked.

Roland froze, his hand stretched out mid-reach for what little remained of Hale's soup.

"Old?" Roland felt sweat on his forehead and armpits.

"You look like you're about eighteen," the retired colonel said. "Given thought to what branch you'll choose when your term comes up?"

"Not the Strike Marines," Standish said. "The recruiter will lie to you. Tell you it's nothing but hanging out on a void ship watching movies and that you'll never have to walk anywhere since you'll be space-borne infantry. They won't mention the face-eating aliens on Nibiru or that you'll have to singlehandedly save Phoenix from being nuked."

"What?" Hale gave Standish a sideways glance. "I thought Bailey and Egan were with you when that—"

"Who's telling the story here, sir? You or me?" Standish shook his head quickly, then wagged a finger at Roland. "Recruiters lie, kid. All of them. Constantly. You'll know what you're qualified for. Don't accept anything less than exactly what you want. That's the first and last time you'll ever get to make a choice in the military. The rest of your time you're stating a preference that will be ignored with a second thought."

"You're still mad I made you go on that first Pathfinder Corps mission with me to the jungle planet?" Hale asked.

"I still have the rash. You want to see it?"

"Some friends from my orphanage went orbital artillery," Roland said as he picked up their plates. "They say it's kind of boring."

"As the former head of the Pathfinder Corps," Hale said, "we always needed motivated individuals to help scout out new planets for colonization."

"And those with the talent to recover alien tech," Standish said.

"Which is why I needed you on those first few missions," Hale said. "You had a reputation for…foraging."

"I regret nothing." Standish raised his nose slightly.

The curtain swept aside and Smith glared daggers at Roland. Jerry was just behind him, his eyes wide with fear.

"I am so sorry, gentlemen," Smith said. "Our staff know better than to—"

"We were the ones bothering him," Standish said. "He's doing a great job. In fact, hold on…" Standish twisted around to the woman. "Julie, do I own this place?"

"Yes, you do, Mr. Standish."

"If Reggie here isn't working until the day he goes to serve his term," Standish said, picking up a fork and tapping it against the tablecloth, "I will be most perturbed. *Capisce?*"

"Of course, Mr. Standish."

"Son," Hale said and Roland turned to him with a jingle of china plates, "good luck out there. Take care of the men and women you serve with and they'll take care of you."

"Thank you, sir."

"Smith," Standish rapped his fork against the side of an empty wine glass. "Break out the Cheval Blanc. My friend's going on a long trip and I'll not have him go thirsty."

****

Roland cleared a table as the last guest for the evening finally left the restaurant, well past midnight. As the premier restaurant in Phoenix, Deco's catered to individuals from across the planet and the solar system, many of whom didn't have their sleep cycles tuned to local time. The restaurant stayed open very late, as no one would pay for dinner while the sun was up.

He set dishes into a cart and wiped his sleeve across his forehead. Standish and Hale had left hours ago, but the encounter was still fresh in his mind. That he was so close to his term of service and had no idea what he wanted to do hadn't concerned him until the two veterans had asked him about it.

Smith rapped a data slate against the hostess station, his signal that the receipts for the evening were tallied and it was time to disperse tips. Jerry, working two tables away, looked at his smart watch and bit his lower lip in anticipation.

Roland felt a slight vibration from his own watch. His total haul for the evening…zero dollars.

"Oh, yeah!" Jerry ran over to Tanya and gave the suddenly pale woman a high five. "Hey, Mr. Smith? I quit!" The now ex-busboy tossed off his apron and strode out the front door, snapping his fingers to a tune only he could hear.

Roland looked across the other tables that were Jerry's responsibility, knowing he'd have to clear all those too.

"Mr. Shaw," Smith said as he walked over.

"Sir."

"We keep our word at Deco's. You promised Jerry your tips. I promised you'd have your job until you leave for your term. See that everything's loaded into the washer before you leave for the evening. See you tomorrow." Smith gave him a nod and walked off.

Roland picked up silverware...and realized he didn't have enough money for bus fare back to the orphanage.

****

Roland walked along the sidewalk, his jacket slung over one shoulder. The air was dry and still oppressively hot, even this late at night. Phoenix summers were relentless, and he wished he'd had enough money to get a few stops closer to the orphanage in an air-conditioned bus. Light from Earth's two full moons, Luna and Ceres, spilled across the city. He looked up at Ceres and got a glint off the Crucible star gate in orbit around the smaller moon. Some nights he could see a flash as the gate opened a wormhole to distant parts of the galaxy, but the gate had been still since he'd left work.

He'd sent a few pleading texts to Jerry for a small loan, but had received only pictures of open bottles of alcohol and scantily clad women from one of the city's more notorious bars. Jerry had turned eighteen a few days ago and was old enough to drink. Roland had yet to go to his first bar, due to a lack of cash, not desire.

"Enjoy your first hangover, buddy," Roland said as a picture of Jerry getting kissed on both cheeks and holding a flute of champagne came across his watch.

Roland turned a corner and slowed to a stop. The street leading through the Remembrance Park was blocked by a holo tape. Law enforcement drones hovered over the perimeter that stretched around the entire park. Inside the park, Armor Square was lit up. Ten life-sized statues of armor soldiers, hewn from marble that gleamed in the light, surrounded a raised dais.

"Oh…great." Roland swiped across his watch and a new route taking him around the park came up. He'd get home just before sunrise.

There was a faint rustle of wind.

"The Remembrance celebration is the same day every year," a woman said.

Roland whirled around. The speaker had ash-colored hair and a well-lined face, but her voice was that of a much younger woman. She wore a simple spacer's jumpsuit. None of the buildings around them were lit up or looked open. Where had she come from?

"I've lived here since I was a kid," he said. "The holiday was just another one of those things. It's so close I never made it a priority to go see it. Crowds. Tourists. Hassle. What're you doing out here so late, ma'am?"

"I'm something of a night owl. What's your excuse? You look dressed for work."

"Just came off shift. I'd take a bus home but...I ran out of money before I ran out of month. I'll chalk this long, hot walk up to a learning experience."

"I knew plenty of junior Marines that never learned that lesson. Want to cut through with me? I have clearance. Name's Sophia."

"That would be incredible. Roland," he said, extending a hand to her. She looked at it for a second then shook his hand. Her grip was like solid iron, and Roland drew his hand back quickly.

Must be a prosthetic, he thought, *but don't most war wounded get vat replacements? Only takes a day or two to grow a new arm.*

Sophia waved a hand across the strips of holo tape and they turned green.

"Come on," she said. "The armor isn't here yet, which is the only reason I'm doing this. It's best not to anger them." She stepped through the perimeter and walked quickly toward the monument.

"Thanks, ma'am, I appreciate this. Is it true that all the armor come here from Mars for the ceremony? I came once on a school trip when I was a kid. Saw them in formation next to the honor guard from the Marines and Army."

"Every armor soldier that isn't deployed off world returns for the Remembrance Day ceremony. Some of them arrive the night before and stand vigil around the monument," she said.

"That vigil—the city's drone cops are all over the place during that. Anyone tries to get close enough for a picture or even see the armor, they'll end up arrested and fined. What do they even do? Have you seen it?"

"They pray—not all of them, just those that keep the Templar creed. The soldiers will leave their armor and spend from sundown to sunup in prayer. It's sacred for them. That's why the security is so high."

They'd come close enough to the monument that Roland could make out details of the ten statues. All were in different poses, each wielding either a sword or a spear and the massive gauss cannons mounted on their forearms. Some had aegis shields braced against an unseen foe.

"This was the moment that won the war, right?" Roland asked. "Ten armor held back the Xaros Masters on their command ship long enough for some kind of bomb to take out all their leadership. Then their drone armadas self-destructed."

"There were more than just the armor there that day," she said, "but what you said is close enough to the truth."

"I haven't served yet," he said, "but I can't imagine how hard that decision must have been. All the armor died when the bomb went off. They knew they were going to die, didn't they?"

"They knew." She nodded slowly. "Armor are a different breed than the other services. They do not fear death. They fear failing each other, their mission. The first anniversary of the war's end, all the surviving armor came here and they...they were mourning. Not for the loss of Elias or Colonel Carius...but that they weren't with them when they died. Now the Templar come back every year to offer penance. Not a year goes by that I don't try to think of some way the ten martyrs could've been saved."

"What? Were you...there?"

"No," she said curtly and walked faster.

"You sure do seem to know the armor pretty

well…you think they'll take me if I volunteer?"

She stopped and looked at him from the corner of her eye.

"Why would you want that?"

"My parents died fighting during the war. They died to keep me—to keep Terra—safe. It wasn't as big a deal as what the armor did, but when I join up, why should I try to go for something safe and easy? That's no way to repay my parents, to honor them." Roland felt his cheeks flush. He'd never shared these feelings with any of his friends, much less a complete stranger he'd met in the dead of night.

"Every life lost in the war mattered equally," she said. "No sacrifice was in vain. Not those left behind on Earth when the Xaros first arrived and wiped almost all of us out, not those who died in the final moments…or as a footnote on some alien world. I'm sorry about your parents."

"Everyone lost someone." Roland shrugged.

Sophia started walking again, leading him past the monument.

"The Armor Corps is always recruiting," she said. "Their numbers have grown slowly over the years. They aren't looking for anyone that can take the plugs…they're looking for someone with iron in their heart."

"How do I know if I've got that? What does that even mean?"

"Their recruiting methods aren't well-known outside Mars, but I know a few people," Sophia said. "If they take you in, they'll find the iron in your soul...or you'll break. Just know that there are easier ways to serve your term."

"You don't think I could do it?"

"Son, one of the best Marines I ever served with failed out of selection. I knew a woman whose body was as frail as a newborn kitten, but when she donned her armor, she became a demon on the battlefield. It takes all types. The only way to know if you've got what it takes is to volunteer."

They walked to the other side of the park and through the perimeter holo tape.

"Ma'am, I appreciate you taking me through...but I'm just as lost about what to do for my term as when we started talking," Roland said.

"Ah, to be young again. Making your own decisions and taking responsibility for your life is what makes you an adult," she said.

"If you don't mind me asking, what did you do during the war?"

"Strike Marines for a while…then I became something else. Good luck. I hope your term of service is quick and uneventful."

"'Quick and uneventful,' that sounds boring."

"War is never something to be enjoyed." She pointed down the street behind him. "That a cab?"

Roland turned around as an auto-cab slowed to a stop next to him. His name popped up on the passenger compartment glass with FARE PAID flashing.

"Ma'am, did you call—" He looked back, but she was gone. "I'm not telling anyone about this," he said. "I'll fail my service psyche eval if I start telling ghost stories. Or if I keep talking to myself."

The cab door popped open.

CHAPTER 2

A bus pulled up to the curb outside a multi-story brick building with neat rows of windows. Full-motion posters extolling the excitement of the Marines, Space Navy and other arms of the Terran military services lined the ground floor on either side of open double doors.

"Welcome to Service Entrance Processing Station – Phoenix" hung in holo letters over the doors.

Roland got out of the side doors on the bus and found his backpack in the open cargo bay. Jerry came down a moment later, his face puffy and blinking hard against the sun's rays. Roland grabbed his friend's bag and swung it gently into his chest.

"Why did I drink so much…and for so long?" Jerry asked.

"You mentioned something about your last gasp at freedom in between barfs in the toilet that we shared in our very small room," Roland said, shouldering his pack. As he watched families cluster around men and women his age along the wide sidewalk outside the SEPS, he felt a tug on his heart, wishing that his parents could've been here to see this.

"For as hard as I partied, I wish I remembered more of it. I think her name was...Dakota?" Jerry blinked hard at his smart watch and swiped to the side. "No, that's Dakota. The one with the expensive taste in everything was Cherry."

"I can't believe you blew through two months' pay in three days. Hope you handle your finances better once we get through this place." Roland gripped the handle on his pack, ready to go inside, but his feet felt glued to the ground.

"I seem to remember you borrowing bus fare from me this morning. You wasted all your money on scout courses and a gym membership. You know the military is about to teach us all that. For free."

Roland took a deep breath and let it out slowly.

"You ready for this?" he asked.

"Service is mandatory...unless you want to run off

44

to a squatter settlement in the Rockies and live on whatever you can grow or catch. The orphanage and busing tables sounds like paradise compared to that. Good luck with…what branch do you want?"

"I'm still not sure."

"Should've figured that out sooner. Just don't let them put you on the Venus terraforming mission. That may be the one place in the solar system worse than Mars." Jerry slapped Roland on the arm. "See you in there. Good luck." He walked into the SEPS building.

Roland looked up and down the row of posters as more people followed Jerry inside. Every branch looked interesting in the three- to five-second looped videos; even Orbital Artillery boasted spectacular views of the outer solar system. But there was one branch he didn't see—Armor.

"Maybe they're not recruiting after all." Roland hiked his pack onto his shoulder and walked inside.

A gust of cool, moist air greeted him as he crossed the threshold. Rows of kiosks, each served by a robot with articulated arms, ran up and down the foyer. A giant flag of the Terran Union stretched almost the entire length of the room: the Western Hemisphere with a star on Phoenix, spread avian wings on either side of Earth over a gray background. One of the feathers was midnight black in remembrance of all who fell to save Earth during the Ember War. Flags of the different branches hung from just below a walkway along the walls. Roland saw the mailed fist clutching a sword blade of the Armor Corps and felt a glimmer of hope. Maybe there was a chance.

He went to a kiosk and pressed his palm to a sensor pad.

"Welcome Shaw, Roland L." The robot's head lifted up and its metal palms touched together twice. "You've arrived on your assigned report date. Well done. Please place your pack into the receptacle."

A panel opened up at the bottom of the kiosk, just large enough for all the personal belongings Roland had been told to bring with him.

"Do you have any items on the restricted list?" the robot asked. "Penalties for failing to declare nonprescription medication, narcotics, alcohol, unauthorized electronic devices—"

"Nothing."

"—living or dead animals, weapons, currency in excess of three hundred Terran dollars or sanctioned enemy material can be punished by assignment to the needs of the service and criminal prosecution."

Roland did a mental repacking. His other set of civilian clothes and a few pictures of his family and one data slate didn't strike him as anything forbidden.

"Nothing," he repeated and put his pack into the box. The panel clicked shut.

"Thank you…Shaw, Roland L. Here is your schedule for the rest of the day at Service Entry Processing Station – Phoenix. This is now your place of duty. Follow the prompts to each evaluation station. Any attempt to leave the building without express authorized permission will be considered an attempt to go Absent Without Leave. Check tab Nine-Yankee for associated penalties. Good luck."

A white data slate rose out of a slot, Roland's name flashing on the screen.

"Wait…when do I get my stuff back?" he asked.

The robot motioned to the slate with one hand, down a hallway with another.

"Mom always said the military life was easy. Just do exactly as you're told and no one will yell at you." He took the slate and directions to the medical evaluation station popped up. He scrolled down, his brow furrowed at the rather long list of places he had to get through by the end of the day.

"At least I've got fifteen minutes for lunch," he said.

****

The auditorium buzzed with hundreds of conversations between nervous recruits, all wearing gray jumpsuits with their names stenciled above a pocket on their chests. Roland caught sight of Jerry sitting in a back row, cradling his face in his palm.

"Hey, how's it going for you?" He took a seat next to his old roommate.

"Doing all this while hung over was a *bad* decision." Jerry turned his head to Roland, then looked back at his feet. "You look good in a uniform. Maybe this is for you."

"Got it at med processing after some robot poked and prodded me. Then it was a dozen more tests for reflexes, spatial awareness, math, history of all things. You get any feedback from any of your tests?"

"Nothing more than a few disapproving glances from the cadre. Did you have to do…room twelve? I got in there and there's some guy in civilian clothes who just started yelling at me. I asked him if that was the room for an argument. He just kept yelling until I left."

"I had the same thing happen to me," Roland said, frowning. "Wasn't in room twelve, though. I kept my mouth shut and left. Then my next assignment popped up on my slate. Weird, right?"

"I'm not entirely sure what're we supposed to be doing here right now. With what looks like every last high school graduate in Phoenix."

Roland swiped his finger over his data slate.

"Pre-assessment briefing…for two hours. Then dinner."

"Two *hours*? How can anything in the military take that long?" Jerry tapped his own data slate. "Of course there're no game apps on this thing."

"Maybe we should pay attention? Could be pretty important for our term."

"Fine. Mr. Responsibility." Jerry leaned back and crossed his arms.

"Excuse me," said a young Asian woman with straight hair, as she stuck her head between the two of them, "either of you have the latest bonus points list?"

"Bonus?" Roland asked.

"For colony assignments. I saw the list from

yesterday, but a friend of mine from an earlier session said everything had changed. Thought maybe you two had heard something," she said.

"Nothing." Jerry shrugged. "I thought off-world colonies were done by lottery."

"There are different pools of lottery," she said. "Haven't you two ever been off world?"

The lights dimmed and rose several times and the room grew quiet.

Roland's slate powered off by itself and he slipped it into a thigh pocket.

A tall woman in a Marine uniform walked out onto the auditorium's stage, her hands clasped behind her back.

"Greetings, recruits." Her voice came from speakers built into the seats, making her words sound like they came from just a few feet away. "I am Captain Grainger, your commanding officer during your time at SEPS-Phoenix. I already had to sign expulsion paperwork on six individuals who thought they could smuggle contraband through the scanners and three more with narcotics in their system. If you're going to do anything stupid during your term of service, do it now. Removing the exceptionally stupid and foolish at the SEPS level saves the Terran Union a significant amount of time and resources."

Jerry laughed…the only one that laughed. Roland leaned away from him, hoping Captain Grainger didn't think he was the mirthful recruit.

"You've all finished your initial evaluations," Grainger said. "You'll receive your scores in a moment, and these scores will be taken into account when you meet with the branch recruiter following this briefing. I highly encourage you to make your decision before your time with the recruiter ends, else you'll be assigned to the needs of the service, and Venus just sent me another labor request."

"I told you," Jerry whispered.

A holo screen materialized over the captain's head and a star chart centered on Earth filled the screen. Icons for settled stars spread from humanity's home toward a yellow shaded region labeled Ruhaald Space to Earth's galactic east.

"The Terran Union is engaged in aggressive colonial expansion to nearby stars and more Earth-like worlds linked to the Crucible jump-gate network. Colonists to higher-priority worlds receive tax breaks, homestead assistance and tuition forgiveness for any and all higher-education expenses. Some colonies are…idyllic," —the holo shifted to a world with azure skies and Hawaiian-like islands— "others, less so. The Marines are currently engaged in a police action to remind the Xie'e that Cardova-II belongs to the Terran Union.

"Those that chose to apply for colonial assignment will receive a preference based on the conditions of their terms of service. The more in demand certain positions, the more preference in the way of points. Consider this when you meet with your recruiter. In addition, the aptitude you've displayed during your civilian schooling and assessment today will determine which positions you can apply for. This is simple. Anyone that asks me to explain it further will be docked five assessment points."

Roland inched away from Jerry again, hoping he didn't consider that last part another joke.

"Good." Grainger raised a hand. "Release the scores."

The slate in Roland's pocket buzzed. He slapped a hand against the slate and gritted his teeth. Much of his future depended on what was waiting for him, and he said a quick prayer to his parents that whatever he was qualified for would manage to honor them. The thought of taking out the trash on a macro-cannon in the far reaches of the Kuiper Belt was nothing to be proud of.

He removed the slate and looked at the screen.

"I got an 88," Roland said. "Is that good?"

"I'm 37?" Jerry frowned. He twisted around to the redhead.

"102." She smiled. "You," she said to Roland, "are about mid-tier for assignments. Your friend…not so much."

Roland touched the screen and a list of positions came up with two columns of numbers. The first was the cutoff score; the second was for colonial weighting. The upper tier of positions were grayed out.

"So much for medical school…or advanced quantum spatial engineer, whatever that is." Roland reorganized the table by colonial weighting. The positions that came with the best chance of moving to a garden world were all combat arms. Marines, Rangers and fighter pilots had the top spots.

"Casualties must be bad," Jerry said. "Why else would they need more people on the front lines?"

"We're not at war with anyone," Roland said, "officially."

"Sanitation engineer?" Jerry sneered at his slate. "Not no, but hell no. I'll be a Marine. See if I ever have to clean up anyone's garbage when I'm doing that."

Roland scrolled through the list again.

"You have armor on your list?" he asked Jerry, who

didn't answer but kept mumbling to himself. Roland repeated the question to the redhead.

"I found it." She flipped her slate around for Roland to see. "It's hidden in another tab. But there must be some mistake...armor is zero-zero. No requirement, no colony points."

"It's almost like they don't want anyone to apply," Roland said.

"My sister tried for armor," she said, "didn't get past the first day of selection. Couldn't tell me anything else, had to sign one hell of a nondisclosure agreement."

"You two can plug yourselves into those tin cans all you want," Jerry said. "The Marines are calling me. Did you know I've met *the* Colonel Hale?" he said to her. "Came to my restaurant a few days ago."

"That's great." She waved a hand at him. "So you're thinking about armor..."

"Roland."

"Masako."

"I was just at the armor monument...I can't think of a better way to serve," he said.

"Well, good luck." Masako gave him a smile and stood up. A room number flashed on her slate. "Looks like I get to see a recruiter now. See you."

"Bet we've got a while to wait," Jerry said. "Hope there will be some Marine slots left by the time I'm called. You really want armor, or were you just trying to impress her?"

"I really want armor."

"What's going to get you more play with the ladies? The Marines' full-dress blues or plugs in the base of your skull? I mean, have you ever even seen an armor soldier outside their walking tanks?"

"Not everything is about sex and money, Jerry."

"If you just had the week I did, you might see things differently."

Roland's slate buzzed with a room number and directions.

"Don't you take the last Marine slot," Jerry hissed at him.

"What would a Marine say about this situation? Survival of the fittest?" Roland got up and gave Jerry a pat on the shoulder.

****

Roland double-checked the room number on a door with the number on his data slate. A nameplate for a Staff

Sergeant Harris was just beneath the brass numerals. Roland knocked.

"Come in!"

He cracked the door open and leaned his head into the office. It was just big enough for a desk at the far end and a single chair canted to the side, ready and welcoming for the regular cycle of recruits. Staff Sergeant Harris leaned his elbows onto the desk, an array of data slates set in front of him.

"Yes, you, Mr. Shaw." Harris motioned to the open seat. "Let's get started."

Roland hurried into the office and sat down. He kept his back straight, fidgeting with his now-dead slate.

Harris swiped his hand over a keyboard and Roland's personnel file came up, complete with an older picture of him taken during a mercifully brief period of time when mullets had come back into fashion.

"You are prepared for your term of service," Harris said. "Too many of your peers come in here without a clue as to what's expected of them. Just because there hasn't been a shot fired in the solar system since the last Xaros attack, they think military service is some sort of hobby the government decides to keep going. You completed your Scout training and evaluations...your instructors even recommended you for Ranger evaluation. Well done. Top quintile for athletic assessment…no surprise. Science, technology, math and engineering scores…are there." He pushed himself away from his desk and looked Roland over like he was evaluating a major purchase.

"Have a preference in mind, son? Terran law requires me to consider your first choice."

"I had a question…about armor. Is it available?"

Harris' face fell.

"Not another one. Look, Mr. Shaw, the Armor Corps gets a lot of interest thanks to their contributions—overstated, in my opinion—to the last war. The Armor Corps is separate from all the other branches and they do things their own way, which don't always make sense to those of us who're in uniform. So understand that some of my information is a bit limited, but I know this: ninety-five percent of those that volunteer for armor never make it to Mars. Two-thirds don't even get past the initial selection at SEPS."

"Is there something in my file that makes you think I won't make it?"

"It's a numbers game, Mr. Shaw. If I bet a day's pay on every armor candidate *not* making it through selection, I'd be a very rich man by now. Armor has no physical or education requirements to start selection. With your scores, I can't get you into the higher-tier engineering or medical fields...but Marines—even Strike Marines—that I can do in a heartbeat. The colony preference points for the Strike Marines is as high as I've ever seen it. If you want to start a new life on a world that makes Phoenix look like a festering dumpster fire in comparison, I can get you there." Harris pushed a data slate, with a Strike Marine that looked suspiciously like a younger Colonel Hale, toward Roland.

Roland looked at the slate, but didn't touch it.

"So I can go armor?" Roland asked.

Harris sighed heavily.

"Of course you can." Harris waved his hand over his keyboard and started typing. "Couple things I'm required to go over with you first. In my official capacity, this question is usually forbidden under the Procedural Persons Act, but it's a medical issue and it's allowed. Are you a true born human being?"

"As far as I know. I thought all the proccies had memories of growing up and families and from before they came out of those tubes. Does any proccie know what they are?"

"You're spot on about the proccies, son," Harris

said. "Ibarra had to grow them fast to rebuild the fleet. Took him nine days to grow an adult body and implant a unique mind from whatever alien sorcery he used to make them all. Millions of people joined the fight against the Xaros that way, their memories no different than someone born on Earth the old-fashioned way. They helped save the Earth, no doubts there."

"Why does it matter if I'm a proccie or not?"

"Armor Corps won't accept them. None of them can take the plugs to connect to the suits. Some sort of side-effect of being grown so fast in a tube. I'm a proc myself, can't say I ever feel any different than the true born that come in here." Harris took out a small cube with a finger hole in one end.

"It's normally strictly illegal to base a government position—or anything, really—on if someone's a proccie or not, but we've got a medical necessity waiver. Please," the recruiter said, and tapped the desk next to the cube.

Roland put a finger into the device, and it lit up. He knew he was born before the war started, that proccies came on line just after Admiral Garret had won the battle that seized the Crucible from the Xaros…he'd never worried that he was anything but true born until this exact moment.

The box blinked on and off.

"Thank you." Harris plucked the box from his finger and put it back in his desk. "Telomere length checks out. You're true born. We'll check off that box. Next, are you aware that armor candidates will undergo cybernetic augmentation as part of their term of service?"

"The plugs in the back of their skulls…I know, but that's not permanent, right?"

"You can ask the doctor when you see her. I don't have that information available. Next point, the term of service for any who complete armor selection is 'for the duration.' Anyone who wants to return to civilian life voluntarily must receive permission from the Armor Corps commander. You go Marines or Ranger, you're out after a few years. You get your plugs with armor and basically the only way to leave is feet-first."

"They don't let anyone out?" Roland's hands clenched into fists and his eyes went to another data slate with a Ranger in a black beret holding a plasma rifle on a desert planet.

"Not exactly. No armor candidate that's ever made it to Mars for the last phase of selection has ever asked to leave the service. Seems they all opt to make a career out of military service. Which does lead to my next point. There is no penalty for non-selection or voluntarily dropping from armor while you're a candidate. If they say no, or you decide it isn't for you, you come back to SEPS with your same scores. Colony points might be different."

"But I drop out of Marine basic training and…"

"'Needs of the service,'" Harris said with a frown. "You don't want to find out what that is."

"Why does the Armor Corps make it so easy to quit? It's almost like they don't want anyone to even try to join them."

"Armor wants a certain kind of person. I'm not privy to their selection methods, but their candidate-to-selectee ratio is terrible. Ninety-five percent don't make it to Mars, remember? You can drop out at any time, no penalty. So, with all these cards on the table" —Harris glanced down at the many data slates on his desk— "you still want to go Armor? Or you want something with a better future at the end of your term?"

Roland picked up the Space Navy slate and scrolled down to a picture of a fleet over Saturn's rings. He remembered when his parents had first told him about moving to Saturn with a colony fleet, about the exciting life he'd live on a space station and the endless opportunities he'd have when he grew up. He remembered how excited they both had been to get away from Earth.

Then he'd lost them both during the war. His father in the battle to retake Ceres and the Crucible jump gate, his mother when the Xaros returned and smashed Luna.

His mind wandered back to his walk past the armor monument and what the strange woman had said about how those ten armor soldiers met their fate.

"I don't want to play it safe, to miss out on what I could be." Roland put the slate back on the desk. "I want armor."

"I hope you make it, Mr. Shaw. If not, I'll see you back here and we'll get you going down another path." Harris typed furiously for a few seconds, then turned off his holo screen with a swipe.

The slate in Roland's lap buzzed.

"Medical evaluation," Harris said. "Get moving."

CHAPTER 3

Roland's chair tilted back and the headrest pressed against the back of his neck. A lamp moved over his face and he closed his eyes against the glare.

"I feel like I'm at the dentist," he said.

"Did they do this at the dentist?" A medical tech pressed a button on her slate and restraints clamped down on his wrists and ankles.

"The doctor will be with you in a moment," she said, and left the room.

"Wait…what's this test even for?" Roland pulled at the restraint on one arm and it tightened even more in response. He let his arm relax, and the cuff loosened.

The room was oddly silent, the oppressive glare from the lamp making him wonder if he'd been sent to a military intelligence evaluation instead. One of his fellow orphanage mates had gone into the espionage field for his term of service and written back with a number of wild stories.

He heard the door open and shut, then an elderly woman with hazel eyes leaned between him and the lamp. The smell of cigarette smoke wafted off her white lab coat.

"I'm Dr. Eeks," she said, "sorry for the wait. You may, at any time you choose, end the testing and be dropped from selection. Ready?"

"What…exactly are you going to do to me?"

"Standard neural profiling. If your body can't take the plugs, then there's no point in doing anything else, is there? You'll feel a slight pinch."

The headrest tightened against his neck and the back of his head. He felt the touch of a small, cold bit of metal against the base of his skull. He squirmed against the restraints, then forced himself to relax, taking measured breaths as the doctor looked at a holo screen projecting off her forearm computer. A body outline filled with red and blue nerves pulsated on the screen.

"Any fear of enclosed spaces?" she asked.

"No, ma'am."

"Any history of neurological issues in your family? Multiple sclerosis, Parkinson's, things like that."

"I don't know. My parents died when I was a kid. We never had a talk about whether any of my uncles were a bit looney."

"Sense of humor while under duress, good." Eeks tapped a pad on the back of her hand and files for Roland's parents came up. "How does a soldier become armor, Roland?"

"I don't...exactly know. There are the brain plugs, right?" The bit of metal against his skull pressed harder. "That's how the soldier moves the armor around. Am I supposed to know this?"

"Soldiers receive a neural shunt that connects them to their armor. The soldier doesn't move the armor around. The soldier *is* the armor. Hold this for me." She pressed a metal rod into his left hand.

"What is it—ah!" The rod sent a shock up his arm, contracting his muscles and tightening his grip. The surge stopped within a second and she plucked the rod out of his hand.

"Sorry about that. Needed a trauma reading...tell me why you want to be armor."

Roland gritted his teeth, his patience wearing thin.

"There's no wrong answer. I ask everyone," she said, her eyes glued to the holo display of Roland's nervous system.

"To make a difference. To honor my parents."

She rubbed her chin, then clicked her tongue a few times.

"At this time, you're eligible to continue selection," she said. The cold metal receded from Roland's neck and the headrest loosened its grip. "We need to continue gathering biometric data, which is where this little gem comes in."

She held up a black hoop with an inch-wide plastic pad attached to it.

"It'll conform to your skin tone once I put it on and you won't even notice it's there after a few hours. Remove this and you'll be dropped from selection, understand?"

The seat back lifted Roland upright.

"What does it do?"

"Collects data. The neural shunt—if you do elect to receive it—has a number of potential…negative side effects. We do our best to screen out those susceptible, but…"

Roland looked at the monitor. The idea of being wired into a medical device was not altogether welcome.

"Plenty of negative side effects of being a Marine or Ranger, right, ma'am? Like bullets and void combat." He lowered his chin to his chest.

"I've not heard it put that way." The doctor pulled the hoop open and slid it around his neck, then pressed the pad against his spine. It tightened around his neck and a shiver went down his back.

"What's it like having the plugs?" Roland asked.

Eeks turned her head to the side and lifted up her hair, revealing a perfectly normal base of her skull.

"Ask your cadre if you get the chance. We need a few more seconds for the monitor to synch with you." She double-tapped the restraint on Roland's wrist, and the chair released him.

"Am I supposed to sign a nondisclosure agreement for this?" He reached to the back of his neck to rub the monitor, then pulled his hand away.

"There's no way to prepare for this part," she said. "Either you're minimally qualified for the plugs or you are not. Don't worry about touching the monitor or showering with it on. Taking it off requires some effort. Do remember that if you remove it, you will be dropped."

Her forearm screen beeped.

"Now you're good. Report to the VR chamber in basement level 1C for your next assessment."

"But it's getting kind of late. When is din—I mean,

yes, ma'am."

Eeks chuckled.

"You remind me of a skinny little Kurdish kid from many years ago. If you really want to be armor, you listen to me. Don't hold back. Don't ever hold back." She gave him a pat on the cheek, then pointed to the door.

"Now get moving. I've got to get through twenty more potentials."

****

Tongea and Gideon stood in a control room, watching a screen where Roland paced back and forth in an empty VR chamber. The lit squares on the floors, walls and ceiling came in and out of focus as the holo projectors compensated for Roland's shifting point of view.

"Eeks has this one down as marginal," Gideon said.

"Marginal med evals make it through fairly regularly. His psych profile concerns me." Tongea touched his forearm screen and Roland's nervous system came up. "Adrenaline elevated…he's ready for a fight."

"I say we cut him now, suggest he reapply after his first term is up." Gideon crossed his arms.

"Colonel Martel sent us here to find armor, not lessen our burden. Let's run him through the canyon. I'll take this one."

CHAPTER 4

Roland reached toward the white abyss surrounding him. The VR chamber hadn't changed since he first walked in. Only his shadow across the floor and the closed door behind him gave him any sense of spatial awareness. He took three steps forward and his fingertips touched the wall, sending ripples away from the impact like a stone dropped in a pond.

The wall shifted to beige and he jerked his hand back. A desert landscape formed around him and he felt a slight vibration from the floor. Dark storm clouds billowed over distant mountains and a gust of hot air washed around him. He turned around, noting that the door was gone.

"Candidate Shaw," came from a speaker in the ceiling, hidden behind a holo panel showing him a deep blue sky. "Take the equipment provided and travel to the location on the map. This is a timed event."

A circle opened in the ceiling and a drone floated down, a combat gauntlet and gauss carbine on top of it. Roland slipped the gauntlet over his left forearm and picked up the carbine. The drone rose back into the opening and vanished behind a sky projection.

Roland removed the magazine from the weapon and did a quick inspection. There was a blue line around the top of the magazine and a thin blue line around the top bullet. Training munitions. He slapped it back into the weapon and cycled a round into the chamber. The battery that would power the magnetic accelerator to propel the cobalt-jacketed tungsten darts read as nearly depleted. He could get a few shots off at most.

"This weapon's more dangerous as a club when it's loaded with training rounds. Why bother giving me a bum battery too?" He raised his gauntlet and a map came up. Although a dot pulsed in the bottom of a canyon, there was no indicator of where he was on the map, but there was a compass wheel.

He turned around and found a distant mountain peak, the spine of the connected range descending to the east. Roland twisted the map around on the gauntlet screen and found a match for the terrain feature. He shot a back azimuth and managed to estimate his location as a few kilometers south of the pulsating dot.

I knew spending those weekends at Scouts would pay off. He ran north, keeping a pace count as he went; the roar of engines rising from behind him. A half-dozen Eagle fighters raced overhead, low enough that Roland could almost read the squadron markings on their tails. The fighters vanished into the approaching storm clouds.

Roland kept running until his chest was heaving and his heartbeat pounded in his skull. Taking a knee beneath the shade of a mesquite tree, he tried to touch it, but his fingers went right through the hologram. He glanced at his gauntlet…and the dot vanished, reappearing farther west. Much farther west.

"You're kidding me." He stood and shot an azimuth to the new location and started jogging at a more even pace.

A hot wind picked up behind him, and blowing sand obscured the distant mountain peaks. He turned just in time to see a wall of sand rushing toward him, and raised his arms over his face out of reflex, but not a single grain of sand touched him within the VR chamber. Everything around him was a brown morass.

I've lived in Phoenix since I was seven. Never seen anything like this. What're they trying to test, how well I do in Alice's Wonderland? he thought.

A ripple of cannon fire rose over the wind, and rounds hit the sand a dozen yards away. The sound of an Eagle and another, higher-pitched, engine swirled above him. Roland lifted his gauntlet up, turned to the west and started running again. Whatever was happening overhead was not something he wanted to be around.

This is crazy, he thought. *I want to be armor. Why are they running me around the desert like it's the last war?*

A thunderclap and a flash of yellow light cut through the sandstorm. A hunk of smoking metal hit the ground and bounced straight toward Roland. He dived to the ground as the debris sailed overhead.

Stupid. None of this is real. He got up and kept moving. The sandstorm abated a few minutes later…and all the mountains he'd used for terrain navigation were gone. Small hills and wide salt plains surrounded him…but there was a billowing parachute a hundred yards away connected to an ejection seat lying on its side.

Roland went for the seat, hoping whatever he found there might help make sense of this whole thing. He approached the ejection seat with the carbine to his shoulder, finger off the trigger. The seat faced away from him, and he heard groaning from the other side.

He sidestepped around and found the pilot slumped against the restraints, his helmet lying in the dirt. Walking closer, Roland bumped his foot against the helmet, sending it tumbling away.

"That's not a hologram?" He tapped his foot against the ejection seat and found it was real too.

Kneeling next to the pilot, he gave his shoulder a gentle shake, and blood leaked out of the side of the pilot's mouth. An ugly rip ran down the side of his flight suit, soaked with deep red blood.

"Hey, can you hear me?" Roland found a bright yellow box beneath the seat and pulled it out. Inside were a med kit, emergency transponder and a food pack.

The pilot groaned and gave a wet cough. Roland removed a quick-clot patch and a suture laser from the med kit, then gingerly pulled back the torn flight suit. Within, a pile of spilled intestines quivered in a pool of blood. He cried out briefly, then pressed the flight suit closed and dropped the patch to the ground.

"Help...me," the pilot said.

Roland wiped blood off his hands and looked around, but there was nothing but the stretch of flat desert. His gauntlet buzzed and a new dot appeared. An icon for a

Mule transport came up beside the dot.

"Help's on the way, buddy. Just let me think for a second." He snatched up the yellow case and fiddled with the transponder. Flicking the plastic cover off a red button, he looked up. A dogfight raged high overhead, the flash of gauss rounds and energy blasts crisscrossing the sky.

"I hit this, and someone will come for you, right?" The pilot answered the question with a groan. A half-dozen scenarios came to Roland—moving the pilot, waiting for help. He looked at his weapon leaning against the ejection seat and wondered if the pilot was mortally wounded and suffering...

"Not that." Roland pressed the transponder button and it began flashing. He put it back into the yellow box, jimmied the box back into the seat and found a gauss pistol within a holster belt. He drew the pistol and pressed it into the pilot's hands, then took the spare battery in the holster and slapped it into his own rifle.

"Help will either come here, or I'll bring it to you." Roland ran for the spot on his map, glancing over his shoulder every few seconds back to the pilot. Ahead of him, he made out a Mule through the heat haze.

The desert faded away and the lit squares of the VR chamber returned. Roland skidded to a halt and thumped into the wall with his shoulder. He whirled around and found the pilot sitting on his ejection seat on the other side of the room. He wiped blood from his face, revealing tribal tattoos on his chin and the side of his face.

"Give me your weapon," Tongea said, holding a hand out, "and your gauntlet."

Roland breathed hard as he walked over. He offered the butt of his carbine to Tongea, then yanked it back. He powered down the weapon and withdrew the magazine, then handed it over. There was a protocol for transferring a weapon from one soldier to another, a painful lesson Roland had learned early on in Scouts when he made the mistake of giving a rifle with a loaded round to a former drill instructor.

"Did I…pass?" Roland removed his gauntlet.

"You completed this training event. If you are dropped from selection, you will be told immediately. Until then, you are under constant evaluation. Understand?"

"Yes, sir."

"Why did you leave me behind?" Tongea gave Roland a hard look.

"You were…dying. Sort of. I couldn't do much for you with what was in the med pack. I figured I could get to the Mule and bring them to you, or you'd get picked up by a search-and-rescue team before I could come back."

"Your mission was to bring the intelligence data to the location provided on your gauntlet. That information could have changed the course of the battle, even the war. Why did you bother to help me at all?"

"I couldn't just leave you there…I tried to find a way to do both. Was I wrong?" Roland asked, flopping his arms against his sides in frustration.

"This was a relatively simple exercise. There will be exponentially more difficult tasks to come," Tongea said. "Do you wish to continue selection?"

"Yes, sir."

"A shower and fresh clothes are down the hall. Third door on your left. Report to the mess hall for dinner. The SEPS computer will assign you a room for the night. You'll learn if you'll continue selection in the morning." Tongea twisted around and pointed a small device at the wall. The door appeared after a click.

Roland got a good look at the plugs at the base of Tongea's skull and his hand went to the back of his own head. He opened his mouth to ask a question…but hesitated.

"This training iteration is complete. Move out." Tongea motioned to the new open door. Roland nodded quickly and left.

Tongea looked up once the door closed.

"He didn't make time," Gideon's voice came through the speakers. "Cut him."

"No. He has the right instincts, held up well under stress. We can work with that."

"He'll drop by morning."

"We shall see."

****

Roland sat on the bed of his one-man room, a Spartan affair with a small wooden desk, a chair and an open closet for his personal items and a spare jumpsuit. Roland's quarters were on the top floor. He'd passed through several open bays of double bunks with recruits destined for the Marines. He'd caught some odd looks and overheard whispers about the device around his neck before he made it to the sequestered barracks for armor candidates. He touched the base of his skull, running his fingertips down the smooth plastic of the monitor.

Suddenly, he burst to his feet and pressed the palms of his hands against the sides of his head.

"I screwed it up," he muttered. "Why didn't I just

leave him and keep running? This isn't going to work. I'll be a jarhead by morning. Why don't I go out there and make friends before they're certain I'm some sort of freak because of the monitor…"

He sank back to the mattress then picked up his personal data slate—a battered model almost five years old with a cracked screen—and connected to a weak civilian data network. Nothing from Jerry, but there was an e-mail from Ms. Gottfried that he didn't want to read. She'd pry, and telling her he was in armor selection felt like a sure way to jinx what little chance he had left.

"Sammy." Roland woke up his data assistant. "Find me an interview with an armor soldier. No earlier than the start of the Ember War."

Video clips of armor fighting Xaros drones during the war popped up around his screen. His eyes lingered on a looped video of armor charging over a trench line on Hawaii, cannons blazing as they counterattacked the Toth landing. The armor moved with a human grace, nothing like the stiff, predictable motions of the humanoid robots toiling around Phoenix.

"Data unavailable," the computer said. "Would you like to watch the special features that came with your purchase of *The Last Stand on Takeni*?"

"I've seen that movie a thousand times. No. Have any armor soldiers mustered out of service since the war ended?"

"Data unavailable."

"Is it restricted or does it not exist?"

"Data unavailable."

He rolled his eyes and almost slapped the slate against the bed frame to punish it for insolence.

"What *is* available about the Armor Corps fortress on Mars? Mount Olympus?"

A pic taken from orbit of the largest mountain in the solar system, a wisp of clouds breaking against the slope, came up. Geologic data scrolled beneath the photo.

"The Terran Union Armor Corps headquarters within Mount Olympus is one of the most active military installations in the solar system," the computer said. "The location sustained damage during the Second Xaros Incursion and is currently off-limits to all civilians."

"How many armor soldiers are there?"

"Data unav—"

"How many casualties did the Armor Corps suffer last year?"

"Data—"

Roland clicked the slate off and tossed it onto the

desk.

"Why am I doing this to myself? If I wanted to do a stint in black ops, I should just try for Intelligence. No spikes in my brain there." He went to the door and hooked a finger beneath the monitor. "Just take it off, go to the robot at the barracks door. Forget all this…" He tugged at the monitor and pushed the door open.

The edge bumped into someone standing just outside his room. Masako, her hand raised to knock, backpedaled away, her eyes squished shut in pain.

Roland froze, his jaw slack.

"Sorry," she said, rubbing a hand against her elbow.

"No, it was me. I didn't know you were out there." He plucked his finger from the monitor and smoothed it shut against his skin.

"Thought I saw you with this thing in the mess hall." She tapped her own monitor. "Guy next door said this was your room, so I…"

"I thought you were going medical?"

"Me too, then I got to thinking that I'd probably never have this chance again… Why go through life wondering 'what if?' If this doesn't work, then medical is still there." She shrugged. "Looks like things are going well for you."

"I don't know about that...you have any idea what's next?"

"Not a clue." She glanced down the hallway, then leaned toward him. "Did you have to do some sort of VR sim in Hawaii?"

"No, I think I was out near the Superstition Mountains, way east of here. There was this pilot and—"

A clearing throat startled Roland bad enough to make him rattle the handle on his door. Gideon stood in the doorway of a room ten feet away; lieutenant rank on his shoulder epaulets, the glistening silver helm Armor Corps badge above rows of ribbons stacked high on his chest.

Roland snapped to his best approximation of the position of attention. Masako clutched her hands to her chest.

"I'm so sorry," she said. "Are we not supposed to—"

"Taps in ten minutes," Gideon said. "I suggest you get as much sleep as possible."

"Yes, sir, thank you sir." Masako pointed to the restrooms down the hallway. "I'll just...and then..."

Gideon shut his door.

"Does he scare you?" she whispered.

"A little. Not as much as the other one."

"Well, good luck tomorrow." She gave him a wink and hurried away.

Roland stumbled with a reply, then retreated into his room. He reached for his monitor…and let his hand flop against his side.

"We'll see how tomorrow goes. At least I'm in good company."

****

Roland woke up to the sound of screaming and the crash of metal on metal. The sound came muffled through the walls, from the open bays on the same floor as his room…and through the floor. He glanced at his slate…the clock read just shy of five in the morning.

Someone moved across the light coming from beneath his door and he heard a slight hiss of paper sliding across the floor—a small envelope, its shadow stretching into the darkness. He put his bare feet on the cold linoleum and stared at the missive for a moment.

"Maybe it says 'read me.'" He picked it up and read CANDIDATE SHAW in the low light. The lights clicked on and a trumpet song blared from speakers in his issued data slate, sitting next to his personal device on the desk.

Ripping the green envelope open with his thumbnail, he removed a folded piece of paper.

"'Room 12A. 0530. In-processing attire.' What?" Roland flipped the paper over, looking for another clue, then heard feet shuffling in the hallway. He cracked the door open and watched as two candidates walked past, both carrying their packs on their shoulders and monitors in hand. One had a crushed red envelope in his fist, muttering to himself as he left.

Masako, her hair a disorganized mess, waggled a green envelope at Roland from her room across the hall. Roland flashed his own and felt his heart beat faster with a touch of hope.

Shutting his door, he heard the screaming coming through his windows. He looked out and saw formations of young men and women engaged in calisthenics, hounded by drill sergeants wearing olive-drab campaign hats, who seemed to grow angrier by the second. He imagined that Jerry was out there in the predawn light and wondered if his friend was more confident than he in his choice of service.

Roland slapped the paper against his palm.

"Maybe what's in this room is worse than the drill instructors."

****

Room 12A held a pair of cubicles. Stepping inside, Roland found a man on one knee, his head bent in prayer; he gulped when he noticed the plugs at the base of the man's skull. The kneeling man held a sword by the hilt, the tip pressed into the carpet by his foot. The pommel was round, with a red Templar cross, and the man spoke in a language Roland didn't understand.

As he glanced at a clock, he found he was a minute early. He raised a hand to knock, but the man stood up exactly at the moment the clock hit 0530.

Tongea reached into a cubicle, brought out a scabbard, slammed the sword home and turned to Roland, who still had his hand ready to knock. Tongea's uniform bore only his nametag, the silver Armor Corps badge and a white circle with a cross identical to the one on the sword just below the armor badge.

"Chin up." Tongea raised his own chin and Roland followed suit. The soldier swiped two fingers across the monitor on Roland's neck and he heard a chirp from a slate in a cubicle. "You're clear to continue. Follow me."

Tongea went down the hallway, Roland a step

behind him.

"Sir…can I ask you a question?"

"You just did."

"Yes. No. I mean can I ask you another question? Not including that one. More questions."

"You can ask, but I will not answer unless it's to clarify my instructions to you," Tongea said. Roland bit his lip, realizing that silence was probably the better option.

Tongea turned down a dimly lit hallway and Roland felt the humidity rise. The smell of saltwater rose as the soldier opened a white door. Inside was a white pod the size of a large coffin. A hatch lifted and light glinted off the water within. A screen separated a bench and shower from the rest of the room.

"Candidate Shaw, you will begin a sensory-deprivation exercise of undetermined length. Should you choose not to participate or to end the exercise early, you will be dropped from selection. Do you have any questions?" Tongea asked.

Roland looked at the pod and got a good smell of the briny water within.

"What do I…do in there?"

"I will explain more once you've begun the exercise." He opened a basket next to the door and handed

Roland a pair of shorts, then pointed to the screen and turned his back to the room.

Roland shrugged and changed behind the screen, then he stuck a foot into the pod and found the water lukewarm. He slid inside and his body floated with ease. A bit of salty water splashed onto his lips, and he spat to drive it away.

"When you said 'undetermined length,' exactly—"

Tongea pressed a hypo injector against Roland's bare chest and Roland felt a chill spread across his sternum and into his stomach.

"Hey, what was that?"

The soldier shut the pod hatch, and lights flickered on. Roland reached up and pushed against the roof. It didn't budge.

"A digestion inhibitor." Tongea's voice came through a speaker behind Roland's head. "The reason for that should be self-evident. The exercise will begin shortly."

"Wait…what am I supposed to do in here?"

"The armor interface nodes are similar to the pods. Candidates must be able to endure such conditions and this exercise will test your mental and physical resilience. You are not required to do anything, but any attempt to open the pod hatch will terminate the exercise and you will be dropped from selection."

Roland sloshed around and felt like a very large fish in a very small tank.

"So just…lay here?"

"Correct."

The lights switched off and Roland found himself in pitch-blackness. His heartbeat thumped in his ears. When he moved a leg to the side and gently pushed against the pod, his head and shoulder bumped against the wall.

Did this thing get smaller? He raised a hand and it touched the roof…mere inches above the waterline.

It definitely got smaller. He let out a slow breath and reminded himself that he wasn't claustrophobic. At all. And this wasn't the time to pick up the phobia.

Of course the armor pilots don't control their suits like they're driving a car or flying a plane. They wouldn't use the plugs if that was the case…so how do they even see in these things? He reached across his chest and pinched a bicep, appreciating the brief moment of discomfort against the otherwise null chamber.

How long will this last? A day? They don't expect me to starve in here…well, I'd probably die of thirst first. Can't drink this water, too salt—wait…who else has used this? Did they pee in here?

He braced his hands against the pod, his heart beating faster until he remembered the digestion inhibitor Tongea had given him.

The absolute isolation of the pod was a different experience. He'd been in the orphanage since he was a child, surrounded by other children constantly. The last time he'd been this alone…was in Utah, during the second Xaros invasion.

He, and dozens of other military children, had been in a bunker hidden within Signal Peak in the mountains outside St. George, one of the few cities partially intact after the alien occupation. He remembered a young woman who had tried to keep him and the other children calm during the attack. He didn't remember her name, but he remembered the fear in her eyes.

An iceberg tip of fear touched his chest as he remembered the lights cutting out after a direct hit to a neighboring bunker…clutching the woman's hand and pretending she was his mother as other children wailed and sobbed around him.

He banished the memory with a shake of his head.

I'm not some terrified child anymore. The war is over. I am here. In Phoenix. This is all just a test.

He forced his mind to replay the last battle of the Smoking Snakes, armor that had held back Xaros forces on Takeni, buying time for a ship full of Dotok refugees to escape from the doomed planet. He knew much of the movie had been "embellished" for morale reasons, but the part where the Smoking Snakes had volunteered without question or coercion to stay behind and give their lives so that the Dotok could escape…no one ever questioned that part.

What makes them that way? How can someone just look certain death in the eye and charge? I don't know if I've got that in me.

He touched the roof, his arm tense, ready to push the hatch up and end what felt more and more like a poor choice.

No. Mom didn't give up. Neither did Dad. He lowered his arm and let it float.

His mind wandered…to memories of armor videos, to Jerry in the Marines, to Masako.

After a while—he had no way of knowing exactly how many hours—shapes appeared in the darkness, roiling black and white fractals swimming across his vision.

"Whoa…" He splashed his legs in the water and the images receded. "That's not normal. Right?" His heart beat faster and a sense of dread came over him…almost like there was something in the tank watching him.

They're messing with me.

He relaxed and concentrated on the feeling of the saltwater climbing up and down the side of his face.

How long do they stay in these tanks anyway? Warship crews, Marines and fighter pilots had fought for several straight days against the Xaros…did the armor ever get out?

A white line appeared across his vision. Roland didn't react, assuming it was another hallucination…until the hatch opened and lights turned on. Tongea reached into the pod and grabbed Roland by the upper arm and helped him sit up.

"How long was that?" Roland asked.

"This training evolution is complete. Get out. Now."

Roland tried to muster the strength, but his muscles were like jelly. He managed to flip over after considerable—and embarrassing—effort. As he swung a leg out, he noticed he wasn't in the same room. The pod sat next to a sparring mat; on the other side was another pod. Gideon stood next to the open hatch, speaking to another candidate who was having as much trouble as Roland.

"You were in the Scout Auxiliary, correct?" Tongea asked.

"Yes, sir." Roland got out of the pod and took a wobbly step.

"Then you're familiar with unarmed combatives rules. None of those apply here. Your next exercise is to retrieve the armor badge in the center of the sparring mat and bring it to me. The other candidate has the same instructions." Tongea pointed to a small bit of silver in the center of the mat. "Go."

The other candidate was half a head taller than Roland, wider at the shoulders and a good deal more muscled. The larger candidate wiped water from his eyes and nodded as Gideon spoke to him.

Roland took an unbalanced step onto the mat, feeling like he'd just woken up from a long night's sleep. The idea of fighting the other man—who was having as much trouble walking as Roland—did not strike him as a winning proposition. He leaned forward and broke into a run, his eyes fixed on the silver badge.

He heard the other candidate's wet feet stomp against the mat as the two closed on the prize.

Roland dove forward…and landed a foot shy of the

badge. Lurching forward, he snatched the silver badge just as the other candidate ran past, his hand scraping against the mat to scoop it up. Roland gripped the badge in his fist, feeling two metal spikes pressing against his palm. He got to his feet and squared off against the other candidate, who stood between Roland and Tongea.

"Give it up now and I won't have to hurt you," said the other man.

"Get out of the way and I won't have to—" Roland ducked under a haymaker and swung a punch into the other man's ribs that landed with a wet smack. He took a counterpunch on the shoulder, a blow that landed with enough force to send a jolt down his arm.

Roland snapped a kick toward his opponent's inner thigh and went almost horizontal as his base foot slipped on the wet mat. Landing with a thud, Roland's skull bounced off the mat. He brought his guard up just as the other fell on top of him. Roland snapped a short punch into his opponent's jaw and knocked the man's face to the side.

The larger man lifted his head back, then slammed his forehead into Roland's face. The blow smacked the back of his head against the mat again, and Roland felt the world start spinning. The man jammed his fingertips into Roland's clenched fist holding the badge and tried to pry the hand open.

Roland released his grip and the badge fell onto his chest. He snatched it up with his other hand.

The other slammed a hand against Roland's neck and tried to rip his monitor away. Roland panicked and let go of the badge. He gripped his opponent by the wrist, twisting his neck side to side to save the monitor. The big man, assisted by Roland's hold, lifted him a foot off the ground, then slammed his head into the mat.

Roland kept his hold, but his arms felt like they belonged to someone else. The big man lifted Roland again and slammed his other hand into Roland's nose, breaking it with a wet crack. He slammed Roland's head down again, and Roland went limp, his eyes lolling in their sockets as he coughed on blood.

The victor picked up the pin and carried it to Gideon, keeping an eye on the semiconscious Roland.

Watching the ceiling lights swirling overhead, Roland tried to remember where he was and exactly what he was supposed to be doing. Tongea leaned over him, speaking into a wrist mic.

"Bring that guy back here!" Roland struggled to sit up, but Tongea gently pushed him back down.

"He's got my…thing." Roland gagged on blood and

rolled onto his side, letting the flow of blood pool on the mat instead of running down his throat.

"Guess he didn't win." Roland recognized Dr. Eeks' voice. He felt a press of a hypo spray against the side of his neck and the world snapped back into focus. Someone pulled him up to a sitting position and guided his head to hang forward. Tongea pressed gauze into his hand and Roland mashed it against his broken nose, feeling cartilage wiggling beneath the skin.

He felt something touch his wrist, then realized his monitor was broken, hanging loosely against his neck.

"No! I didn't take it off," Roland said, his eyes wide with panic. "I still want to be here. I still want to do this. Don't cut me. I didn't—"

"I saw everything, candidate," Tongea said. "You didn't take it off. You're still in selection."

Eeks clenched a fist twice, then her fingertips lit up. She waved her hand across Roland's face and glanced down at her forearm screen.

"Minor concussion…but the CSF injection's mitigated the effects." She snapped her fingers, and her fingertips went dim. "Don't need fifteen years of medical school to know his nose is broken. I'll take him to medical for a new monitor."

"What about my nose?" Roland swallowed hard, sending a very unfortunate amount of blood to his stomach.

"It's on almost sideways now. I think it's an improvement," Eeks said.

Roland blinked hard, wondering just how hard he'd hit his head.

"And I'll fix your nose too. Demands, demands, demands." She and Tongea lifted him onto his feet.

"We have a schedule," Tongea said.

"Not my first rodeo, Tongea, I'll be back in time for the next victim," Eeks snapped. She led Roland out a door and into a brightly lit hallway. He kept the gauze pressed to his nose, trying to keep the blood from dripping onto the floor.

"I'm a washout," he said. "I didn't get the badge to him."

"Did you quit?" Eeks asked.

"No. I got my ass kicked."

"Then I think you'll be all right. Armor Corps needs a certain kind of person, and if we insisted on candidates that were undefeated champions in everything ever…we wouldn't have anyone. You'd be surprised how many candidates quit the moment they realize they're going to have to struggle. We can teach you to win a fight, but we need to know you have the resolve to learn."

"Are the lessons always this painful?" Roland asked as they passed by a group of female recruits. That he was in a bathing suit, wet and bloody, got him a few comments and giggles as he went by.

"Son, you're just getting started," Eeks said.

CHAPTER 5

Roland sat at a round table in the mess hall, staring at his tray. His nose, reset and repaired by an auto-surgeon, throbbed with pain. His new monitor felt tighter than the last one, but he put that to swelling from the other candidate's grip. He touched his nose and winced. The robot that fixed him said the pain would go away in a day or so…pain that couldn't be dampened with anything stronger than aspirin, as medication interfered with the monitors.

A chair scraped against the floor next to him and Masako sat down. She looked tired, the black ring of bruised flesh and a split lip accentuating the fatigue on her face.

"This was *not* in the recruiting commercial," she said.

"Do you know how long we were in the tank?" he

asked.

"Must have been...twelve hours. We got in before breakfast, got out and then beatings commenced and now its dinnertime. Did you win?"

"No. You?"

"I got the badge to the cadre with the face tats." She stuck her fork into a plate of shrimp scampi and frowned. "I haven't seen the girl I fought."

Someone large came up to Roland's other side, casting a shadow over them both.

"Hey, Roland," said the man who had beat him so soundly, holding a tray with a steaming bowl on it. "It's Roland, right? I...I'm sorry about that. Didn't mean to hurt you so bad. Adrenaline. If it makes you feel better, you broke two of my ribs. Name's Burke."

"You broke my face." Roland put his foot on the open seat next to him and pushed it aside for Burke.

"Thanks. I get the weirdest looks because of the monitor." Burke set his tray down and gave Roland a thump on his shoulder.

"Wait a minute...you two are friends all the sudden?" Masako asked.

"It wasn't like we were fighting 'cause we're sore with each other," Burke said, biting into a slice of corn bread, "just fighting for fighting. He got some good hits in."

"He showed me that the mat is not my friend." Roland cut off a piece of breaded chicken and forced himself to take a small bite.

"Men…" Masako said, shaking her head. "When women fight each other, we become enemies for life."

"You see the fruit salad of ribbons on that one cadre?" Burke asked. "He's got the Cygnus campaign ribbon. That fight just ended. Bet he's got some stories to tell."

"The other's got a new vat-grown arm," Roland said. "Looks older than the other, but no ribbons. Seem odd to you?"

"Either of you have the guts to ask him about it?" Masako slipped a spoonful of chopped vegetables into the undamaged side of her mouth.

The two men shook their heads.

"Me neither," Masako admitted.

****

Gideon swiped his hand across a holo screen and the image flipped over to a Ranger standing in line for at food combiner.

"This one?" he asked Tongea.

"He had a borderline panic attack three hours into the pod test." The Maori tapped a screen on their control station and the Ranger's service record came up. "He received a Bronze Star on Victoria after digging out his sister squad from a building collapse. His psych profile had a marked shift after that."

"He was hesitant during the combatives assessment. Drop without prejudice. Let him try again after another term." Gideon crossed his arms in front of his chest.

"I agree. He'll get his envelope in the morning. Next."

The holo jumped to Masako, Burke and Roland sitting in the mess hall.

"One has a high risk of plug rejection," Gideon said.

"There's always risk. We send them all to Knox for the next phase and Eeks can get a better neural workup. They all volunteered. They'll all know the risk before they reach Mars. If any of them reach Mars."

"None of them were as good as my old lance," Gideon said.

"They're un-tempered. It is our duty to forge them

into armor."

"They're cherries, all three of them. You know the success rate compared to those that have done a term, that have experience."

"And you know that some of the greatest of us went straight to Knox for the trials." Tongea touched his forehead then crossed himself.

"I don't keep to your faith. Just because one woman made it through against the odds doesn't mean everyone else deserves the same chance. Don't let the cross of yours cloud your judgement. We take these cherries to Knox, they'll drop for loss of motivation. That's a drop with prejudice, never get a shot again. We send them to the Marines or the Fleet for a few years, then one of them has a decent chance of making the cut."

"The Saint's path was as her own, just as these three will have their chance to prove themselves," Tongea said.

"I'll save an 'I told you so' for when the last of them drops. Send the notice. Let's get out of Phoenix," Gideon said.

Tongea tapped at a control pad and the three candidates on the screen looked down at their slates, and then at each other. They shrugged their shoulders and began eating as fast as they could.

CHAPTER 6

A miniature auto-bus pulled up next to a Mule transport ship, its ramp down and engines idling. Roland and a dozen other candidates piled out of the bus and stared at the Mule. He'd seen the plane in countless videos, played with them as toys, and even flown a small RC version during a Christmas when a foster family took him in for the holiday.

Roland had never been to the military terminal of the Phoenix spaceport, only ever caught glimpses through the outer fences while traveling through the city. Being so close to an actual Mule, feeling the hot exhaust from the jets and smelling the ozone from the anti-gravity thrusters was almost a dream come true. Larger Destrier transports and Eagle fighters flew overhead. A pair of the air/void supremacy fighters angled up and roared to the heavens.

Tongea came down the ramp. Not bothering to try to speak over the engines, he pointed at the candidates with a knife hand, then to the ramp.

Roland found his pack in the cargo compartment in the side of the bus then raced up the ramp. A long, thigh-high pallet with a top over it was secured to one side of the deck near a row of seats. Roland went to an open seat on the other side where a group of men and women in army and navy fatigues were already seated. Roland guessed there must have been a reason they were all on that side of the Mule and sat down next to a soldier in his early twenties.

"Hi," Roland said. The soldier looked at him out of the corner of his eye.

"Put your pack under your seat." The words sounded artificial, like they were coming from a speaker, and the soldier's mouth hadn't moved. He shoved his pack into webbing beneath his seat then stuck a fingertip into his ear and wiggled it.

Engine noise, or maybe getting my clock cleaned messed up my hearing, he thought.

The rest of the candidates boarded the Mule, and most ended up on the other side where the long pallet offered very little in the way of leg room.

"Guess you're on to something," Roland said. The soldier to his left ignored him.

A flight tech came from around a bulkhead separating the cockpit from the cargo bay.

"If this is your first flight in a Mule, then you'd better listen up," she said. "The Terran Union builds these for form and function, never comfort. So if you think I'm going to bring you a bag of peanuts—or anything but the stink eye—you are wrong. Strap in. Our pilot is either incredibly talented or a maniac, depends who you ask. Either way, this won't be a smooth trip. The restraints are so easy a child could figure them out. Tell me if you're having trouble so I can come and mock you. My name is Fitzsimmons. Don't bother me."

Roland put his arms through the shoulder straps and buckled the two sides together and it tightened automatically against his chest.

"Waist strap," came the speaker voice. Roland looked around for the source, then stretched a hand down the lip of his seat and found a third strap.

The soldier sitting next to him lifted his right hand, and the fingers snapped open with a click. He put his fingertips against his shoulder strap and his fingers clamped together, missing the strap. He tried again, his hands just as stiff and mechanical as the last time.

The engines whined louder.

"Can I help you?" Roland asked.

The soldier looked at him, his jaw set, then nodded quickly. Roland got out of his seat and got the other man buckled in. He looked up and saw a small speaker embedded in the base of his throat.

"Thank you," the soldier said, his words natural, but dissociated.

Roland got back into his seat as Fitzsimmons glared at him from the edge of the ramp, her hands on her hips. She tapped a panel on her gauntlet, and a hatch opened on the ceiling. A short ladder descended from a ball turret. Gideon ran up the ramp and jumped onto the ladder. He climbed into the turret, and the hatch sealed him away from the rest of the Mule.

"Riding turret comes with the best view," the soldier said, "unless you're getting shot at, then the novelty wears off real quick." He extended a fist to Roland and his hand popped open, ready to be shaken.

Roland gave the hand a gentle shake and felt servos beneath the plastic skin.

"Jonas Aignar," the soldier said.

"Roland Shaw, sir," he said.

"Don't 'sir' me. I used to be a sergeant. Besides, the Armor Corps makes us all privates until we get our plugs or we wash out." Aignar's jaw never opened as he spoke, nor did his mouth move at all. "First time on a Mule? Same with all the others?"

"That's right for me. Probably the others." Roland shrugged.

A twinkle came to Aignar's eye as Fitzsimmons raised the ramp.

"Something I should know?" Roland asked.

"Get sleep if you can." Aignar rolled his shoulders forward, then snuggled his head against his seat.

The Mule lifted off suddenly, and Roland felt g-forces push him against the back of his seat, then slide him against the candidate to his right, who seemed to have missed his last three chances at a shower.

A few harrowing minutes later, the Mule levelled off. Fitzsimmons left her seat near the ramp, went to a hatch in the floor, pulled a lever and lifted it up. Roland watched as another turret descended and locked into place against the bottom hull. Through the turret glass, he made out city lights below.

Tongea came out from the cockpit and jumped into the turret.

"Think we're in for trouble?" Roland asked Aignar, but he was fast asleep.

Catching Burke's eye across the cargo bay, he gave him a wave. Burke waved back, then kicked his feet up on the pallet.

Roland tapped his fingers against his thighs, wondering just how long this flight would last. At least there was a good deal more to look at than the inside of a sensory-deprivation pod.

After a half hour, Fitzsimmons stumbled out of the cockpit, one hand against her stomach. She put a hand on Aignar's knee to steady herself as she made her way back to her seat. Aignar sat up and rubbed sleep from his eyes.

"Who the hell...oh, I know," Aignar said.

"What? Something wrong?" Roland asked.

Fitzsimmons jammed an airsickness bag against her mouth and vomited. Loudly. Conversation died away and everyone stared at the flight tech as she threw up again. She wiped green liquid from her mouth, then sealed the bag with trembling fingers. She passed the bag to the candidate to her left, then gestured to the front of the cargo bay, shaking her head furiously.

The candidate held the bag with his fingertips, then passed it toward the front of the cargo bay.

The bag came to Roland, held by trembling fingers from the man to his right.

"Tell them to trash it. Hurry!" the other candidate said, nose pressed to his elbow.

Roland grimaced, took it and reached across Aignar's chest to the woman in black navy fatigues.

Aignar laughed, a simple, robotic "Ha ha ha."

"I think I'm going to be sick." Roland swallowed hard as turbulence rattled the deck.

The sick bag made it to the last person on Roland's side of the cargo bay, another flight tech. The tech got out of his chair, bag in hand, and went to a garbage chute in the middle of the forward bulkhead. He opened the chute, then sniffed at the bag.

"What is wrong with him?" Roland felt blood drain from his face.

The tech took a long-handled spoon from a pocket, opened the sick bag…and started eating.

Cries of shock and horror erupted from the candidates as the tech licked his fingers. The veterans began laughing hysterically.

Roland dry-heaved and looked away from the horror show.

"You puke on me and I will beat your ass," Aignar

said.

Roland put his hand to his mouth and clenched his stomach.

"Soup. It's just pea soup, you damned cherry," Aignar said. "Fitzsimmons dumped it in the bag. Other tech's in on the joke. Calm down."

Roland's revulsion subsided. Across the cargo bay, Masako and another candidate both had sick bags to their mouths.

"You're serious?" Roland asked.

"Yes." Aignar looked at him, his jaw perfectly set, his eyes alight with mischief. "This is my serious face."

"Who does this kind of thing? Pretending to eat— urk." Roland squeezed his eyes shut.

"That joke's almost as old as flight. They'll be rolling for days if any of you actually puke."

"Any other pranks I should know about?"

"No, that's the only one there is."

Roland gave Aignar a dirty look, not believing a word he had just said.

"Don't suppose you know where we're going?" Roland asked.

"Fort Knox, out in the wildlands that used to be Kentucky. Old home of the Atlantic Union Armor Corps. I heard Louisville was resettled. Maybe they'll let us out for a pass, but I doubt it. You've been in the service for what, three days?"

"That's right...what's going to happen when we get there?"

"Your guess is as good as mine. I was infantry for three years; details on armor were few and far between. All the brass ever told us was to stay the hell out of their way and how to recover one of them out of a downed suit." Aignar looked away, his gaze unfocused.

"Why all the secrets? Doesn't that hurt their recruiting efforts?"

"If you knew the answer, would it matter?"

"Well...might help me figure out what they want from me."

"And you'd act differently. It wouldn't be the real you. Ranger selection is similar. Same with the Strike Marines. Stress and uncertainty will bring out what they're looking for, or it'll break you."

"So I may not have it...great."

"You're on a bird to Knox, cherry. It means you've gone farther than sixty percent of other applicants. I think you're doing all right."

Roland felt a shift in his seat as the Mule began its

descent. A few minutes later, the craft slowed to a stop midair and set down with a bone-jarring thump. Roland made out little more than darkness beyond the windows.

"Stay seated!" Fitzsimmons ordered as she lowered the ramp.

Gideon and Tongea emerged from the turrets and removed the tarp from the long pallet. Beneath was a long box of folded machinery and armor plating. With a cadre member on either side, the box rose on anti-grav suspensors and they carried it down the ramp and clear of the Mule.

Gears on the box came to life and mechanical arms unfolded from the sides. A fist slammed to the ground and a torso rose up. A helm fashioned after the knights of old emerged from the shoulders, optics flashing beneath a visor slit. The full suit stood up, dark panels of armor plating sliding into place over the entire fifteen-foot-tall frame and locking together with a click.

Roland's jaw hung agape. The rest of the candidates stared on in silence.

The armor looked down at Tongea and Gideon, then slammed a fist against its breastplate with a ring of metal on metal. Tongea looked over his shoulder to Fitzsimmons.

"Up and out!" She lifted her hands over her shoulders several times for emphasis.

Roland hurried out of his seat, helped Aignar with his buckle, then raced down the ramp with his pack over his shoulder and fell into a line of candidates forming in front of Gideon. A dark forest surrounded the landing pad, and humid air enveloped him like a fist. The armor looked over each of the candidates, the massive helm turning from side to side.

"Which of you" —the words boomed from speakers embedded in the armor's shoulders— "which of you maggots put your feet on me?"

Fear rose in Roland's chest, even though he knew he was innocent.

The armor swung its helm to Tongea.

"They're going to make me ask twice?"

"Me!" Burke squeaked. Roland's fear grew, as Burke was standing right next to him. "It was me, sir...or ma'am. I didn't know that you were—"

The armor stomped over to Burke's place in line, growls emanating from the speakers. It leaned forward and slowly extended a fist the size of an engine block toward Burke's face. A metal finger the thickness of Roland's arm snapped open to the exact width of Burke's head. The armor snapped his grip into a fist, earning a whimper from Burke.

"Find your iron." The armor stepped back as its legs transformed into treads, and it rolled away toward a gap in the tree line.

"Candidates," Gideon said, snapping on a flashlight and pointing it after the armor and into the forest, "follow me."

****

Roland wasn't sure which was worse—the high heat and humidity or the mosquitos that constantly attacked his exposed skin. They'd hiked up and down hills for the better part of an hour in the moonlit night without a word from the two cadre. He shifted his pack against his shoulder, surprised at just how heavy so little gear could get.

"Think I see some light," Burke said from behind him. "Over the top of this hill, which is number nine thousand and twelve by my count."

"Yeah, there's a glow." Roland wiped a sleeve across his forehead.

"Light at the end of the tunnel. You think it's a train?" Burke asked.

"Shh!" Masako hissed. "You think maybe there's a

good reason no one else is talking?"

"Cadre have us wired up," Burke said, tapping his monitor. "I don't think idle conversation is something to keep hidden."

"Talking…" Roland grimaced as a blister on the side of his foot sent a sting of pain up his leg, "talking makes these hills a little harder. Yes?"

"Navy doesn't have to walk anywhere. Just sayin', is all," Burke muttered.

Gideon stopped just as he crested the hill. Down the slope, Fort Knox spread out along a valley. Rows and rows of warehouse-sized buildings were laid out in a grid, all lit by flood lamps. A perimeter of tall, reinforced fencing patrolled by small drones and armed security bots surrounded the base. Smaller, two-story buildings that looked like something out of a black-and-white video from the Second World War clustered next to a larger square building with a lit sign atop oversized doorways.

Gideon took a deep breath through his nose. "Candidates, welcome to Fort Knox, the first home of the Armor Corps."

He led them down the hill, which Roland found to somehow be worse on his knees, through the outer fence and down a roadway lined with tanks on either side, toward the large building Roland had seen from the hilltop. The tanks were re-creations—the Xaros had left nothing behind beyond a few cities in the American West—of armor from the turn of the twentieth century to the last version of the vaunted M1 Abrams, and they led to the glass doorway.

A soldier with an anti-grav pallet collected their packs as they came inside. The entrance was mercifully air-conditioned and another soldier passed out paper cups full of orange liquid.

A suit of armor stood motionless near the entrance, a brass plaque on a stand near its feet. The armor's limbs were metal frames, the torso a cage around a mannequin sitting inside, holding controls in both hands, a sensory helmet over the top of its head.

"This is the Mark I," Tongea said, holding up an open hand to the crude armor. "Ibarra Industries created the first suits during the early days of the Great Pacific War with China in 2058. The next version," he said as he walked over to another suit fully enclosed in metal plates, a massive belt-fed rifle larger than Roland in its hands, "saw combat across Australia and the Pacific Isles. Designed solely for terrestrial combat."

Across the hallway, Roland recognized the next model: a double-barreled gauss cannon mounted on one arm, the twin vanes of a rail cannon on its back, a Gatling gun on the other shoulder. One hand was withdrawn into the forearm casing, the tip of a spike in its place.

The suit was pockmarked, lines of welds and repair epoxy marring the armor like old scars. An iron-colored heart was below a stenciled name on the breastplate that read: ELIAS.

"The Mark III's and IV's fought in the Ember War. This is an earlier suit, before the aegis plating was implemented," Tongea said and turned to face the gaggle of candidates hanging on his every word. "The latest models are on Mars or deployed."

A set of double doors behind him opened to an auditorium. He led the candidates inside, where half the seats were already full of new recruits and a smattering of veterans.

"Take your seats. Fill in from the front." Tongea stepped aside.

The wooden stage held three flags: the Terran Union; a stained-glass image of an alien world from orbit set to cloth; and the flag of the Armor Corps. Roland followed Masako down a row, then froze as he did a double-take.

At the far end of a row, a half-dozen aliens sat next

to each other. The upper halves of their blue-gray heads were almost human, but they had blunted beaks for mouths and jaws. Thick black quills ran from their foreheads to the backs of their skulls. They chatted among themselves, quick clicks and muted squawks.

Burke gave Roland a gentle push.

"Move it. You act like you've never seen a Dotari before," Burke said.

Roland shuffled forward and sat next to Masako.

"On screen, not in person," Roland said, "and they're called Dotok."

"They changed soon as they got their home world back," Masako said. "The etymology of 'Dotok' in their language means 'one cut off from home.' Now they're 'of home' and Dotari." She shrugged. "We're the Terran Union now."

"How do you know all this?" Roland asked.

"Military Intelligence was my next choice after medical," she said. "I studied up just in case things didn't work out."

"Why do we need intelligence on our allies? Never mind. Why are there Dotari here?" Roland leaned over his seat to get a better look at the aliens.

"You know two of the armor in Memorial Square

were Dotari, don't you?" Masako shook her head at him. "What were you doing in high school?"

"Not paying enough attention," Roland said.

The lights dimmed and brightened several times and conversations died away.

A soldier walked onto the stage and clicked his heels together.

"Room! Atten-tion!"

The veterans snapped to their feet, and the new recruits stood up quickly, but not nearly as fast.

An army captain came onto the stage, his hands clasped behind his back.

"Be seated," he said. "I am Captain Perez, your company commander at Fort Knox. While you are here, you will be evaluated for mental and physical suitability to serve in the Armor Corps. You have all been officially accessed into the Corps on a probationary basis as privates—any rank you held before today is gone. You may choose to drop from training at any time, and I will return you to Phoenix for reassignment without any adverse action on your personnel file. Do not remove your monitors. Do not speak with candidates in other training cycles."

When he paced to the other side of the stage, Roland saw that the back of his head was normal. No plugs.

"All candidates who've completed a tour of duty, stand up and exit to the door to my right." Perez waited as the dozen veterans and all the Dotari left the room.

"The rest of you will now meet your drill instructors."

Doors on the other side of the auditorium opened with the force of a bomb blast. Soldiers in campaign hats swarmed into the room like sharks tearing into a wounded whale, bellowing orders at the top of their lungs.

One of the drill instructors grabbed Roland by the front of his uniform and hauled him to his feet, commenting on his parentage and lack of motivation and questioning if his IQ was above room temperature.

****

Roland pushed the door to his barracks room open, fell onto his hands and knees, twisted around and shut the door as quickly, and as quietly, as he could, while the shouts from drill instructors echoed up and down the hallway. He slumped to the ground, sweating buckets as his arms quivered with exhaustion.

"Good times?" Aignar asked from the back of the room.

Roland's head shot up and he froze like a deer caught in headlights. The room had two beds along the walls, small closets and desks, and a single sink. Aignar sat behind his desk, wearing a gray issued exercise T-shirt and holding a slate.

"They're all so…angry." Roland went to the sink and drank straight from the faucet. "I never knew there was a correct way to turn left and right, or around, or walk with people who don't know their left from their right."

"Drill and ceremonies…good times." Aignar set one edge of his slate on the desk, then dropped it as his fingers snapped open.

"Why was it just us newbies out there getting yelled at?" Roland opened the closet on his side of the room and found uniforms with his name on them hung up, each hanger equally spaced away from the others.

"Everyone with a complete term has already done basic training. The Air Force weenies had it easy compared to the rest of us—some things never change. You cherries need that same baseline." He gestured a stiff hand toward a slate on Roland's desk. "Training schedule is out. Looks like you have an additional hour of training at the beginning and end of every day."

The two beds were made, the corners folded into

forty-five-degree angles and the sheets pulled so tight that Roland wasn't sure if he was supposed to sleep under them.

"Did you...do all this?" Roland looked under his bed at a neat line of unpolished shoes and boots with straps instead of laces.

"I'm selfish that way," Aignar said. "If DIs come in here and see you're a soup sandwich, they'll crush me too. Now that you're here, I suggest you get through the assigned reading. I need some rack time."

When he stood up and walked around the desk, Roland saw that both his legs from the knee down were bionic. Gears in his metal and composite-plastic feet whirred with each step. Black rings circled his forearms close to the elbows, marking where the prosthetics ended and his flesh began.

Aignar sat on his bed and looked at Roland. "Just ask."

"About...what?" Roland turned his gaze to the floor.

"I got hit on Cygnus. First week of the campaign, too. Years of training and then a Vishrakath razor-wire grenade brought my Ranger career to a screeching halt. Trauma systems in my armor kept me from bleeding to death. Then I find out I'm something of a medical phenomenon—one of a very small percentage of human beings that can't take vat-grown organ replacements. Took six transplants to figure that out." Aignar's eyes flashed with pain for a moment.

"They offered me a discharge, full benefits and pension…but I'm not ready to be a cubicle mushroom. Armor will take anyone that can pass the screening, so here I am. I'm not the first broke dick to come through these halls. I won't be the last."

"If I can help you somehow…"

"They didn't let me leave the hospital on Maui until I could take care of myself." Aignar leaned forward and twisted the top of the prosthetic on one leg. His knee came out with a pop, leaving the shin and foot on the ground. He removed his other leg and shifted over on the mattress.

As he pressed one finger to the side of his jaw, there was an audible pop as Aignar's mouth snapped open a quarter inch.

"Now the tricky part." Aignar grabbed one arm and removed it with a snap. He put it on the desk behind the head of his bed, then looked at his still-attached arm, then to the one on the desk. "You mind?"

"Yes. I mean no. I mean sure." Roland stood up and rubbed his palms down his sides. "I need to…"

Aignar held his hand out to Roland.

"Just twist it to the left."

The faux-skin felt like thin leather as Roland gripped it. He grimaced and turned it slowly. The prosthetic popped free of the socket and Roland stepped back, holding the arm up to get a closer look.

The thing came alive and grabbed him by the wrist.

"Jesus Christ!" Roland tossed his hands up in shock and the prosthetic clattered to the floor as Aignar's monotone HA HA HA filled the room.

"Sorry," Aignar said, one elbow slapping against his side, "the look on your face. I'm sorry."

"You want help like this again? Not the way you're going to get it!" Roland crossed his arms over his chest, more embarrassed than angry.

"Really, I'm sorry." Aignar gestured to the arm on the ground with his chin. "Would you put it on the desk?"

Roland touched the prosthetic, snatched his hand back like it was a live wire and then set it next to the other arm.

Aignar got under his sheets and rolled over to face the wall.

"Roland, let me tell you something," he said as he nuzzled his head against his pillow. "Secret to happiness in the military is getting enough sleep."

Roland sat at his desk and looked over the slate. The schedule for the next day began entirely too early with physical training, then there was a long block of empty space until another period of physical training and drill instruction.

"Why's there nothing else on here? Shouldn't there be a plan?" Roland asked.

"One of two things." Aignar yawned. "Either the cadre have no idea what they're doing and they turn candidates into armor by accident, or they want us off balance to get used to working in a chaotic environment. Which do you think it is?"

"Latter." Roland went to the next tab and found his assigned reading: History of Armor during the Australian Conflict. "I thought I was done with homework after high school."

Aignar snored softly.

CHAPTER 7

Roland sat in a small classroom, his muscles aching from the physical training session with the drill instructors earlier. He thought sitting would help him feel better, but all it did was give his legs the opportunity to cramp up.

Gideon stood behind a small lectern, a thin metal pointer in one hand. He snapped the tip against a map of Australia covered in red and blue symbols, a snapshot in time from the Australian theater of the war between China and the Atlantic Union in the middle of the twenty-first century.

Roland rubbed his calf and glanced at the two Dotari a few seats from him. The aliens had been in the classroom when he and a dozen others arrived. Neither had spoken yet.

"Colonel Carius committed the 4th Regiment to the envelopment effort just north of Brisbane," Gideon said.

"What was the effect on the Chinese 3rd Army…Burke."
He leveled the pointer at the candidate's chest like he was a
fencer about to lunge forward and impale him.

Burke stood up and scratched at his monitor.

"The Chinese…got their asses kicked, sir," Burke
said.

Gideon snapped the pointer to his side. He
narrowed his eyes at the candidate.

"'Got their asses kicked' is not how we speak in the
Armor Corps. We use military terms and phrases from
doctrine whenever and wherever possible. Radioing your
commander and telling him there's a shitpot full of Ruhaald
guys with rifles attacking you is not as useful as saying a
battalion of dismounted infantry have engaged from the
ridgeline to your east. The proper terminology was in your
reading from last night. I'll see that you receive an
additional assignment tonight. Sit."

"The Chinese advance halted," Masako said. "The
Atlantic Union armor broke through their lines in a
double…envelopment. Chinese casualties were high."

"And why was Colonel Carius so successful?
Analog armor units—crewed tanks with turrets and
treads—from the American 1st Cavalry Division had
attacked through the same terrain days before with limited

success." Gideon looked over the candidates before tapping his pointer on Roland's desk.

"It was the first time armor, our kind of armor, was ever massed on the battlefield," Roland said, racing to pull up snippets from his fuzzy memory. "Before, they'd been used in four suit units called lances. So many used in one attack was too much for the Chinese to handle."

"Decent, but wrong." Gideon flicked his pointer to the wall behind his lectern, and a holo screen came to life. A highway, the shoulders crammed with civilian cars bulldozed off the road, stretched into the distance. Squat tanks and armored personnel carriers took up the road, spaced a dozen yards apart. The camera, which must have been ten feet off the ground, bounced along with the stomp of metal footfalls on the asphalt.

An armored fist smashed into the driver's hatch of the Chinese tank, and the turret swung toward the armor slowly. The armor jammed his belt-fed rifle into the gap between the turret and the hull and fired twice, the back of the tank exploding into flame as the ammunition cooked off. The armor charged through the flames and slammed hands down on the front of a personnel transport. The fingers crumpled the hull, then hefted the vehicle up onto its side. The armor shoved it over with a crunch of breaking antennae and abused metal.

A door on the overturned carrier popped open and a Chinese soldier scrambled out. He looked up at the armor, dropped his weapon and ran with a frightened yelp. The armor snatched the fleeing soldier by the leg and lifted him into the air.

"Sha xi ni!" boomed from the armor's speakers.

Bullets snapped through the air. The armor turned around and faced three more Chinese that had escaped their stricken APC. The armor raised the terrified soldier in his grip, then swung him like a club into his fellows.

Roland winced as the video captured the sound of breaking bones.

One Chinese, his arm badly broken from the impact, cowered against the side of the APC. The armor crushed him with a stomp, then flung the dead soldier in his hand down the highway, the corpse skipping like a stone over a pond until it came to a messy stop against another Chinese tank.

"Sha xi ni!" The armor charged toward the tank, firing its massive rifle from the hip. More armor suits joined the charge, all broadcasting the same message.

Gideon froze the replay just as a helicopter came around a hillside and exploded, the victim of massed fire from several armor soldiers.

"What were they saying?" the cadre asked.

The candidates shifted in their seats as more than one looked queasy from the brutality they'd just witnessed. Roland glanced at the two Dotari, but if they knew the answer, he couldn't tell.

"There are only a handful of native Chinese speakers left on the planet, prisoners of war picked up in the last few hours before the Xaros attack, and none of them are in this room," Gideon said. "But if you had to guess what was said...Yanagi?"

Masako tugged at her lip.

"Well, sir, it's not 'surrender.'"

"Prepare to die," a Dotari said. Roland assumed the alien was a she, given the mammary glands on her chest and slight stature compared to her broad-shouldered companion. "Or words to that effect. Your prewar languages are difficult for us."

"Sha xi ni," Gideon said as he whacked his pointer against the chair of a candidate dangerously close to nodding off, "roughly translates to 'I will kill you.' Did these words make a difference in the battle? Anyone?"

"It was the fear," the same Dotari said. "These other humans had never faced armor before. To come beak to beak with something so brutal while confined to those metal boxes, death must have seemed inevitable."

"Your name?" Gideon asked.

"Sub-Lieutenant Cha'ril," she said.

"And what gives you this insight, Sub-Lieutenant?"

"Dotari armor fought at the Battle of Firebase X-Ray, during the brief conflict with the Ruhaald and Naroosha. The Ruhaald, even though they had rudimentary armor of their own, were...intimidated by the Terran and Dotari armor."

The cadre touched a screen on the back of his hand and the holo changed to a painting. An armor soldier, an aegis shield mounted to a forearm, faced an alien tank shaped like a scorpion. Another suit of armor leaped through the air, a lance gripped in both hands angled down at the enemy tank. The artist had added semiopaque feathered hooks to the back of the airborne suit and a ray of sunlight that glittered off the lance.

"Fear." Gideon paced back and forth across the classroom. "Violence of action...*élan,* effective against the Chinese—against enemies that have the biological capacity for an ingrained resistance to death, these are useful tools. Tools you will learn to use. Armor, Terran and Dotari, have many roles to fill on the battlefield. Fire support with our rail cannons. Action in environments too hazardous for normal troops. All of this will be taught to you, but when it comes to instilling fear…you must find that iron within you."

"We're to be terror weapons?" Masako asked. "Did Ibarra have that in mind when he invented the suits?"

"Ibarra?" Cha'ril asked.

"Marc Ibarra," Gideon said, setting his pointer on the lectern, "was an inventor, businessman…and a manipulator. He had advance warning—decades in advance—of the Xaros invasions. Decades he used to engineer a solution to the overwhelming drone armada. A solution that led to the deaths of every man, woman and child in the solar system that wasn't part of his Saturn Colonization fleet the moment it sidestepped the invasion. That humanity survived, and won the war against the Xaros, is largely thanks to him. The Armor Corps is part of his legacy."

Gideon swiped a finger across his forearm screen and an oblong drone with bent spikes protruding from its surface came up on the screen. The drone's surface swirled with deep-gray fractals. Roland felt ice in his stomach as he looked upon a monster from childhood nightmares.

"This is a Xaros drone. It did not feel fear, or

remorse. It carried out programming to destroy and eradicate any and all intelligent life it encountered, and to build Crucible gates in systems with worlds habitable by the now-dead Xaros Masters. Ibarra knew what they were, their weaknesses. Why did he bother to create armor to fight them?"

"Didn't the drones hack almost every computer when they first attacked the system?" Burke asked. "The armor had someone inside, hardwired to the suit. There was nothing to hack. I'd rather be in armor fighting those things than in this," he said, patting his uniform.

"Sir, why don't we just ask Ibarra all this?" Masako half-raised her hand with the question. "I know he turned himself into some sort of hologram to survive the invasion. Where is he?"

"Marc Ibarra has…retired from public life." Gideon's hands balled into fists. "Let me ask you all this: if the armor was created to counter the Xaros, and the Xaros are gone, why do the Terran Union and the Dotari Hegemony maintain their own Armor Corps?"

"The final battle against the Xaros," Roland said. "When President Garret dedicated the monument to the ten armor that died, he said there would be an Armor Corps for the next five hundred years because of their sacrifice."

"I'm afraid it takes more than a politician's promise to make something a reality, Candidate Shaw." Gideon shook his head.

"I was on Cygnus," Aignar said, the speaker in his neck straining to match the volume he wanted. "I think I saw you there." He pointed a stiff hand toward the black-and-yellow patch on Gideon's right shoulder. "Saw you take out a platoon of Vish tanks with your bare hands, then wreck one of their gunships when you threw a hunk of metal through the cockpit. That was you?"

"I fought at the Briar Patch," Gideon said.

"We have armor because they make a difference on the battlefield," Aignar said. "There was only one phrase we infantry loved to hear on the radio, and that was 'armor in support.'"

"The Armor Corps is the force of decision," Gideon said. "Commanders will send you to the heaviest fighting, on the most dangerous missions, because they know we will not fail. We will not falter. That we are…armor. You are all here to find your iron."

Gideon picked up his pointer and collapsed it to the size of a pen.

"Time to lose your monitors," he said. "Dr. Eeks is waiting for you all in medical. On your feet."

****

A single auto-doc robot dominated the small surgical suite. The machine, which looked like a hunched-over beetle to Roland, was bolted to the floor. A half-dozen thin arms were folded against it, boxes full of medical equipment in antiseptic tubes forming a ring around the robot.

The smell of iodine was thick in the air. Roland rubbed his nose, unsure why such a modern marvel of engineering would have such a stench. He sat topless on a gurney with an opening on one end large enough for his face. Roland bumped his heels against the gurney's frame, wondering if the cold air and the wait were just another test.

Dr. Eeks strode into the room, her eyes fixed on her forearm screen, a vapor tube in her other hand.

"All right, Mr. Shaw." She took a puff on the tube and exhaled steam from her nose. The doctor twisted her tube around and offered it to Roland. "Take the edge off?"

"What? No…I don't…can you smoke in here?"

"Evidently," she said as she slipped the tube into the front of her lab coat. "Terrible habit to pick up. I practically had to beg Ibarra to get a new tobacco farm going in North

Carolina. I swear the old bastard dragged his holographic heels just to spite me for being able to enjoy my body. Take your monitor off."

She went to the auto-doc and brought up a holo screen showing Roland's body, his nervous system pulsing in blue beneath his skin.

"Won't I drop from the training if I do that?"

"Sharp cookie! I had one kid pee himself a little when he fell for that. No, won't drop you. You're about to get an upgrade." She double-tapped a button on the screen and the monitor around his neck loosened.

Roland rubbed the now-exposed flesh, relishing the feel of the cool air against his skin.

"I'm getting my plugs?"

"Ha! That comes later, much later. You are getting neural Tachikoma shunts—or nubs, if you don't want to be all medical like me." She took a small, clear box from a pocket and handed it to Roland.

Inside were four small, brass-colored pins with long spikes.

"They'll go into the base of your brain stem." She flicked her wrist twice, and her fingertips lit up. She wrapped a cold hand around the back of his neck and pressed her fingertips up and down his spine. "Everything looks normal. Questions?"

"Why can I ask you questions...but the rest of the cadre look like they want to rip my face off if I get curious about anything?"

Eeks gave him a gentle pat on the cheek.

"All of this is voluntary, you know that. Two of your buddies dropped out the moment I handed them their nubs. The idea of undergoing cybernetic augmentation is easy to accept," she said, jerking a thumb at the auto-doc. "Letting Boris over there start poking things into your gray matter is another reality entirely. It's important that you understand what's happening to you because if the nubs are too much to handle, then the plugs are beyond you."

"How're these different than the monitor...and the plugs?" Roland turned the case over in his hands.

"The nubs tap directly into your nerves and interface into the rigs. You can, if you choose, remove the nubs with a quick tug. Same consequences as removing the monitor. The plugs...are about half the size of an old railroad spike, and tie directly into your cerebellum. That augmentation is permanent."

"What if someone wants to leave the Corps? Go be a civilian...family and all that?"

"The rest of your biology works just fine." Eeks

suppressed a smile. "But ever since the Corps formed during the war with the Chinese, no one has ever chosen to leave. Those that end their watch are all sent to Olympus. Well, that's not entirely true. But we don't know where they went, so it's entirely possible that they—" Eeks froze, then turned her attention back to the auto-doc.

"Doctor? What're you talking about?"

"Casualties, my boy. Casualties," she said very quickly. "Redliners, killed in action. They're all interred beneath the mountain. If they even find their suits."

"Not that, who went where?"

Eeks brandished a finger at him, her demeanor now serious.

"No. I didn't say anything. You understand?" She looked at him hard with her pale blue eyes.

"I must have misheard you." Roland looked down at his knees.

"Facedown." She took the nubs from him. "You ready for this?" The happier Dr. Eeks had returned.

Roland wiggled his face into the opening and tried to make himself comfortable. The floor moved beneath him as Eeks brought the gurney to the auto-doc.

"The nubs are temporary, right?" he asked.

The gurney stopped.

"Mr. Shaw, if you've any doubts, we can stop the procedure and I can bring a cadre member to speak with you." She put a gentle hand on his shoulder. "I've been doing this for a long time, son. No soldier who's ever gone on to get their plugs and earn their spurs has ever told me they regret the decision. I carry the regret, for all those I send to war who never come back."

Roland propped himself up on his elbows and looked at her.

"There's a suit in the front hall," he said. "Name on it was Elias. He's one of the statues in Memorial Square. Did you know him?"

"That's an odd question to ask at a time like this."

"The last time I was there, this...lady talked about him. Seemed to think he was more important than the colonel that was in charge when the Xaros were defeated. Colonels are supposed to be brave, no fear. What about Elias? Who was he? Was he...scared when this happened to him?"

"I knew Elias," she said sadly. "I tried to help him after his redline, but it took someone stronger than me to save him. He wanted his plugs more than any candidate I've ever met. You'd think he was fearless, but I could see beneath the surface." She tapped her forearm screen. "Elias was afraid, but he never let his fear stop him. He was the best of us, and we are less without him. You make it to Mars and maybe the Templar will teach you more about him. So what'll it be?"

Roland lay down.

"Will this hurt?"

"We'll put you under a bit of local anesthesia. Can't have you scratch an itch while we're in your spinal cord. Before that, you might feel a slight pinch." Eeks wheeled him over and he heard the auto-doc come to life. There was a spritz of cold against the back of his neck and he squeezed his eyes shut.

****

The Fort Knox mess hall was different from the one at SEPS for one single reason—assigned seating. Roland's meal came with a small map showing where each candidate class was to sit. The classes that had arrived before him were down to one or two tables each.

He carried his tray past the more senior candidates, none of whom bothered to even look at him. With drill instructors waiting in the wings like tigers ready to pounce, Roland wanted to get seated before he gave one of them an excuse to come for him.

One of his tables was open, but it was mostly full of Dotari, all seated shoulder to shoulder and eating from bowls in the middle of the table. Cha'ril put a blue, walnut-looking bit of food into her beak and chomped down, snapping the shell. She nodded to Roland.

Roland stopped behind an open seat and asked, "Am I allowed to—"

"Sit down, Shaw!" a drill instructor shouted.

Roland sat down and hunched over his tray. There were two feet between him and Cha'ril to one side. The rest of the Dotari stopped eating and stared at him.

"Sorry," Roland half-whispered. "When they start yelling, things only get worse."

"Do you dislike us?" a Dotari asked.

"No. Why?"

Cha'ril grabbed the bottom of his chair and pulled him over with surprisingly little effort. He found himself shoulder to shoulder with the alien, his tray of food still where he'd left it.

"Why do Terrans sit so far from each other?" she asked. "The separate food…do you think the others will try to take yours away?"

"We just…um…" Roland slid his tray over. He

tried to shy away from Cha'ril's shoulder, but she—and the rest of the Dotari—swayed toward him. He sat up straight, wondering why the Armor Corps hadn't bothered to teach him anything about Dotari culture before this moment.

"How can you eat that mush?" Cha'ril plucked a steaming nut from a bowl and cracked it between her beak. She set it on Roland's tray; the white flesh inside the shell looked like a walnut to him.

"Dotari newborns have lips like yours," she said. "Our beaks do not form until partway through childhood. Try the *gar'udda*. They're fresh from home."

"Thank…you." Roland stuck a fork into the nut and pulled out a piece. *If I'm brave enough to get spikes put into my spinal column, then I can eat this.* He shoved the nut into his mouth and chewed while the Dotari watched him.

He took a sip of water and swallowed hard.

"It tastes like chalk. Very bitter chalk." He looked down at his tray.

"Another?" Cha'ril asked.

"No. Thank you."

Cha'ril's hand hovered over Roland's plate of chicken and rice mixed with an orange-colored sauce. The milky-white pointed nails on her thumb, pointer, and middle fingers clicked together, then she stuck a nail into a lump of Roland's chicken and popped it into her mouth.

She chewed a couple bites quickly, paused, then chewed again. Roland looked at his knife and fork, then at her fingers.

"What is this?" she asked.

"Chicken tikka," Roland said and paused, wondering just how avian the Dotari were, "imitation chicken. All the meat comes from a tube and...do you like it?"

"Too spicy." Cha'ril's flat nose flared slightly. She leaned close to his ear, examining the organ so different from the simple hole in the side of her head. She set her palm onto the top of his head and gently ruffled his short hair. Roland stayed still, unsure just how normal this sort of thing was among the Dotari.

"I've never seen a Terran up close before," she said.

"No kidding."

She sniffed the side of his neck, then spoke to the other aliens in their own language. They watched Roland while he ate as fast as he could swallow.

CHAPTER 8

Roland pressed his knuckles against the seal on his body glove and ran his fist down his side. The suit tightened around his legs and torso, leaving his hands, feet and neck uncovered. Burke struck bodybuilder poses in front of the locker next to Roland.

"Feel like a superhero in these tights," Burke said.

The sound of metal footsteps rang out on the other side of the lockers and Aignar walked around the corner. His bodysuit flapped open above his knees where the metal met flesh.

"You two going to make the cadre wait for us?" Aignar asked.

"Cadre are a lot easier to deal with than the DIs," Burke said. "The cadre act like they don't even care about us. The DIs know when I'm thinking the wrong thoughts." He tapped at the nubs on the back of his neck. "I swear they've got their own feed."

Other candidates in the same body gloves walked past them and out of the locker room.

"Get moving." Aignar jabbed a stiff hand toward Burke and slammed his locker shut.

"Guess it's tank time again." Burke elbowed Roland. "Good luck."

Roland cringed at the memory of the test in Phoenix and felt the new bruises Burke had given to him during the combatives training the night before.

On the other side of the door was a room with a dozen pods, all smaller than what Roland had experienced in Phoenix. Roland fell into the second row of candidates forming in front of Gideon and Tongea. An emergency medical robot stood against the wall, the status lights on its chassis blinking amber.

"Candidates," Tongea began. He stepped up onto a small platform with a holo control panel as Gideon went down the line, touching the side of each candidate's neck with a hypo injector. "This assessment will measure your physical suitability and mental fortitude. These tanks are a close match for the wombs used within the suits. You will be fully submerged within amniosis for an unspecified length of time. Any request to leave the pod early will result in termination. Any questions?"

"Sir?" Masako raised her hand.

"Stop raising your hand and just ask, Candidate Yanagi," Tongea said.

"How do we breathe if we're fully submerged?" she asked.

"Amniosis—the fluid within the womb—is hyper-oxygenated and serves as a life-support system in conjunction with the wombs. Your lungs and stomach will fill with the amniosis, rendering you less susceptible to shock and acceleration. Reaching equilibrium with your womb feels, until you get used to it, similar to drowning," Tongea said.

Gideon stopped in front of a wide-eyed and suddenly pale Roland. The cadre looked down at his forearm screen, then adjusted the dosage on the hypo injector. He pressed it to Roland's neck and the candidate felt something like ice water running from the injection site through his veins.

"As armor, you will be expected to endure high g-forces and jump directly into combat from orbit or from air assets." Tongea picked up an open can from the control station. "If your body is not in equilibrium with the womb, the effect is similar to this."

He dropped a pebble into the can and shook it, rattling the rock inside.

"How long can we last in there?" Burke asked.

"With regular amniosis replenishment," Tongea said, directing a candidate in the front rank to a pod, "a soldier can survive almost indefinitely. Most can't go more than a few months before the wither sets in. Without fresh amniosis, no more than ten days. After that, you will die from lack of oxygen."

Roland waited until Tongea pointed him to the seventh pod. The floor beneath his feet was ice-cold, and he wasn't sure if the shiver in his shoulders was from the cold or fear. The pod hatch opened with a snap, revealing a body-contoured space within. He'd seen coffins with more breathing room.

"Candidates, enter the pod," Tongea said.

Roland put a foot onto the pod. The lining was tepid and slick against his bare skin. He lay down and the shivering got worse. Tongea came over a moment later with a small earpiece. He attached it to Roland and pressed a button that stuck to his skin against the front of his throat.

"Speak normally once you've reached equilibrium," the cadre said.

"Do you use the same thing in the real armor?"

"We don't need it." He tapped the plugs at the base of his skull. "Cross your arms over your chest." Opening a panel just behind Roland's head, Tongea removed a hose tipped with a mouthpiece. "This makes it easier. Trust me."

Roland, his body shivering, opened up and bit down on the mouthpiece, remembering an orphanage trip to Lake Havasu where he'd gone snorkeling several times a day. The memory of watching fish swim along the lake bottom was a momentary comfort, then Tongea closed the lid.

The darkness pressed around him. He heard Tongea's footfalls through the pod as the cadre went to the next candidate.

"Shaw," Gideon's word came through the earpiece and Roland bumped his head against the roof in surprise.

"Shaw, your parasympathetic system is on fire. You're scared. Do you wish to end this evaluation?"

Roland tried to speak, but his jaw refused to open.

"Nod your head if you're done with this. Last chance before things become unpleasant."

Roland shook his head furiously.

Warm liquid filled the base of the pod and rose up his body.

Just breathe…somehow.

The amniosis crept past his eyes and nose, smelling

of sugar water before it filled his nostrils. The mouthpiece fed him air for a few seconds, then there was a click.

Warm fluid filled his mouth and ran down his throat. He tried to spit the mouthpiece out, but his jaw and mouth refused to comply. The pod squeezed against his body, stopping him from moving more than a finger's breadth in any direction. He fought the urge to throw up as his stomach filled with amniosis.

Roland struggled against the smothering grip of the pod, his body in full-scale panic as his lungs lost their air to the crush and the liquid flooded his chest, which felt like it was burning, suffocating him until...nothing.

The pod pressed against his abdomen, regulating the rhythm of his diaphragm as fluid moved into and out of his body.

"Candidate Shaw," Gideon said through the earpiece, "can you hear me?"

"Yes, sir." Roland froze, unsure how he'd managed the word without moving air across his voice box.

"The modulator's working well. Good. How do you feel? Answer quickly and honestly."

"I...have to pee." Roland noted that he sounded an awful lot like Aignar as he spoke.

"Normal reaction to equilibrium. It will pass. Why

are you here?"

Roland's brow furrowed in confusion. This was a level of interest the cadre had never shown before.

"Sorry, sir. Are you…are you talking to me?"

"Yes, candidate, I am."

"Just an odd time to make conversation…sir. I'm an orphan. Lost my parents to the Xaros. This is how I want to honor them." He pushed a foot against the end of the pod and felt water swirl up his leg.

"I don't believe you," Gideon said. Roland opened his eyes in shock, though he saw the same inky darkness as when they were shut.

"Your parents were both in the navy," Gideon said. "Armor is far from that. We do not speak of our deeds outside the Corps. Only in death is your name made known beyond the Corps. I've never met a parent that wanted their child to have a shorter life span. Your reason doesn't pass muster. Tell me the truth."

"I…" Roland squirmed against the pod, which felt tighter since Gideon had spoken to him. "Do you know what it's like growing up in an orphanage? No one cares. The people that ran my place were not a mother or father to me. I was a just another thing to be managed. Sent to school, monitored. I didn't matter. To anyone.

"Then I'm walking home one night and this strange woman pops out of nowhere when I'm at the Armor Square and tells me a story about all the armor that died that day. People don't just volunteer to die beside one another unless there's a damn good reason. Unless they care about each other. Unless they have something worth fighting for. The Templars, the Iron Hearts and the Hussars, they all found something. I'm not going to quit until I do too."

"Who told you this story?" Gideon asked.

"Some old lady with enough influence to get through the perimeter security. Said her name was Sophia."

"You met the Minder of the Crucible. Impressive."

"What who of the what, sir?" Roland waited a moment, then repeated the question. Gideon didn't answer.

Roland turned his focus to the warmth and closeness of the pod walls.

I wonder if this is what it's like being a mummy, he thought. *So warm and cramped...maybe this is what the womb—Mom's womb—was like. Sure wasn't breathing air in there. Just add a heartbeat and this might be just like it.*

What would she think of this? Did Gideon call me on my answer because he can see God-knows-what through the nubs, or was it just that weak?

The question stayed with him as the long dark

continued.

"Shaw." Gideon snapped the candidate out of his wandering state. "The exercise is over. We're taking you out of equilibrium."

Lights filled the pod, wavering through the amniosis. The liquid drained quickly, but air didn't return to his lungs.

The pod opened and Tongea pulled out Roland's mouthpiece. The cadre flipped the candidate on his side and amniosis came rushing out of his nose and mouth in waves onto the floor.

"That was horrible." Roland stayed on his side and wiped a trembling hand across his mouth. "I see why they didn't mention this part back in Phoenix."

The other pods were open; most held recovering candidates. Two were empty.

Roland struggled to sit up, his muscles trembling and his ears ringing.

"The first time is the worst." Tongea shined a penlight into Roland's eyes. "Your body will adapt after more sessions. You won't need the mouthpiece or forced evacuation after a few months."

Roland blew air out of his mouth, trying to rid himself of the taste. He looked around the room, wondering who he might have to fight in the next few minutes.

"Sir, where's Burke?"

"That candidate voluntarily dropped from selection four hours ago," Gideon said. "You and the other basics are due for a drill instructor–led road march in twenty-seven minutes. I suggest you shower and change into your kit." He pointed back to the locker room.

"Burke...quit?"

Tongea nodded and looked back to the locker room door.

Roland swung his feet onto the floor and took a few unsure steps on half-numb legs. If Burke, who'd never struggled with anything since he entered selection with Roland, couldn't make it, Roland wasn't sure how much longer he'd last.

****

When Roland finally got into one of the large warehouses he'd seen when he first arrived at Fort Knox, he expected to find the buildings brimming with advanced equipment to train him into an armor soldier. But when he and the rest of his class entered one of the buildings, he found it rather underwhelming.

The warehouse was nearly empty. The floor was raised a few feet off the ground, and he marched up a short flight of stairs with the rest of his class and stopped in front of Gideon. The walls and deck were gently lit holo panels, and the uniform glow played with Roland's sense of distance.

Gideon paced back and forth along the line as he spoke. "Candidates, today you will receive your rigs. They are a step down from full armor, but the tactics and techniques you learn in the rigs are the same as what you'll use in armor."

Double doors on the opposite side of the warehouse opened, and Tongea strode in, clad in an exoskeleton that left much of his body exposed. The rig moved like simple cargo robots Roland had seen around spaceports and construction sites—graceless and slow. Empty rigs followed Tongea, each with a mock-up rotary cannon on the right shoulder, forearm-mounted gauss weapon, and electromagnetic rail vanes on their backs.

A smile crept across Roland's face. Finally.

"Mount up," Gideon said.

Roland ran to an empty rig and looked it over. The footrests and straps were easy enough to grasp, but there were no control sticks or keypads anywhere. A brass plate against the back of the rig at neck level glinted in the light, and Roland's excitement waned.

"What're you waiting for?" Masako asked as she climbed into the rig next to his. "We're finally in the crawl phase of crawl-walk-run."

"Haven't had my brain waves turned into motion before." He put a foot onto a stirrup and stepped up into the rig. Straps came out of the rig and went over his thighs, chest and shoulders, pulling him taut against thinly padded backing.

After spending so much time in the equilibrium pods, being sewn into the rig didn't feel that awkward.

"Press your nubs against the receiver plate," Gideon said. "This will feel a little odd."

Roland leaned his head back to the padded headrest. He felt a tremor go down his neck, then there was a whirr of servos. A visor snapped over his face and pressed against his forehead. Everything went dark for a moment, then a screen came to life, showing him the same view he'd had before. He reached up to adjust the fit…and the rig's mechanical hand came into view.

Roland stretched his arm forward, and the rig mimed the gesture. He looked down…and found his arm was still at his side.

"What the hell?" He looked over at Masako, and the rig swung a foot forward to face her rig.

"The rigs are responding to the commands your brain sends to your body," Gideon said. The cadre looked at his forearm screen, then to Masako, and frowned. "The neural bridge isn't as efficient as the plugs and"—there was a crash of metal as a candidate and rig fell to the ground—"there will be an adjustment period."

"Roland," Masako said as Gideon and Tongea went over to their felled classmate, "you getting a weird taste in your mouth?"

"No...but my feet are tingling a little bit."

"Candidates..." Gideon touched his forearm screen and several floor panels sank down and moved beneath the rest of the floor. A lift holding dented and splintered wooden blocks rose up.

"Time to build a house," Gideon said.

****

The M-99 gauss cannon was a weapon exclusive to armor, who carried the double-barreled weapon system mounted to their right forearms. Roland looked at the one on the workbench in front of him, armored access panels raised up to expose the inner workings, and put his hands on his hips.

"They've got to be messing with us," he said. A group of candidates was behind him, examining schematics on an oversized tablet. Several teams worked on different cannons throughout the maintenance bay. "Why do we need to know how to fix this thing? Don't we have maintenance bots? Service crews? Do the cadre spend a lot of time elbow-deep in…grunt work?"

"Think trouble-shooting is beneath you?" Aignar asked. The veteran snapped his cybernetic fingers around a wrench and brought it over to the weapon.

"Hardly, I just don't know when we—the armor— would ever do such a thing."

Aignar leaned his head into the weapon, which was almost the size of a small refrigerator, and tapped the wrench against a component.

"What will you do when your ship full of maintainers and robots gets blown out of the sky?" Aignar asked. "And then your ammo feeder breaks. What'll you do? Shrug your shoulders and tell the enemy that we can't play war until everything's in working order?"

"Guess I didn't think of that." Roland felt his cheeks flush in embarrassment. "Was the fighting that bad on Cygnus? Everything I saw on the net said it was a 'low-intensity' conflict."

Aignar lifted up one of his cybernetic hands and let it fall heavily onto the top of the cannon with a ring of metal on metal.

"No such thing as 'low intensity' when you're getting shot at," Aignar said. "A battalion gets chewed up by Vish over the course of a month or in a day, doesn't make the casualties any less dead."

"I think the problem's in the mag coils," Masako said. She carried the tablet with her and held it between Roland and the weapon. The screen projected a wire diagram of the weapon's interior, the innermost working flashing orange. She held the screen up for a moment, then her hands began to tremble.

"You okay?" Roland took the tablet before she could drop it.

"Feels like pins and needles." She winced and squeezed her hands shut.

"Should we tell the cadre?" Roland asked quietly. "Get you to sick call?"

"Why? So they can find some excuse to drop me? No. The feeling comes and goes," she said.

Aignar tapped his wrench against the cannon's

inches-thick metal case.

"Might be the mag coils," Roland said, swiping across the screen, "which means we need to open access panel D9...then remove coupling H22-b...wasn't the original design of the M-99 Swedish? Didn't they use to make furniture so simple to put together the instructions didn't have words? Now we've got this thing and...wait."

Masako reached into a panel and flipped a switch. The back of the casing fell open, and the metal swung against the hinges and smacked against the table. She grabbed the pair of handles and pulled the inner workings out on a set of rails built into the bottom of the case.

"Didn't you do the reading last night?" she asked Roland.

"Someone was up until 'Taps' putting his side of the room back together again after the DIs found his closet unsecured," Aignar said.

"I swear they give us thirty hours of work for a twenty-four-hour day," Roland said.

"Aignar, did the higher-ups even tell you why you were fighting on Cygnus?" Masako asked.

"Something about the Crucible network. I was more focused on my little piece of the orbital assault than the reasoning." Aignar reached for the magnetic coils and his hand smacked against the housing. Stuck. He tried to pull it back, but it wouldn't budge.

"Well…shit," he said.

Roland and Masako traded worried looks.

"The coils will hold a charge even after being powered off," Tongea said as he came over, Cha'ril a step behind him.

"Sir, should we get another unit with reverse polarity to…" Masako swiped the tablet and trailed off into a murmur.

Tongea took the wrench from Aignar's hand and hit it against the coil housing. Aignar's hand popped away.

"Guess that part wasn't in the reading," Roland said. Masako took a deep breath through her nose, her face trembling with anger.

"Candidate Shaw, why were Terran forces fighting on Cygnus?" the cadre asked.

"Sir…it was something to do with the Crucible network, right?"

"Are you asking me or telling me?"

Roland opened his mouth to answer, then stopped, unsure what kind of logical conundrum he'd stumbled into.

"Cygnus' Crucible gate fell within Earth's sphere of influence," Cha'ril said. "The jump gate could open a wormhole within a light-year of Earth, depending on gravity tides, but that gave the Terran Union a priority claim on the world by the Hale Treaty."

"Did you all understand that answer?" Tongea asked. The three human candidates shook their heads.

"Any Crucible gate can access any other gate the Xaros built across the galaxy," Cha'ril said. "The gates can also open a wormhole within a certain range, depending on the amount of energy stored in the gates and quantum gravity fluctuations in the target—Roland, your eyes are glazing over. Any gate can provide one-way travel from it to a limited area."

"Any gate that can open a portal to within a light-year of Earth is a danger to us," Tongea said. "Why, Candidate Yanagi?"

"A hostile species could send an invasion fleet through," she said. "Might take them a while to get to Earth, but they could still make it. Or they could send a mass driver through at high velocity. The math is complex, but doable. If a rock the size of a battleship moving at a significant percentage of the speed of light hits a habitable world…the effect would be disastrous."

"Is this why the colonial administration was so hell-bent on settling worlds after the Ember War?" Roland asked.

"Quite right, candidate," Tongea said. "The first phase of settlement went to gate systems that could launch an indirect assault on Earth. The second phase will secure the stars around *those* worlds."

"Then why wasn't Cygnus settled immediately?" Aignar asked. "It wasn't exactly a top-tier world before the Vish tried to poison it, but the place didn't need much in the way of terraforming."

"The stars are ever moving," Cha'ril said. "A small black hole a couple of light years away ingested a brown dwarf, sending a graviton wave that—Roland, your eyes again...do you need medical attention?"

"No!" Roland's face perked up. "Just fine."

"The disturbance changed the range on Cygnus' Crucible. The Vishrakath could have used the gate to launch an attack on Earth. They are well-known for their use of asteroids as ships and as weapons," the Dotari said.

"It was ours by the Hale Treaty," Masako said. "Why didn't they just leave?"

"The Vishrakath demanded time to recover the resources used to establish their colony before they left," Tongea said. "Phoenix agreed, and the aliens used the time to poison the well, as it was. While there are billions of stars in the galaxy, the percentage of stars with habitable worlds is almost insignificant. A planet that doesn't require terraforming is a jewel beyond price for humanity—and our allies. That we abandoned colonies on three worlds per the Hale Treaty without razing them, and the Vishrakath did not return the favor, put us in conflict."

"Why didn't we just declare war on all the Vish?" Aignar asked. "The Xaros hit them hard toward the end of the war. We could have ended them quickly."

"The Vishrakath were very influential on Bastion before it was destroyed," Cha'ril said. "They maintained a network of alliances. A vast network."

"We fought on Cygnus as the situation there was something of a gray area in the Hale Treaty," Tongea said. "Attacking the Vishrakath directly would lead to a much wider war. One we might not win."

"What's to stop them from using one of their allies to hurt us again?" Roland asked. "The Ruhaald are at least cordial with us now. We haven't heard from the Naroosha and the Toth since the last time they attacked us. Whatever happened to them?"

"The Naroosha refuse to have any diplomatic contact with us," Tongea said.

"And the Toth? I've heard rumors some of them

survived the attack on Earth and live in the unsettled territories," Masako said.

"I cannot speak of them." Tongea touched the timer on his forearm screen and walked off.

Aignar rapped a knuckle against the coil housing.

"There's still a pull," he said. "One of you open this up."

"Anyone else find it odd that Tongea doesn't want to talk about the Toth?" Roland picked up a motorized screwdriver and went to work on the housing.

"Never had a threat briefing about them in training," Aignar said, shrugging.

"They were not present at Bastion when the technology to create Crucible gates was shared," Cha'ril said. "They may be confined to their own world."

"Then why doesn't Tongea just say that about the Toth?" Roland plucked a screw off the end of his tool. "What's the big secret?"

"You want the Toth to show up and fix this cannon for you?" Aignar asked. "Stop goldbricking and let's finish this job."

****

Sweat ran down the back of Roland's neck and into his soaked-through fatigues. Moisture collected around the edges of his Heads Up Display glasses. That he was unable to wipe them clean while in his rig was infuriating, like being pestered by a mosquito while his hands were tied behind his back.

Roland scanned the top of the tree line just beyond the last range markers of the firing range. A target drone sailed up, and he focused his vision on the spinning cube. His HUD locked on and the gauss cannons on his extended arm barked twice. The target cube bobbed in the air, untouched.

Other cubes over the tree line burst apart as the other candidates found better aim than he did.

"What is wrong with you, Shaw?" Cha'ril asked from the firing position to his left. "Your marksmanship has decreased our average by nine points. *Nine* points. Recalibrate your HUD and learn to function."

"My HUD is fine. It's not using manual aim that's throwing me off," Roland said.

"So the issue is talent, not technical." Cha'ril blasted the next target a split second after it bobbed over the tree line. Roland fired three times and managed to clip his cube. The score tally on his HUD didn't register the point.

"Cease-fire. Cease-fire," Gideon's voice boomed over a loudspeaker. "All candidates lock and clear your weapons and return to the base of the tower to be cleared from the range. Lane seven, you failed to qualify. Stand fast."

Roland bit his lip in frustration. He was on lane seven.

Cha'ril let out a brief hiss as she strode past him in her rig. He kept his gaze downrange, avoiding looks from the rest of the more successful candidates as they made their way back to the wonderfully air-conditioned maintenance bay to drop their rigs and enjoy a few minutes of rest and relaxation.

The humid air felt more oppressive as Roland waited. He had grown up in Phoenix, where hot, dry air was the norm. The weather around Fort Knox was a special kind of misery for him. He would take the Arizona sun over this Kentucky soup any day of the week. Shifting in his rig, he felt his damp uniform pull away from his skin as he tried to scratch an itch on his back.

"Candidate," Gideon said as he walked up to him, dressed in simple fatigues.

"Sir," Roland said, swallowing hard.

"You were in the Scout Auxiliaries before enlisting, correct? You learned to shoot over iron and holographic sites?"

"That's right, sir." Roland squeezed his fist tighter, his hands essentially useless in the rig, buried in the metal frame's forearms and bound shut.

"Your muscle memory is getting in the way," Gideon said. "You see a target and your brain wants to press a rifle against your shoulder. Your fingers want to squeeze a trigger. You're thinking about proper breath control. Rig and armor weapons don't work this way. You mark the target with focus"—he tapped the side of his head—"and let the armor work out the firing solution. When you try to use your old training, you engage the manual fire controls and this throws off your targeting. Do you understand where you're going wrong?"

"I understand the concept, sir, but the instincts of how I used to shoot are dying hard."

"You dissociate when you're in the sensory-deprivation pods. I know you do—I've seen your brain waves. Do the same here. Don't aim and fire. Target and fire, all in your mind. It's easier once you have the plugs and the HUD is in your visual cortex, but you can do it here," Gideon said, and tapped his gauntlet.

"Engage." Gideon slapped a pair of sound bafflers over his ears.

A round target snapped up downrange. Roland marked it with a moment's concentration and his gauss cannons snapped. The target slid down, a hit marker on his HUD. He engaged the next two targets, then scanned the tree line for the pop-ups. Two cubes bobbed up. He marked them both and his weapon arm seemed to move on its own to adjust the aim.

"Cease-fire!" Gideon shouted and waved a hand up and down in front of his face.

Roland pulled his arm back and pinpricks of pain ran up his arm as his rig and his brain moved out of synch.

"Sir?" Roland asked.

Gideon took his bafflers off and pointed to the right. At the edge of the cleared range, a herd of deer trotted out and began nibbling the neatly trimmed grass.

"Perimeter drones should have scared them off." Gideon tapped at his gauntlet. "Damn stupid animals. You'd think after a couple were 'accidentally' hit during a live fire, the rest would get the message, but range control frowns on that sort of thing, as they have to clean up the mess. Hold fast. They'll be gone in a few minutes."

Roland kept his smoking gauss cannon oriented

downrange, but aimed at the dirt. Gideon crossed his arms over his chest and shook his head at the deer as they spread across the range.

Glancing at the fleur-de-lis patch on the cadre's right shoulder, Roland said, "Sir, I've noticed fully qualified armor—like you—have very different shoulder patches. Why is that?"

"Back when the Armor Corps first formed, lances and platoons were formed from individual countries in the Atlantic Union. They kept a good deal of their own traditions and history. Smoking Snakes from Brazil. Hussars from Poland. Zoaves from France. Highlanders from Scotland. One of the American army lances took their colors from the old Second Cavalry, the Dragoons."

Gideon's heel ground into the dirt as he continued. "Records of the first Xaros attack are incomplete, but the Dragoons were at the last stand on Phoenix. Hale and his team came across their dead armor when they pulled Ibarra out from beneath Euskal Tower. Once recruitment started going again after the Toth invasion, Colonel Carius brought back the Dragoons, rechristened them Iron Dragoons in memory of their last battle."

"Why do so many cadre have those red crosses, like Tongea?"

Gideon huffed. "Religion. Nothing I've ever cared for. Some armor choose to associate with their creed instead of their unit's lineage."

"If the Iron Dragoons came back as a unit, what about the armor from Memorial Square? Iron Hearts, right?"

"No…Colonel Martel, General Laran, they'll never break out the Iron Hearts' colors. No one can live up to their memory." Gideon ran a finger down the wide scar on his face. "I saw them once, all three Iron Hearts. Was a Marine in the trenches around Mauna Kea on Hawaii when the Toth came crawling out of the ocean. Me and a bunch of doughboys were holding on by our fingernails, up to our knees in dead lizards, when Elias steps over our trench, cannons blazing. Saw him rip the head off a Toth warrior without missing a beat. Then Hale orders everyone over the top to push them back into the sea.

"I got about a hundred yards when a Toth warrior I thought was dead reaches up and rips me open from my hairline to my waist." Gideon closed one eye, the right side of his face twitching.

"Put in for armor selection while I was in the hospital," Gideon said. "I caught a glimpse of the Iron Hearts once or twice after I earned my plugs. Never had the guts to tell Elias he was the reason I joined…There we go. Deer are getting chased off. You're staying here with me until you qualify, candidate."

Aiming his weapon arm downrange, Roland let out a breath as he tried to clear his mind of Gideon's story.

CHAPTER 9

Roland opened the door to his barracks room and walked in, bent under a rucksack bulging with gear. Sweat soaked through his fatigues and he groaned as he leaned back and hit a release on his straps. The pack slapped against the floor, and Roland rubbed his sore shoulders.

"There. Feels so much lighter now. Bad enough we've got classroom time, homework, rig training, then I get worked over by the DIs before and after the day's other fun." He pressed his hands against the small of his back and straightened up.

Aignar knelt beside his bed, his arms on the mattress, his head bowed in prayer, his metal feet creaking against the floor. A data slate with a picture of a smiling Aignar and a tallow-haired boy sat on the bed next to a small porcelain figure.

Roland quietly set his ruck into his closet, then went to the sink and rubbed water on his head and neck.

Aignar perked up, his eyes widening at Roland. The veteran grabbed at the small statue, but his cyborg fingers closed too quickly and sent it bouncing off the floor with a ring. Aignar let off a panicked grunt and lurched forward to catch the statue.

It bounced twice, then landed in Roland's palm. He held it up in front of his face. The figure was of a woman in a wheelchair, her hands folded in her lap, her head tilted slightly to one side. A red Templar cross was painted on her chest.

"Give. It. Back!" Aignar clamped a hand onto Roland's forearm and squeezed. Roland tried to pull his arm back, but Aignar held on like a vice.

"Ow! What the hell?" Roland held the figure up and Aignar carefully plucked it out of his fingers. The grip on Roland's arm went away with a whine of servos.

"I'm...sorry, Roland." Aignar clutched the figure to his chest and took it back to his desk, his bare metal feet clicking against the floor. "My hands are not my own. Controlling them is a struggle even on the best days." He opened a drawer and put the woman's statue into a felt-lined box.

"What's the big deal? It's not like that's contraband. Is it?"

"You don't have much in the way of faith, do you?" Aignar sank onto a chair.

"I soured on church after a priest tried to explain that my parents' dying in the war was all part of God's plan." Roland shook out the hand Aignar had nearly crushed and drank from a canteen near the sink.

"That there are no atheists in a foxhole is mostly true," Aignar said, "at least for me. I didn't care for religion through most of my life. The night before the big drop on Cygnus, some of the armor held a vigil. The damnedest thing, seeing them outside their armor, kneeling against their swords. At the end, they swear an oath to not leave their armor until the battle is won. Death before dismount, an old tradition from the days of tracked tanks. They'll let anyone join them in prayer…I thought about it, but was more focused on every last little detail before the drop."

"Did you find them again after you went dirtside?"

"Not exactly. The first two weeks were a hard fight. Rangers and Marines started talking about…visions. Guys claiming they saw a woman in a wheelchair after they'd been wounded. Being told just when to duck before a Vish bombardment was about to hit. I thought it was just stress.

173

Too much adrenaline and fear for too long does things to the mind, power of suggestion…then I got hit."

Aignar rubbed a knuckle under an eye.

"I was lying there dying," he said, looking at a hand, the fingers twitching of their own accord, "then I heard a voice telling me to hold on. I saw her face and she told me I wasn't done yet…I was in a bad way for a while. When I finally came to on the *Denver*, that statue was beside my bed. Nurse said one of the armor mechanics brought it to me."

"Who is she?"

"They just call her the Saint. Word was, she died fighting on Mars. Soldiers ask her for protection, courage. I hear most navy ships have little shrines to her. Most everyone thinks she was armor. How else was somebody supposed to take on the Xaros if they're in a wheelchair?"

"All this started on Cygnus? No offense, but this seems a little…cult-y."

"There's nothing much in the way of organized religion anymore," Aignar said. "All the church hierarchies were wiped out when the Xaros erased us from the solar system. Faith isn't confined to dogma as much as it used to be. There are clergy out there, but they're all derived from the old military chaplains. That was more about counseling and spiritual growth than 'thou shall' or 'thou shall not' before the war."

"It's your business." Roland shrugged and pointed to the slate on Aignar's bed. "You want your slate or will you feed me one of my fingers for touching it?"

"I said I was sorry." Aignar looked away, his eyes filled with shame.

"Accident, I get it." Roland picked up the slate. His thumb swiped against the screen and another photo came up—Aignar in uniform and the Ranger's black beret and the same boy on his shoulders.

"That's Joshua," Aignar said. "He's almost nine."

"You're married?"

"Was. Got hitched two weeks before I enlisted and I knocked her up with Joshua during the honeymoon. You make a lot of poor decisions when you're eighteen and coming face-to-face with all the stress of serving. You seem smarter than a lot of privates I met in basic training. Anyway, Rangers aren't home much, which takes a toll on spur-of-the-moment marriages. Josh and his mother live near San Diego, the air base on Coronado Island."

"Get to see him much?"

"Only once since…" Aignar rubbed the back of his hand against his fake jaw.

"You're like an old man compared to me," Roland said. "Done everything and been everywhere."

"Kid, you have yet to begin making stupid decisions. I'd give you shit about going armor, but here I am next to you. Why don't you get your stanky ass into the showers so we can—"

Two loud knocks hit the door and they both snapped to the position of attention.

"Enter, sir or ma'am," Roland said.

Tongea opened the door and pointed a knife hand at Roland's chest.

"Candidates," the cadre said as he shifted his hand to Aignar, "you will both come with me for sensory-deprivation exercise. Be outside this room in three minutes. Fatigues." He closed the door.

"The fun never stops." Roland grabbed a meal replacement bar from his desk and wolfed it down as he changed clothes.

CHAPTER 10

Roland's mind drifted, his body floating in the amniosis and touching the tight confines of the pod when his limbs flexed. He'd cramped up a few weeks ago and found stretching and isometric exercise staved off the spasms of underutilized muscles.

He heard footsteps through the pod.

"Shaw...why are we still bothering with him?" Gideon's voice came through the amniosis, low and muffled.

"His test scores and rig performance are marginal. If you and I both recommend cutting him at the next review, he'll be gone," Tongea said.

Roland's eyes popped open and his heart began to pound. Did they think he couldn't hear them in the pod? He moved a hand through the thick fluid to the transmitter on his neck, but didn't activate it.

"We don't have to wait until the next review. Pull him out now and we can focus more time on candidates with half a chance. Shaw will never wear the armor. He doesn't have it in him," Gideon said.

"We cut him, he can come back after his first tour. We wait for him to crack in the pod, he'll be a loss-of-motivation drop. Barred from the Corps forever. What do you want to do?"

"Let him stew until he's an LOM. It's kinder to let an impossible dream die than string him along for years only to crush his hopes the next time he applies," Gideon said.

"Agreed. His amniosis has eighty more hours of oxygen. I doubt he'll last another twelve."

"I'll have his paperwork done before he gets out. Knew we should've left him back in Phoenix…" Gideon's voice faded as the two walked away.

Roland felt a new weight in his chest. A swell of emotion threatened to rise up and overwhelm him, and he wished the pod had enough room that he could curl into a ball.

Screw them, he thought. *I've done every last stupid Zen bullcrap thing they wanted* and *dealt with the drill instructors hounding my ass for every last detail. They think I'll give up? I'll stay right here. They'll have to pry me out of this pod and then I'll be back. Someone in the Marines knows what the armor wants of me. Maybe I'll find an armor soldier that doesn't have a stick so far up their...*

He felt his clenched fists press against his sides. Blood rushed through his head as the anger grew.

If I spin myself into a frenzy, I'll lose it. I am here. I'm not leaving.

He let the rampant thoughts exhaust themselves and returned to the drift…until red lights flooded the pod and a buzzer went off so loud that it rattled Roland's teeth.

EMERGENCY PURGE flashed on the inside of the pod. He felt a tug against his body as the amniosis exited through a valve near his feet. Blunt nozzles extended from the pod and air forced its way into Roland's chamber. The fluid sank past his face and ears, and the buzzing grew more intense as freezing cold replaced the warm embrace of the hyper-oxygenated liquid.

A line of light traced around the interior of the pod, then the lid burst open and Roland fell into a world of light. He landed hard on his hands and knees, his eyes burning against the sudden bright onslaught. He punched himself in the stomach and a glut of amniosis exited his mouth. He heaved, spewing out more liquid.

Taking in a wet lungful of air, Roland fell onto his side, his shoulder and hip settling into coarse sand.

"Miserable...I know why they never mention that part...to candidates." Roland blinked hard, and his eyes finally recovered from the long dark. He lay in dirt colored burnt-orange; he grabbed a handful, letting the parts that didn't congeal into mud on his wet hands fall between his fingers.

A scrub desert stretched out around him, tufts of grass and a few low trees. Distant bald rock formations wavered in the haze of hot air.

He spat and pushed himself up onto his knees.

"What in the hell?"

He leaned back and bumped into something metal and unyielding.

A suit of armor knelt in the sand, one fist planted into the earth, its breastplate and inner womb wide open. One arm was missing, ripped away at the shoulder. Scorch marks and impact dents marred the surface, and the top half of the helm had been blown away.

"OK...this is..."—he touched the cold nubs on the back of his neck—"training. Has to be training. They wouldn't kick me out and dump me in the middle of—"

The bit of grass near him rustled and a small lizard the size of his hand scurried out. Its skin was covered in thorny protrusions, and lines of deep orange ran down its tan body. It ran over to the base of a tree shrouded in thin needles.

"—wherever I am. Not Phoenix, that's for sure."

Heat from the sand burned his bare feet as he stood up. Roland found a latch on the armor's inner left leg and stepped back as the armor plate swung open. Just beneath the servos and hydraulics of the limb, he found a bright-yellow case with a red handle.

Pulling it free, he opened it on the ground. The emergency case held tightly packed rations, survival gear and a single gauss pistol. Taking a small roll of fabric, Roland peeled off a strip and put it on his foot like a sock, where it molded into a hard-bottomed boot. Once he had his other foot shod, he stood up and touched a control panel inside the open breastplate. The suit didn't respond.

"No power at all...so no commo, and the distress beacon is missing from the suit and the survival pack. Great." Roland secured the gauss holster to his hip and attached a hose from the case to a node on his lower back, running the line over his shoulder. Fixing it beneath a clip, he took a sip of water from the end. His skin suit would recycle sweat and residual amniosis into drinking water. He didn't want to consider the other options his suit provided to stay hydrated.

Taking a quick inventory of the pack, Roland found a thin gauntlet beneath food packs. He slipped it over his left arm, and it came to life, showing a contoured elevation map. He tapped at the screen, but couldn't access any other functions.

"This again." Roland pressed a palm to the survival pack and it changed color to match the sand. The rigid frame softened and Roland shook out a set of straps, then swung the pack onto his back. Drawing the gauss pistol, he released the magazine. The bullets were real and the weapon had a full charge.

"Huh. A little different from last time." He looked at the map on his gauntlet, tugged the screen from side to side with a fingertip and stopped. A road ran parallel to a mountain range, ending in a small cluster of buildings with a landing pad nearby.

Looking to the northeast, he found the line of mountains on the horizon.

"Maybe the town is prewar and the Xaros never got around to erasing it…or it's new and someone will be there. Time to become a desert creature. Not like I have a lot of options right now." He took off at a slow jog, then stopped.

"What am I forgetting?" He looked back at the damaged armor, then snapped his fingers. Roland made a large arrow in the sand pointing toward the distant mountains and filled it in with bits of grass and rock. If someone did come across his suit, they'd know where he was heading.

He left the suit behind at a walk, deciding to conserve energy and water. Maybe there would be a town with people and a way out of wherever he was…maybe not.

As the sun rose higher, the heat became worse. Roland frowned at the tufts of grass and small patches of yellow wildflowers as he marched on. The flora was a far cry from the mesquite and cottonwood trees near Phoenix. A black-and-white bird the size of a crow flew in front of him and landed in the branches of a squat tree with spare branches. The bird tilted its head at Roland, then flew off.

Roland put a hand to his pistol. Since the war's end, much of the Earth was still unpopulated. Although humanity had fortified mountain ranges across the continents before the second Xaros assault, the migration from the cramped confines of the mountains to more traditional city locations had been slow. Every city but Phoenix was essentially recreated from scratch, and construction had been slow as the Terran government's focus was to reestablish the solar system's defenses from Mercury to the distant dwarf planet Eris and colonize Earth-like worlds found through the Crucible network.

More than one person had floated the theory that the Phoenix government dragged their feet rebuilding Earth's cities to encourage off-world migration, yet some cities had returned: Los Angeles, Seattle, Vienna, Milan, Munich, Sydney. The survivors of the war had been part of the old Atlantic Union (which included Australia for reasons no schoolteacher could ever explain to Roland), and those that resettled old cities went through great effort to rebuild what they remembered, choosing to have the same architecture and monuments instead of more modern buildings.

Despite Earth's population edging over two billion souls, much of the planet remained uninhabited. Throughout the wild spaces, the years without any human influence had led to a return of predator species. Packs of wolves and coyotes were a constant problem around Phoenix. Lions had spread through Africa and the Indian sub-continent was rife with tigers.

Roland patted his pistol. Wherever he was, a gauss

pistol was more than enough to handle any animal…assuming he saw it before it attacked. With multiple generations of a human-free environment, animals had lost their ingrained fear of people. A predator might catch a whiff of Roland and decide he was dinner, and not a danger.

Wiping sweat from his brow, he took a break in the scant shade of a tree, fished a food bar out of the pack and looked over the wrapper.

"Fruitcake…yum. Guess it'll taste better as I get hungrier." He put it back and found another bar. "Oatmeal it is." He ripped the corner away and took a bite. After who knows how long he'd spent in the pod subsisting on the nutrients added to the amniosis, chewing his food felt a little odd.

Through a nearby bush, a shadow moved in. Roland drew his pistol and aimed, the bar still in his mouth. At first, the animal that rose up looked like a giant rabbit, then it reared up onto its hind legs. The kangaroo wiggled its nose at him, then hopped away.

"Australia…great." Roland gnawed off a corner of his meal. "Bunch of poisonous snakes, giant spiders and crocodiles. Really wish I was in my rig right now."

He got back up as thunder boomed to the south.

Dark clouds trailing sheets of rain swept across the sky and a gust of moist air promised a radical change to the weather in the near future. After consistent training with the drill instructors in the forests around Fort Knox—rain or shine—Roland accepted that Mother Nature was fickle and did as she pleased, no matter how much he cursed or prayed.

He shouldered his pack, and froze. A set of tracks led northeast. Something with three large toes and a stubby rear claw had left deep prints near a muddy puddle. Smaller prints from feet the same shape peppered the damp soil nearby.

"Thought crocs had five toes." Roland looked at the larger footprint and wondered about the size of a crocodile with feet almost eighteen inches long. The rumble of approaching thunder got him moving again.

With the storm closing fast, Roland searched for anyplace to take shelter. Spotting a knot of trees near several boulders, he changed direction. As he got closer, the smell of smoke grew. He was a hundred yards from the trees when he found tire tracks in the dirt.

"Here we go." Roland followed the tracks into the trees, and the smoke took on a scent of burnt meat. His uneasiness grew as he got closer. He didn't hear an idling engine or anyone moving around inside the copse of trees. Drawing his pistol, he crouched against a boulder.

Looking over the top of the rock, he found a jeep next to a pond. A black scar ran down one side of the vehicle, and the entire front end was burnt, pitched forward into the edge of the water on collapsed tires. The charred remains of the driver were still in the front seat.

Roland ducked and put his finger to the pistol's trigger. The jeep looked like it had been hit by a plasma weapon—and recently, judging by the smell and heat emanating off the wreck. He crept toward the other side of the boulder and looked again.

His breath caught as a creature came to the edge of the pond. It was reptilian, with neon-green skin, a pointed snout and exposed needle-sharp teeth. Wearing the tattered remains of a silver uniform, it dragged a dead kangaroo to the water, then dipped its snout toward the pond. A gust of air blew from behind Roland and into the oasis.

The creature raised its nose, sniffing. Roland ducked back behind the rock.

Can't be, he thought. *Is that a…Toth?*

A glob of thick liquid fell onto his pistol and Roland looked up and found the Toth clutching the top of the boulder. Hissing sharply, it snapped at his face.

Roland fell back and swung his pistol toward the alien. It slapped the weapon out of Roland's hand, then leaped onto him, sharp claws biting into Roland's shoulders and hips.

"Meat! Meat!" the Toth spat.

Roland bashed a fist against the Toth's head and it squealed in pain. He pulled an arm free of the creature's grasp just as it bit down toward his face. Roland caught the alien by the neck and squeezed.

The Toth ripped claws down Roland's arm, tearing the fabric of his body glove. Its hind claws slashed at Roland's stomach, ripping furrows from his solar plexus to his waist. Roland rolled over and pinned the Toth to the ground, his grip tight around the alien's throat and his longer arms keeping the Toth from reaching his face.

A foot away from the squirming Toth's head was a rock. Roland lifted the alien's head up and slammed it against the rock, causing it to fight harder, digging a claw through his gauntlet's screen and into the flesh of his forearm. Roland fought a scream and hit the alien's head against the rock again. Its eyes bulged in panic.

Lifting it higher yet, he crushed the back of the alien's skull against the rock. Cool yellow blood spurted onto Roland's hands, and the alien went into tremors. He tossed the dying Toth aside and found his pistol in the dirt.

Rolling over, he aimed the weapon at the Toth, but it was still. Roland got up and gave it a kick: no reaction.

Roland grimaced as the pain in his arm broke through the combat adrenaline. Blood dripped down his arm and off his fingers.

"Son of a bitch." He cradled his injured arm to his side and shrugged the survival pack off his shoulder. Abrasions up and down his torso hurt, but they weren't bleeding. He found a spray can of Quick Clot and pulled the cap off with his teeth.

A twig snapped behind him.

Roland rolled to the ground and aimed his weapon straight at Cha'ril, Masako and Aignar, all in their skin suits and wielding pistols.

Roland raised his pistol to his shoulder and sank into a patch of tall grass.

"They never did teach us to sneak up on an armed guard at Knox," Roland said.

Masako found his spray can in the dirt and extended Roland's arm.

"We thought there were more Toth nearby," she said. "Didn't want to spook them too."

"More?"

"We tracked the pack to here," Cha'ril said, sniffing the air and looking at the smoldering jeep. "The menials are too small to carry a Toth blaster. There has to be a warrior out there somewhere."

Masako lifted the edge of Roland's torn sleeve and a sheet of blood dripped from his wrist.

"Don't look at it," she said as she stuck the nozzle into the wound. Roland snarled as a hiss of air sent smart platelets into the wound. The bleeding stopped almost instantly. He held up his hand and slowly opened and closed his fist.

"It feels…cool," he said.

"That's good. Means the artery wasn't damaged. If it starts burning, you need a tourniquet." Masako slapped him on the shoulder and helped him up to a sitting position.

Aignar went to the jeep and looked into the backseat. Gripping the door with a cyborg hand, he ripped it off the hinges.

"Why are there Toth in Australia?" Roland asked. "I thought the only place they made landfall was Hawaii."

"They suffered a number of casualties during their orbital assault," Cha'ril said. "Evidently some managed to crash-land here and survive."

"How did no one ever notice? It's been years since

190

the Toth incursion," Masako said. "Why the hell would the cadre send us all out on a survival exercise if they knew the place was crawling with Toth?"

"Perhaps our class is too large and they needed a higher attrition rate. Voluntary or not." Cha'ril's quills rustled against her head.

"Severe injury and death are never acceptable in training," Aignar said. "You all need to see this." He motioned toward the jeep with a nod of his head.

"Can you walk?" Masako asked Roland.

"A hand up, if you please." Roland grabbed her arm with his good hand and got to his feet.

The dead Toth's limbs had pulled into a fetal curl. Flies buzzed nearby, but didn't land on the corpse.

"We found the tracks not far from here," she said. "Cha'ril's father was Dotari militia on Hawaii, told her a bunch of stories about hunting Toth through the entire island chain. Seems the Toth were excellent swimmers."

"Why were you three looking for this damn thing— especially if there's a warrior with them? The big ones could rip us in half." He looked at his suddenly inadequate pistol and holstered it.

"Because of this…" Masako reached into her survival pack and pulled out a ripped piece of fabric the size of her palm. Sewn to the cloth was a bloodstained patch with a crown and rising sunburst. "Aignar says it's Australian infantry. We found it near another jeep, crashed into a ravine and surrounded by Toth footprints."

"They have prisoners," Roland said.

"You two done over there?" Aignar called out.

A fat raindrop hit Roland's shoulder and he looked up as the forward edge of the storm eclipsed the sun. Rain spattered down around them.

"There were four in the jeep," Aignar said as Masako and Roland got closer. Masako turned away at the sight of the charred remains, one hand to her mouth.

"Four rucks in the trunk." The veteran tapped a metal knuckle above the rear wheel. "Most of their gear's still in there."

Each of the backpacks had been torn open. Spare clothing and toiletries were strewn around the trunk.

"They wouldn't have left this all behind," Roland said. "What happened?"

"Never met an infantryman that didn't carry plenty of pogie bait out into the field," Aignar said. "The Toth took their food."

"I assume the dead one killed that marsupial." Cha'ril pointed to the dead kangaroo.

"That Toth wasn't part of the group that ambushed the jeep," Roland said. Rain fell harder, hissing as it struck the fire-blackened front end of the vehicle. "Why keep hunting if you've got plenty of food?"

"Their nest must be nearby," Cha'ril said. "My father never found a menial beyond keening range of the alpha warrior."

"Keening? Could your father—and could you—hear it?" Aignar asked.

"No," Cha'ril said, shaking her head. "He had one of the Karigole advisors with him during the hunts. They were most motivated to kill Toth and their senses were far superior to Terran and Dotari."

"This rain isn't helping." Aignar turned his face up and closed his eyes as the shower intensified.

"There's a town not far from here," Roland said. "We get there, we can call for help. Get someone armed with something better than pistols to help with the search. Couple seeker drones should be all we need."

"I'm certain the soldiers came from that village," Cha'ril said. "If the Toth are bold enough to strike here, they may have the strength to attack a larger target, especially if the town just lost a significant amount of manpower."

"Then we need to get there sooner rather than later." Wind ripped through the trees and Roland raised an arm to shield his face as the rain came in harder.

"Any idea how long this storm will last?" Masako ducked beneath Roland's arm, using him as shelter.

"We don't have time to wait," Aignar said. "The Toth will either take shelter or keep moving with their prisoners. They shelter, we move and get ahead of them. They keep moving, we risk falling behind by staying here."

Roland shook his head at his shattered gauntlet.

"Sure hope one of you has a compass and map working," he said.

"I do." Cha'ril pointed over the pond, its surface jumping as raindrops landed. "Follow me."

"Keep close," Aignar said. "Too easy to get lost in this mess."

As the four marched into the desert, Roland's feet squishing into the mud as they went, he could see barely more than a few dozen yards ahead of them. His injured arm and hand still felt cold, like he'd forgotten to wear a glove on a winter's day.

"There was talk of the Dotari settling this continent," Cha'ril said. "My father and some of the other militia scouted the eastern coast, then one of the high listers was nearly eaten by some sort of fish the size of a void fighter and another was poisoned by a water invertebrate. My father said this was a cursed land and that only the strongest humans could survive here. Now I truly appreciate the stories."

Thunder broke overhead and Roland reflexively hunched his shoulders. Aignar seemed undisturbed.

"Aignar, how much of you is metal?" Roland asked.

"Why?"

"Lightning."

The veteran lifted a hand to his face.

"Down! Keep them down!" Masako shouted. "You're enough of a lightning rod as it is without tempting fate."

"Cha'ril," Aignar said, "can you go faster?"

"Can you keep up?" The Dotari hurried into a run, her feet splashing through puddles.

****

The rain had lessened to a sprinkle once they found the town. Most of the buildings were single-story and 3D-printed from concrete. A single taller building with large garage doors was at the bottom of a cul-de-sac connected to a paved road leading north.

Roland ducked through a barbed-wire fence and crouched in waist-high grass running along a stream almost ready to spill over its banks. Aignar knelt in the grass, his eyes locked on the town.

"No movement," the veteran said. "No lights. Nothing."

"Doesn't look like it's been attacked," Roland said.

"You want to go knock on a door and see if a Toth answers?"

"Not really, but what if it is full of aliens? There's a road, but who knows how far we are from the next settlement."

"We get more information, then we'll decide," Aignar said. "We keep making the best decisions we can until we have this situation figured out. Not much else we can do."

Cha'ril and Masako crawled through the fence and joined the two men.

Aignar grabbed a foot and bent it at the ankle with a creak.

"Damn it," he said. "Thing's not designed for hiking."

"Can you walk?" Masako asked.

"I can limp at a good pace," he said, "until the other one gives out and then I've got the dexterity of a drunk toddler."

"We can't see much from here," Cha'ril said. "Roland, come with me to the western side. We should be able to see through the large structure's windows from there."

"I'll go. He's hurt," Masako said.

"Roland consistently scores higher than you on all movement-to-contact exercises," Cha'ril said. "Your marksmanship skills are better than his. Our chance of survival is better with you on overwatch."

"And here I was thinking you were starting to like me," Roland said.

Cha'ril took in several snorts of air, almost like the staccato purr of a cat.

"Are you...laughing?" Roland asked.

"Not the time." Cha'ril shook her head. "If we have to retreat, return to the oasis where we found Roland. Let's go."

Roland followed her through the tall grass, crawling on his hands and knees through the mud and rising to a low crouch when the grass was high enough.

Cha'ril stopped and sank low.

"What?" Roland whispered.

"To the right, fence line." She pointed with her pistol.

He craned his neck up, bringing his eyes just above the swaying grass. An enormous quadruped Toth with thick arms and a scarred snout that looked like it could take off Roland's head with a single bite marched toward the town. Six human prisoners followed, all bound at the hands. Ropes hewn from strips of tree bark led from their restraints to the larger Toth's hand.

Smaller Toth menials ran around the warrior, ducking between its limbs without any hint of worry at being crushed. They snapped at the prisoners, shouting high-pitched expletives in English.

"What are they going to do to them?" Roland asked.

"The Toth are carnivores," she said. "Why keep them alive when they could escape or fight back?"

"Just because they look like predators doesn't mean they only care about eating," he said. "Maybe they want to trade hostages for a ship. Get back to their home world."

"Then this is not the time for bravery," she said. "Wait for them to start negotiations, we link up with whoever comes and provide intelligence."

"Then Bob's your uncle," Roland said.

"Bob?"

One of the tall garage doors opened, and a thing of nightmares came out—a tank full of bubbling liquid carried on a mechanical body with four legs, a disembodied brain and sinuous nervous system floating within.

The Toth gave off an ululating cry that sent a chill down Roland's spine.

The prisoners tried to run, but the warrior yanked them all off their feet with a single tug of their ropes. The menials fell on the prisoners, punching and kicking them.

"By the old ones, that's an overlord," Cha'ril said.

"What the hell is it doing here?" Roland pressed his thumb against the side of his pistol and a bolt cycled into the chamber.

A mechanical arm extended from beneath the overlord's tank, the spiked tip reaching toward the prisoners as the menials dragged them, kicking and screaming, into the town.

"My father…he said that the overlords fed on neural energy," Cha'ril said. "The Toth *are* hungry."

"I really don't want to find out how they eat neural energy, but I'm not sure we even have enough bullets for them all." Roland tried to count the menials, but they swarmed around the prisoners like flies around a rotting corpse.

"The small ones are cowards. Shoot the big ones and the rest will scatter." Cha'ril extended her pistol through the blowing grass toward the Toth.

The warrior tossed a prisoner to the ground in front of the overlord. One of the arms grabbed the man by the neck and hoisted him into the air.

"Aim dead center," Roland said as he aimed at the overlord. Nerve tendrils caressed the inside of the tank as the man struggled in the overlord's grasp.

They fired their pistols within an instant of each other. Twin spider webs broke out across the overlord's tank and it stumbled back toward the open garage. The prisoner fell free and scrambled away.

The Toth warrior leaped between the two and the overlord.

"Think he saw us?" Roland asked, just before the warrior pointed into the grass and bellowed a command. The smaller aliens raced toward them.

"Definitely saw us," Cha'ril said.

"Bounding retreat, ten meters, you first." Roland stood up and fired at the approaching disturbances in the grass marking the Toth approach. A menial leaped into the air when struck, its snout biting at the wound along its flank.

As Cha'ril ran back toward Aignar and Masako, Roland let off two shots toward a rustle in the grass and earned a screech. He heard Cha'ril's pistol snapping and he took the cue to retreat.

Grass swished across his legs and thighs as he ran. There was a growl from behind, and a Toth leaped up and slammed into his back. Roland went face-first into the ground, his face scraping over pebbles before he slid to a stop.

He looked up and saw his pistol just out of reach. Stretching out, he missed it completely as a Toth took him by the ankle and dragged him backwards. Roland dug his fingers into the ground, but the Toth that had him was strong and determined. Wet earth came loose beneath his hands, providing no anchor.

Gauss bullets snapped overhead. Roland's panic grew as he was certain whoever was shooting certainly couldn't see him in the grass. He came to a stop, snatched up a rock and rolled over, only to find a shadow looming over him. The Toth warrior slammed a massive paw around Roland's head, shutting off the rest of the world but for a smell of spoiled milk off the alien's flesh.

The warrior lifted him up and clutched him under

an arm. Roland felt the alien's body heat, the smell of old dough from its palm nearly smothering him as it carried him away.

All of a sudden, Roland fell to a concrete floor, gasping for air. He lay on his stomach, looking at the warrior's clawed feet. Turning his head, he saw the overlord's mechanical legs, then a metal claw clamped down on his shoulder and lifted him up.

The overlord's brain floated in the cracked tank, fluid seeping from the bullet impacts and dribbling down the side.

"Hello…meat," came from the base of the tank. "How many are you?"

"Hundreds. We've got this whole town surrounded. You give up now and maybe we'll let you catch a ride back to your favorite fish tank," Roland said.

The grip on his shoulder tightened like a vice. Pain wracked his face, but he didn't scream.

A spike rose in front of Roland's face. It split open and tiny tendrils reached out, caressing his forehead.

"True mind…true body," the overlord said, its nerve endings rubbing together, "a treat I've not had in years. Maybe just a taste, yes? Know the truth before I send my thralls out to find the rest. A feast for the Toth. Your mind for me. Your body for them. Or tell me how many you are and where they're hiding. I'll spare you if it brings me more sustenance."

Roland swung his feet back and kicked the tank.

"You will get nothing from me!"

The spike inched closer to Roland's face. He spat on the tank…and the Toth froze. The bubbles in the tank slowed, and every last twitching nerve ending stopped in place. The claw opened and Roland fell to the ground in a heap.

The warrior behind him also locked in place.

Roland crawled toward a door to the side of the overlord and felt a hand on his shoulder. He shouted, struck out…and hit nothing.

Light wavered, running in a rainbow sheen down a humanoid shape. Tongea materialized out of thin air.

"Candidate Shaw, this training exercise is over," the Maori said.

Roland rolled onto his back and propped himself up on his elbows. He looked from the overlord to the cadre several times.

"Android replicas," Tongea said. "There are no real Toth on Earth. You're safe."

Roland felt every last scrape and bruise budding

around his shoulder. Groaning, he got to his feet, favoring one side of his body.

"What…what was all this about?" he asked.

"There are medical personnel waiting for you behind that door." Tongea pointed behind Roland. "Your exercise is over. Candidate Cha'ril has been 'captured' and will be here in a few minutes. You need to be out of sight."

Roland felt anger building in his chest. That the cadre would dump him into the wilderness with no warning and send him through this sort of a wringer…his trust in them felt betrayed. He reached his good hand toward the nubs on the back of his neck, the urge to remove them and toss them at Tongea's tattooed face almost overwhelming.

He touched the nubs, then let his hand fall.

Tongea reached out and touched him on the shoulder. The older man's face cracked a slight smile, and he gave Roland a nod.

"Is that iron I see in you?" the cadre asked.

"If you call pissed off, in pain and confused 'iron,' then yes, sir."

"See the docs. Hurry." Tongea touched his gauntlet screen and a cloak field enveloped him.

Roland stepped through the doorway and saw Gideon standing in front of a bank of monitors. Screens showed a struggling Dotari as Toth dragged her into the building, an empty firehouse. The other cadre gave Roland a dispassionate glance, then turned his attention back to the screens.

A pair of medics sat Roland down on a bench. One pressed a hypo against his neck and the pain over much of his body subsided. Another, a rather pretty woman with blue eyes and a kind smile, gave him a cup of juice and patted him on the cheek.

"Hello, Digger," she said, "bloody ace out there. We'll have you topped off with the bottler meds and then she'll be apples. No worries, eh?"

"Miss, I have no idea what you just said, but I'm okay with it." Roland kicked back the last of the juice and wondered if Jerry was having an easier time in the Marines.

CHAPTER 11

Roland strode through the hallway of the Fort Sydney transient barracks in his physical training shorts and T-shirt, his wet flip-flops squeaking against the linoleum floors. Carrying a towel on his shoulder, he relished the feeling of his skin recovering from a too-hot shower. As he shouldered his way into his assigned room, he scrubbed the towel over his face and head.

"Aignar, you're full of crap. The water doesn't spin the other way going down the drain just because we're in Australia." He removed his towel and found Cha'ril and Aignar staring at him, Aignar wearing knee-length jeans and a bowling shirt, Cha'ril in a flower-print blouse and loose pants.

"What gives?" Roland asked.

"Our shuttle back to Knox was delayed," Aignar

said. "Typhoon over Okinawa. We got ourselves a six-hour pass. Just have to be back in the barracks by midnight."

"So we can just...walk out of here? Go looking around Sydney and do whatever we want? No cadre?"

"That's what a pass means, Roland. The leash is off. Let's go be adults."

Roland raised his arms over his head then flexed into a crab pose.

"Whoo!" Roland clapped his hands, then went to high-five Cha'ril. She looked at his palm, then to Aignar.

"You said he'd do this." Cha'ril clicked her beak.

"Where are we going to go? To eat? Do they have beer in Australia? Legal age is eighteen down here, right? What am I going to wear?"

"I secured outerwear for you," Cha'ril said, pointing to a plastic-wrapped bundle on Roland's bed. "I cross-referenced popular fashion with the seasonal data and camera footage from the target neighborhood for us to better assimilate."

Roland took out a pair of shorts and a button shirt.

"Wait, what's she talking about?" Roland asked.

"She wants to go to a local hotspot that's not in any of the guides," Aignar said. "The place is also on the list of off-limits establishments—well, it's the only off-limits establishment in the whole city for military."

"Being 'off-limits' sounds like we'd get into even more trouble for sneaking in there. Why are we—no, you—taking this risk? Let's all go anyplace else," Roland said.

"If challenged, we are going to Papa Sam's Pizzeria," the Dotari said. "It is across the street and is well-known for using kangaroo-meat sausage as a topping. One of us—I suggest you, Roland—will confuse the street address, giving us plausible deniability for being at Bloke's Bar and Grill."

"Do you understand the difference between plausible deniability and conspiracy?" Roland asked. "Don't do this. Seriously."

Aignar rolled his eyes.

"Masako is coming with us."

"Oh…well, OK then." Roland unfolded the shorts, then looked at Cha'ril. "You mind? A little privacy."

"Are you ashamed of nudity?" the alien asked. "Masako has no issue with disrobing while I'm in the room with her."

"She's a girl and so are you," Roland sputtered. "Just turn around. Cover your eyes. Something."

"Wait…is it true that your genitals are outside your body?" she asked.

"I am not having this conversation with you, Cha'ril." Roland waved a finger in the air. "Not now. Not ever."

Aignar let off his monotone laugh and slapped his knee.

Cha'ril buried her eyes into the crook of her arm.

Roland swapped out his shirt.

"Cha'ril, how do you think you're going to blend in like you mentioned earlier? I thought the only Dotari on Earth were at the embassy in Phoenix," he said.

"Dotari Marines practice orbital jumps from the nearby spaceport," she said. Roland took off his PT shorts and bent over to pick up the bottoms Cha'ril had chosen for him.

"Hey, guys!" Masako burst into the room and got an eyeful of Roland's bare backside.

As Masako slammed the door, Roland looked up at Aignar, who was laughing so hard that he had to hold on to the wall for support. Roland, his face beet-red, quickly put his shorts on.

"Does Aignar require medical attention?" Cha'ril asked, her face still buried in her arm.

"That asshole will if he doesn't stop laughing!"

Aignar tapped his throat microphone and the sound

cut off.

A few tepid knocks rapped on the door.

"Come. In." Roland turned to the door and crossed his arms.

Masako, in a loose skirt and a blouse with rolled-up sleeves, entered, biting her bottom lip and refusing to make eye contact with Roland.

"Are we...ready?" she asked.

"Does Roland still have his genitals on display?" Cha'ril asked.

"Put your arm down," Roland said, shaking his head. "Let's just get going."

****

Bloke's Bar and Grill sat on a corner next to an industrial recycling center. Puddles from the last rainstorm dotted the sidewalks and streets. Sprinkles flitted through streetlights, and on the holo sign for the bar, the final 'l' sputtered on and off.

Music and the clink of beer bottles spilled into the early evening.

A driverless taxi pulled up across the street and the four armor candidates got out. Aignar swiped a credit fob over the taxi's pay reader as the others formed a loose perimeter around him, all facing out, hands clenched for a fight.

"All of you need to calm down," Aignar said. "We're in Sydney, not a VR chamber at Knox."

A pair of men stumbled out of the bar, each cursing and swinging drunken punches at the other. One took a kick to the stomach and bounced off a parked car, leaving a dent.

"Oi!" A third man ran from the bar, an empty bottle in hand. "That's my ride, you dick heads!"

The original pair of combatants didn't seem to notice when the third man jumped into fight, and the brawl continued up the street.

"We're in a rough part of Sydney," Aignar said. "Just be polite."

"Why does it smell like pee out here?" Masako wafted her hand in front of her nose.

"Five and a half hours of our pass left," Roland said, tapping his watch. "Let's get in, get out and get somewhere that doesn't look like it has a medic on staff. You ready, Cha'ril?"

The Dotari touched a bulge in her pocket, then furled her quills for a moment. She looked up the road to their departing taxi.

"Perhaps this is a mistake," she said. "What if we go to the place with congealed mammary gland secretions and mashed fruit pulp? It is Friday. I understand humans enjoy fermented beverages in combination."

"Pizza and beer can wait," Aignar said. "You said this was important to you. Time to buck up."

Cha'ril let off a trill and marched into the bar.

"Roland," Masako said, grabbing him by the arm, "if anyone asks, you're my boyfriend. Got it?"

"Can do! Should I…" He lifted an arm to go over her shoulder, but she held up a hand.

"Let's not complicate this," she said.

"Right." His arm fell to his side.

They followed Aignar inside. Almost two dozen patrons, most of them men, crowded around the bar and a dartboard. Roland felt his shoes stick against the floor that looked like it hadn't been mopped since the place was built. The air smelled of stale beer and vaporizer nicotine steam. Screens on the wall replayed rugby matches from long before the war ended.

A heavyset man in a sleeveless shirt and a two-day beard leaned away from the bar and looked over the new arrivals.

"Hey, Dav-o, looks like we got some lost little sheep come our way." He stumbled off his bar stool and slapped the tattooed arm of the man next to him. "Should we show 'em what happens to buggers that don't know they're in the wrong paddock?"

"Stop taking the piss, Wayne." Dav-o said turning around and looking the four over through a black and swollen eye. "They're looking drier than the Nullarbor desert, even the Dotty one. Let 'em have a brew."

"Fair dinkum, they'll get the Sheila in trouble again," Wayne said. "Can't have that mate. This is the only boozer in staggering distance from me yard that doesn't water down its piss!"

The bartender stood up from behind the bar with a cricket bat in his hand.

"There's my 'behave yourself,'" he said. The man's nose looked like it had been broken several times and an ugly scar ran along his hairline. Taking one look at the four of them, he shook his head, pointed the club at Aignar and waved him over to an open space at the bar.

"What're you four drop kicks doing in here?" he asked Aignar. "We're all ex-service. You think we can't smell a bunch of cherry AJ's like you from a mile away?"

"What did you call me?" Aignar lifted his chin

slightly, letting the tall bartender see the speaker in his neck.

"Ah sorry, mate." The bartender set the club down. "Your mates are so new they squeak. Can always tell when newbies come round for a sticky beak. Can't serve anyone from the base, might cost the boss her license."

Roland looked over the barman's head to a rail rifle mounted onto the wall. Faded pictures of a short female Marine posing with other Marines and soldiers hung next to the rifle, more than one askew. One photo had the short woman with a rail rifle resting against her shoulder, a Marine Roland recognized from all the Standish Liquors commercials, Hale, Standish, a scowling Hispanic Marine and a tall blond woman, all clustered around a scaly-skinned alien that looked as if humor was an impossible concept.

"I need to see Bailey," Cha'ril said. "I...have something for her."

"The missus doesn't do selfies, autographs or act out any scenes from the pile of dog vomit of a movie that's on the telly all the time," the bartender said. "Now I've asked you to piss off nicely, just like my court appoint shrink says I have to. So I suggest you drongos be on your way before the boys lose their rag with you."

"We are awful thirsty." Aignar tapped his credit fob to a reader next to the barman and dropped a substantial tip.

The bartender worked his thick jaw from side to side.

"Well in that case, what'll be drinking?"

"Two shots of whiskey, and an old-fashioned…with a straw," Aignar said.

"Thought you said you were thirsty." The barman put six plastic shot cups between Aignar and Cha'ril and poured whiskey from a bottle with a ripped-off label. He came back a moment later with a drink in a wide-mouthed glass and a plastic straw.

"I'll see if the missus is interested in a chat," the barman said, nodding at Cha'ril. "Don't get Dotties in here much anymore."

Aignar raised his drink to him, then took a hard look at the orange slice in his drink. He gave it a sniff, then tossed it to the floor.

"A toast to a—" Aignar turned back to Roland and Masako. Four of the six shot glasses were empty. They each held a shot, a look of disgust on their faces.

"Have you two never drank before?" Aignar asked.

"Not me," Masako said.

"Nope. This is not as awesome as I thought it would

be," Roland said.

"The more you drink, the better it tastes." Aignar opened his bottom jaw a notch with a touch beneath an ear. His top lip formed a seal around the straw and he took a long sip. "I suggest you two—" He set his drink on the bar and shook his head as Masako and Roland tossed back their third shot.

"I should've started them out on Shirley Temples," Aignar said.

"Do you think she's here?" Cha'ril shifted her weight from foot to foot, her eyes on the door the bartender had gone through.

"I feel kind of warm," Masako said, grabbing on to the bar and bracing herself. She shook her head slightly. "Now that's different."

"It is a little hot in here." Roland rocked back and bumped into Wayne, his elbow knocking the other man's drink over.

"Oi! You see there's a beverage here, right?" Wayne asked, shoving Roland forward. He bumped into Aignar, who raised his drink and kept from spilling a drop.

Roland whirled around, swaying on his feet.

"Sorry. The room is a little…spinny." Roland widened his stance and teetered back and forth.

"Bloody oath! This wombat looks like he's about to chunder. What say we give this Yank a bit of barroom etiquette," Wayne said, nudging Dav-o, who flashed a semi-toothed smile.

"None of that, you two bogans." A short, sturdy woman put herself between the locals and Roland. "Don't you know armor soldiers when you see them?"

"We're still Nubbies, lady—" Roland stopped talking when the woman grabbed a handful of his shirt and pushed him against the bar.

"Dickhead spilled my drink," Wayne said.

"Get another on the house. Just get it on the other end of the bar, you pair of footy hooligans," she said.

"What? I can take them," Roland slurred. The woman twisted her grip on his shirt and yanked him down to look her eye to eye.

"I've seen armor rip aliens apart faster than you can blink. But you know what you are outside your suit? A sack of meat ready for a good kicking. I'll give it to you myself if the lot of you aren't out of my establishment in five minutes," she said.

"You're Diana Bailey?" Cha'ril asked. "Of the *Breitenfeld*?"

Bailey pushed Roland up and away from her, but

kept her grip on his shirt.

"Any of you shits pulls out a phone for a picture and you'll eat it. You think I'm kidding?"

"High List Bailey, you saved me on Takeni," Cha'ril said. "When the Xaros came, my mother—"

"I know what happened on Takeni, Sheila. I was bloody there—damn stupid movie had me in it without my permission. Other than that, I've got the scars and the nightmares to prove I was there. Just because the *Breitenfeld* helped pull your asses out of the fire doesn't mean I had anything to do with every last one of you. Now get these lightweights out of my bar before they throw up on it."

Cha'ril took Bailey's hand.

"I was born in Usonvi. My mother got separated from the rest of the village when the banshees came for us. They almost caught up to her, then you sent a bullet over her head and killed the abomination. You saved both our lives. Do you remember? The plateau where—"

Bailey let Roland go. The former Marine's face twitched and she put a hand to her side.

"That part wasn't in the movie, but I remember," Bailey said. "Your mother running for dear life, a baby in her arms. That was you?"

Cha'ril nodded furiously.

"I earned me a Purple Heart that day. Wasn't my first. Wasn't my last, but it's the only one I didn't regret. We lost a fine Marine on that plateau where we evacced most of your village, good woman named Torni. I was too busy bleeding to death to help her."

"We remember her," Cha'ril said. "A *ganii* tree grows in her honor on Dotari." She removed a cloth-wrapped object from her pocket and gave it to Bailey. "For you."

The former Marine unwrapped a glossy ball the size of a walnut, Dotari writing scrolled along the shell.

"A *ganii* seed with my family lineage carved into it," Cha'ril said. "My father wished to bring it to you, but his duty in the Scout Corps kept him away from Earth."

"His name was…Un'qu? He fought beside me on the walls when that swarm of Banshees broke through, good fighter."

"Because of you, our family survived. If you plant the seed, it will grow well in this climate. Our gratitude will always—"

"All right, calm down." Bailey slapped her hands to the bar and climbed over. "You get me all misty in front of the boys and I'll have to kick all their asses to respect me again. Let me show you how we say thanks in my bar."

She reached under the bar and brought out a cowbell. She rang it twice.

"Shot on the house!"

Patrons cheered and rapped beer mugs against the bar.

"I want another shot!" Masako said and leaned against Roland. She looked up at him and tried to reach for his face, but missed completely.

"Could we get two shots?" Roland slurred.

"God damn it. I'm in for a long night." Aignar took a sip from his old-fashioned.

Bailey poured the two drunks shots of vodka, and they drank before Aignar could interfere.

"Why armor?" the former Marine asked Cha'ril. "That's a hard life."

"For my father," the Dotari said. "For my people."

"The Lord bless you and keep you," Bailey said, squeezing Cha'ril's hand. "I was there when we lost the Iron Hearts. I hope you never have a fight like that. Maybe the days of that kind of war are over. I'd tell you to stay safe, but that's not what armor's for."

****

Aignar half-supported, half-dragged Roland down the hallway to their room.

"Aussie Aussie Aussie!" Roland pumped a fist into the air as Aignar's hand, pressed against his chest, kept him from falling onto his face.

"Oi oi oi!" Masako came stumbling around the corner, Cha'ril chasing after her. "Hey…Rolly. I saw the back. How about I see the front too?"

Roland tottered around, but Aignar pushed him into a complete 360.

"What? She just wants to see something…" Roland tried to wiggle out of Aignar's grasp, but his cyborg hands were clamped tight on his arm.

"Are they going to copulate?" Cha'ril asked.

"No! They'll have enough to regret in the morning as it is." Aignar shook his head.

Masako bumped into a wall and slid down to a seated position, raising a woozy hand over her head.

"I want another drink!" Her hand bounced off her head and her chin fell to her chest.

Aignar shoved Roland into their room and turned back to Cha'ril.

"Remember. Have her drink water and put her to

bed facedown," he said.

"Are humans always like this when they drink alcohol?"

"This is pretty standard for the first time. Tomorrow there will be many promises to never drink again, promises I doubt they'll keep."

Cha'ril grabbed Masako by the wrists and dragged her into their room.

"Get Rolly," Masako mumbled.

Aignar got Roland into bed and met the Dotari in the hallway a few minutes later. The alien sniffed at her hands.

"Are you aware of the excretions you make when intoxicated?" she asked.

"It'll be worse by morning."

"I hope this isn't a regular occurrence. Dealing with those two is like handling toddlers."

"This'll be a learning experience for them both. Did you say everything you needed to say to Bailey?"

Cha'ril's quills rustled slightly.

"She was not open to speaking more of what happened on Takeni, but she was interested in the Dotari return to our home world. I told her she would be welcomed as a hero if she ever came to visit, but she was not interested."

"Don't take it personal. Veterans deal with a war's aftermath in their own way. Few are ever eager to relive old battles."

"Aignar…why did you help me, help convince Roland to come with us? We have not gotten along during training."

"We are a team, and anyone willing to shed their blood with me is my brother. Getting you to see Bailey was a hell of a lot more important than whatever else we could have done during our time off. I think Roland has that figured out by now."

"Taps" played through the hallway and the lights dimmed.

"Good night, Aignar."

He gave her a nod and went back to his room.

****

As a Mule idled on a flight pad, Gideon marked off candidates on his gauntlet as they filed up the ramp and into the aircraft.

"Candidate Shaw!" Gideon pointed a knife hand at Roland before he could set foot on the ramp. Roland hurried over and snapped to attention, swaying slightly and mashing an eye closed against the sun's rays.

"Candidate Shaw," Gideon said, far louder than needed, "did you enjoy your pass?" He leaned toward Roland and sniffed at the odor emanating from the younger man's body.

"Yes, sir. We…took in some local attractions."

"What do you think of Australia, candidate?" Gideon's voice was on the edge of shouting and Roland winced harder.

"Friendly people. Lovely scenery, sir."

"How about the food?"

Roland choked slightly and Gideon stepped back.

"Get aboard." The cadre jerked a thumb toward the Mule. "Candidate Yanagi," he said, chopping his knife hand toward her, "get over here!"

CHAPTER 12

Within a cavernous VR chamber, Roland raised his rig's foot off the ground and a spike the size of his fist popped out of the heel. As he stomped it into a blinking panel on the floor, his HUD glasses showed him the anchor's progress, twisting into the simulated earth.

"Hurry up!" Cha'ril said, firing around a barricade toward the onrushing horde of gangly limbed aliens in armored environmental suits, all armed with long rifles. Aignar, Masako and a handful of other candidates in their rigs formed a perimeter around Roland as he readied his shot.

"Anchor set!" Roland raised a pair of rail gun vanes off his back and tilted them over his shoulder. He swung the weapon toward an alien ship shaped like a flattened diamond high overhead as it burned along its descent through Earth's atmosphere. Icons flashed green across his HUD.

Firing a rail cannon in atmosphere was dangerous for any nearby individuals not within the confines of a full suit of armor. The concussion of the rail-cannon bullet shattering the sound barrier could prove deadly for even a Marine or Ranger in their combat gear.

In the simulated environment of the VR chamber, Roland's rail cannon crackled with electricity, then went dead. A burning line of air traced through the screens along the ceiling, the simulated shell ripping through the alien ship, breaking it into a thousand flaming pieces.

"You did it," Cha'ril said. "I have lost a bet."

The VR chamber went dark, then reset to neutral. Barricades sank back into the floor and Roland withdrew his anchor.

Tongea came out of a side room in a rig. The candidates fell into a formation, ready for their evaluation.

"Candidates," Tongea said, "an armor soldier must be dangerous at every range. Your rail cannons can destroy starships from thousands of miles away. Gauss and rotary weapons can handle anything a step closer. Now you must close the final gap."

He punched his right arm toward Masako and a

blade snapped out of his forearm housing, stopping a hand's breadth from her throat.

"There are times when it is necessary to close with and destroy the enemy at such range. Boarding parties. Tunnels. Every race we've encountered that evolved on a planet with predator species has an instinctive fear of blades, of being stabbed and ripped apart. The threat of bullets has a degree of separation—it won't be you that gets hit. When confronted by an enemy close enough to ram a weapon through their body, fear takes over. You will learn to use this fear against your enemy. You will learn to control that fear in yourself. You are armor. You are the fear. Spread out. We begin with simple thrusts."

Roland's HUD pinged with a new icon, the blade within his forearm housing. He twisted his wrist aside twice and the blade snapped out.

"Sir," Masako asked Tongea, "there's no targeting routine for this weapon in our rigs. I assume there won't be one in our armor either. Why is that?"

"This is not a ballistics equation," Tongea said. "When you receive your plugs, you won't suddenly know Kung Fu or any of the European martial arts traditions. If you will learn to wield this weapon with any degree of skill, it will take time and practice. Match my movements.

This is high guard."

Roland brought his blade over his head to match the cadre member. It struck him as odd that he, training to fight inside an advanced suit of armor carrying multiple ranged weapons, would ever have to use something so basic as a sharpened length of metal. Then he remembered the statues at Memorial Square, and that every one of the armor at that battle wielded a sword or a spear.

What kind of enemy do we have to kill in hand-to-hand combat? he thought. After the first hour of practice, he stopped worrying and did his best to follow Tongea's instruction without accidentally stabbing himself.

****

Gideon ran a finger down a candidate's neural data. "Marginal," he said to Tongea.

"Mars," the Maori said.

"You and I just agreed to cut three candidates with significantly higher synch ratings," Gideon said. "Why keep this one?"

"Because synch ratings are not the measure of a warrior." Tongea flexed his replacement arm. The skin had darkened slightly to match his natural tone and the muscles were nearly a match for his other appendage. "We cannot train heart, aggression. A candidate without iron makes a hollow suit."

"Don't quote Carius at me," Gideon said. "I sat through all the same lectures you did."

"Then why do I have to remind you? You'll form your lance from these candidates. Would you trust that one to fight by your side, even with the marginal data?"

"The chance of a redline is too high. Simply getting the plugs might prove disastrous." Gideon ran a fingertip down the scar on his face. "But leading soldiers into battle is risk. How can I expect three soldiers to follow me into a fight when I won't even carry them to Mars because of risk?"

"Martel was right. You are ready for a lance," Tongea said.

"We'll have Eeks counsel this one and all the marginals before we leave. We'll see which of them decide to stay on," Gideon said.

"All of them will choose Mars over failure. I know it."

Gideon swiped across the screen.

"Cut," he said. "Too hesitant in hand-to-hand combat. Gunnery skills are subpar."

"Cut," Tongea said, "without prejudice. Let him try again in a few years."

Gideon swiped again.

****

Roland had his hands and feet braced against the floor as he pushed up and bent at the hips, sweat running down his face.

"Thirty seconds to go," Aignar said from his desk, "eight more push-ups to max the PT test."

Roland dropped his hips down into a plank position and did two more repetitions. His arms shook halfway through the third and he collapsed against the floor.

"Last one didn't count," Aignar said.

"You think?" Roland mumbled into the floor.

A pair of white envelopes slid beneath their door and a shadow moved in the hallway on the other side.

"Uh oh…" Roland pushed himself up and wiped sweat from his forehead. Aignar walked over, the bare metal of his cyborg feet clicking against the floor.

"Staring at them won't change what's inside," Aignar said. "But you read yours first."

"No, you read *yours* first. You're a damn robo-jock

in the rigs. They wouldn't cut you."

"I know. That's why I want you to read yours first. You stay on to the next phase of training, I know I'm good to go."

"We read them at the same time." Roland picked up the thin envelopes and ripped open Aignar's before he handed it over.

Roland turned the small paper square over in his hands. Every last mistake he'd made in the past months replayed through his mind. No matter what was in the envelope, at least he'd made it further than he ever thought possible.

"Here goes," Roland said, tearing off a side and plucking out the folded message. He read it with one eye shut, then looked up at Aignar.

"I'm going to Mars," Aignar said.

"So am I." Roland let out a deep sigh.

"Hot damn," Aignar said and extended a fist to his roommate. Roland smacked his knuckles against Aignar's and pulled back his hand with a yelp of pain. Shaking his hand out, he cursed through gritted teeth.

"Dumbass," Aignar said. "If you just broke your hand, I'll bet the cadre will change their minds."

Roland opened and closed his fingers and shook his

hand again as he glanced at the letter.

"We're leaving tomorrow out of Phoenix? Guess we'd better pack," Roland said.

"Phoenix…" Aignar looked over his message, then typed out an email on his slate.

CHAPTER 13

At a food truck on the corner of Thomas and Arcadia, a robot sprinkled cilantro over three small chicken and onion soft tacos and handed the plate to Cha'ril. She joined Masako and Roland—both of whom were already eating—at a nearby bench. The three wore the Armor Corps Class A uniforms: deep-green jackets and trousers with a Sam Brown leather belt around their waist and a strap over one shoulder.

"You don't have any problem eating chicken, Cha'ril?" Roland asked.

"Why would I?" She rolled her taco tight and ripped half of it away with her beak. "Because I share avian characteristics? You have carne asada. Masako has the adobo pork special. Both of you are eating mammals—or you would be, if any of this was actually meat."

"She's got us there," Masako said.

"Roland is correct that this is a superior mobile kitchen," Cha'ril said. "You are an adequate guide."

"Wow, faint praise from Cha'ril, I'm moving up in the world," Roland said. "The owner grows his own vegetables, a step up from the ersatz stuff out of the nutrient factories."

"Our last day on Earth for who knows how long," Masako said. "What else does Phoenix have to offer?"

"You two should overconsume alcohol again," Cha'ril said. "The other Dotari are most curious as to this human behavior."

"No," Roland and Masako said together.

Masako put her half-finished plate aside and touched her stomach.

A dozen yards away, a stretch limo came to a stop and the driver door opened. A woman in a neat suit, hair tied into a severe bun, and sunglasses walked toward them and Roland thought he recognized her from somewhere.

"Excuse me," she said to Roland in a firm voice, "but are you a former employee of Deco's?"

Roland swallowed a bite of carne asada—hard. "Yes, I was."

"Mr. Standish would like to have a word with you."

She pointed back to the limousine.

"Standish?" Cha'ril's eyebrows perked up.

"You're all welcome," the woman said.

"Can we—" Masako stood up, still holding her food.

"Food is expressly forbidden within the vehicle," she snapped.

"Julie!" Standish called from an open window. "Stop scaring them."

"Can't a girl just be a little hungry?" Masako left her lunch on the bench and walked to the limo with Cha'ril and Roland. The door slid open to a leather couch stretching around the interior of the vehicle.

Standish, wearing an Italian-cut suit and shoes that looked like they cost more than Roland would ever make in the military, waved them inside.

"Yes, darling," Standish said into a phone pressed to his ear, "I'm sure we need the bathroom redone in Art Deco...What karat gold plating? How about twelve...Because it's not the guest bathroom, that's why...Does it have to be off-world marble? OK. OK. I've got a meeting with some clients...Love you too. Kisses." He pulled the phone away, gave off a long sigh and pointed a finger at Roland. "Never argue with a woman when it comes to her nest. Just smile and nod and pretend you're interested."

Standish rapped on the glass partition behind him. "Julie. To Vinny's."

Masako sat with her hands clenched tight to her waist, staring at Standish, almost starstruck. Roland and Cha'ril looked around the limousine, admiring the deep leather seats and golden embossed ceiling.

"Well, would you look at you," Standish said to Roland. "Made Armor Corps. Well done, kiddo. Well done."

"Thank you, Mr. Standish. You didn't have anything to do with me getting in, did you?"

"Ha!" Standish stomped a foot to the floor. "You think I'd risk pissing off the Corps by putting my thumb on the scale? Good way to get your head crushed like a grape, doesn't matter who you are. No, my boy, you've got no one to blame but yourself for where you're at today. Good luck on Mars. The easy part's almost over."

Standish leaned toward Cha'ril. "Now, a little birdy told me someone from Takeni came to visit her." He raised an eyebrow. "Someone with a father that has a good deal of clout with the Council of Firsts."

"Yes..." Cha'ril's quills bristled slightly. "If that

was improper, I meant no—"

"Where is my statue?" Standish asked. "I sent one to the Dotari almost two years ago. Nice one. Twenty feet tall. Italian marble. Why don't I see it anywhere on the news feeds from New Abhaile? Where did they put it?"

"Sir, you sent a statue…of yourself…to the Dotari?" Roland asked.

"Is there some reason they wouldn't want one? You have seen the remastered cut of *Last Stand on Takeni* with yours truly in it?"

"Of course," Roland said. Masako elbowed him in the side. "Much better than the original."

"My father did mention this," Cha'ril said. "The Dotari don't erect…statues. We do not honor the living that way, but a memorial *ganii* tree would be appropriate. Later."

"How much later?"

"After you've died."

"Then where the hell is my statue?"

"Still in the shipping container, I believe."

Standish threw his hands in the air and sank against the couch.

"After all I did for the Dotari…my own fault for not knowing the culture. Guess I'll have it brought back to

Earth and set up next to the lap pool."

"Mr. Standish," Masako said, "we've heard some stories about you."

"If you're working with a lawyer, I will neither confirm nor deny anything."

"No, sir, nothing like that. Did you know the Iron Hearts?"

"Knew them? They saved my bacon on more than one occasion. When Kallen and Bodel decided they were going to pull Elias out of his redline, they came to me for help. There were some allegations of grand theft, kidnapping, misappropriation of military hardware after that, but none of it was ever proven," Standish said, wagging a finger at her.

"Saw Elias and Bodel with the rest of the armor in that circle around the bomb that ended the war," he continued. "Don't think I've ever had a prouder—or sadder—moment in my life. What do you want to know?"

"What were they like?" Roland asked.

"Never met a group of people more devoted to each other than the Iron Hearts," Standish said. "You three are going to be armor once you reach Mars. Maybe there you'll figure out what made them like that, because for all my years as a Marine, I never saw anything like what Kallen did for Elias." He tapped his temple with a finger. "She went into his mind and pulled him out of the darkness.

"I know one other person who was that far gone but made it back, but we don't speak about that. You all still hungry? We're going to my favorite hole-in-the-wall Italian place."

****

Aignar sat on a park bench in his Class A's, looking across Memorial Square. Passersby noticed him, their eyes lingering on his ribbons and the speaker embedded in his neck. Unable to smile in return, Aignar nodded to those whose gaze lingered.

"Dad?" a young voice asked.

A light-haired boy with blue eyes leaned over the bench.

"Joshua." He opened his arms and the nine-year-old ran around the bench to hug his father. Aignar enclosed the child inside his arms, but didn't press his artificial hands to the boy's back.

"You look…better." Joshua shied away from his father and sat on the bench, kicking his dangling feet and staring out across the park.

Aignar squeezed his hands into fists, the servos whining.

"Better prosthetics, more lifelike. Not like when you saw me in the hospital with the metal fingers. I know they scared you."

"I was seven. Now that I'm nine I'm not afraid of little-kid stuff."

"This is as good as its going to get," Aignar said. "The doctors can't fix me anymore."

"Why are you still in the army?" Joshua asked. "Mom says they'll let you go. You could get a job in San Diego near us. We could be together all the time. Did Mom tell you I'm in soccer? I'm the best goalie in the league."

Aignar felt a swell in his chest.

"I can't leave yet, son. There's still more I have to do."

"What? You went and fought those Vishy aliens. They hurt you…why do you want to go back out there? What can you do?" Joshua looked at his father's prosthetics and crossed his arms.

"You remember what I told you? Before I left for Cygnus with the Rangers?"

"That there are monsters out there like the Xaros that killed Grandma and Grandpa…and you're going to make sure they never come to Earth."

"I have to go back out there, son. For you. For your mother. For everyone."

"When will you come home for good?"

"I don't know, son. But I'll come back to Earth and see you whenever I can."

"What will you even do?" Joshua tapped a foot against his father's metal shin.

"Come with me." He stood up and motioned to the armor statues in Memorial Square. "I'll tell you a story."

CHAPTER 14

Sol Conveyance–class ships, like most everything in the Terran military, were not built for comfort. The mass-produced cargo and personnel ships were nearly fully automated. The small handful of crew spent their time monitoring the robots and computer systems that ran the ship, and supervising the robots and computer systems that fixed the other robots and systems when those broke down. The ships were assembled by the dozens in the shipyards locked in Mercury's shadow, and dispatched across the solar system.

The fleet of ships connected every planet on an established timetable like busses in a busy city, which made the Terran Logistic Command's job a good deal easier.

Roland and the rest of his class had boarded *Aries 12-12* a few hours ago, and sat through a somewhat dated presentation on safety and emergency procedures before being released to their bunks and the rec room full of aged board games and a sputtering holo big-screen.

One of the few redeeming qualities of the *Conveyance*-class ships was the forward observation deck located over the prow. The crews normally kept them shuttered to cut down on micro-meteor strikes (which they'd have to repair), but a pleasant smile and kind request from Masako had convinced the sailors to open the deck for the armor candidates.

Roland stood close to the curved glass that wrapped around the deck, one hand clenched on a handlebar as he watched the Earth turn. The edge of a swirling hurricane stretched over Florida. Running lights flickered in the distance from shuttles rising out of the planet's gravity well to Titan Station as it rose over the horizon.

"First time in orbit?" Masako asked.

"That's right. You?"

"My parents took us on a family trip to Luna when we were kids. Nothing like the threat of dying in hard vacuum to make a six-year-old learn to love the void," she said.

"You see it in vids and pictures all the time," Roland said, "but like this…it's beautiful."

"Curious that humans developed on a planet with so much water," Cha'ril said. "The Ruhaald home world has even more land mass than Earth, and they came from a very different evolutionary background."

"You're lots of fun to have around, Cha'ril," Aignar said. "There a way to translate 'Debbie Downer' into Dotari?"

"I am not moved to poetry," she said. "The view from my arrival to Earth was very similar to this."

The ship turned to port, and Ceres came into view with the Crucible star gate.

"There it is, boys and girls," Aignar said, "our key to the rest of the galaxy."

"How many times have you been through?" Roland asked.

"Four…" Aignar touched his faux-chin with the back of his hand. "Three that I remember. Traveling through a quantum wormhole is not fun."

"It takes some getting used to," Tongea said from the doorway behind them.

The candidates snapped to attention.

"Shaw, zoom in on the Crucible," the cadre ordered.

Roland touched his index fingers to the glass and pulled them away from each other, magnifying on the

Crucible. Tongea came over and adjusted the view screen. Up close, the Crucible was basalt-colored spikes, each hundreds of miles long, formed into a giant crown of thorns. The thorns moved against each other, forever in motion like a sea urchin in a tide pool.

"Why does it do…that?" Roland asked.

"The individual thorns manipulate the quantum field within the gate," Tongea said. "This gate is connected to all the others across the galaxy, to include the new ones built by the races that were part of the old Alliance. The Minder also uses the gate to create a wave fluctuation that stops other gates from opening a wormhole too close to the system or from using our gate. Our ships on other worlds transmit codes to come through."

"A 'Minder'?" Masako asked.

"That's what she calls herself," Tongea said. "Deck. Lights."

The observation deck went dark. After a few seconds, Roland's eyes adjusted and he could see the deep field of stars beyond Ceres. A crushing sense of smallness came over him as he realized just how far the universe reached, and just how insignificant he was in comparison.

Masako gave his hand a quick squeeze, then pulled away.

"What did we ever learn about the Xaros?" Masako asked. "They were technologically advanced enough to build giant drone swarms that wiped out most of humanity, moved Ceres into orbit around Earth, and built the Crucible gate network. Is there really nothing left of them after the war?"

"According to the Minder, the Xaros fled their home galaxy after some sort of a cosmologic disaster," Tongea said. "They sent their drones to cleanse the Milky Way of all intelligent life before their world ship arrived. The *Breitenfeld* and armor," Tongea touched his knuckles to his lips, "destroyed the world ship and the Xaros Masters. We've found no trace of the drones or their leadership since then, but the Crucible gates remain. The only direct interaction we ever had with their masters was in combat. The Iron Hearts defeated a master called the General, killed it during their second battle."

"Did you know them?" Cha'ril asked. "Or the pair of Dotari who joined their lance at the end of the war?"

"I knew them. Fought beside them in Australia before they'd earned their spurs. I volunteered for the final mission to the Xaros world ship, but old Colonel Carius didn't choose me or my lance."

"Did you know it was a suicide mission when you

volunteered?" Roland asked.

"Every armor soldier volunteered for that mission. Carius took only the best of us—his Templars, the Hussars...and the Iron Hearts." Tongea's face fell. "We are less without them."

A tremor passed through the Crucible.

"Watch," Tongea said. "See how the spikes are moving now?"

A white point of light formed in the center of the gate and blossomed into a thin field. A battle cruiser and several smaller escorts materialized out of the wormhole and arced away from Ceres toward Earth.

"The *Nixon*," Tongea said, "back from her recon mission so soon?"

"What was she looking for?" Cha'ril asked.

"Lost souls." Tongea stepped away from the glass and hurried out of the room.

"Should we be worried?" Roland asked. "He seemed...concerned."

"Perhaps the *Nixon* found an answer to the roster discrepancy of some years ago," Cha'ril said. "The Terran and Dotari have a mutual-defense treaty, and we share a great deal of information with each other. After the Hale Treaty was signed several years ago, a battle group from your 9th Fleet was deleted from the roster. According to my father, the Terran High Command said the ships were 'declared overdue.' That no other details were forthcoming was rather odd."

"Did your father ever find anything else?" Masako asked.

"Those that asked were told to 'keep their nose out of it,' which is ridiculous. We have beaks."

"Aignar? Ever hear of a ghost fleet?" Roland asked.

"I was a Ranger. The only thing we cared about with the navy was them getting us to the fight and not blasting us into paste if they screwed up an orbital fire-support mission. I never heard anything."

"But Tongea knows something," Masako said.

"I'd rather not piss him off," Roland said. "If the Dotari got told to pound sand over this, imagine what'll happen to us if we stick our nose—or beak—where it doesn't belong. We have enough to worry—"

"*All candidates,*" Gideon's voice came from their gauntlets, "*report to cargo bay seven. Full combatives gear.*"

"No breaks during this trip," Masako said.

"We had eight whole hours to ourselves back at Phoenix," Roland said. "How could we ask for more?"

"If I get you on the mat, I'm going for your kidneys," she said.

****

A Mule shuttle flew from the *Verdun*, one of the many orbital fortresses around Mars, and dove toward the red planet. Roland swung his turret around, his hands gripping the gauss cannon controls tightly. Riding in the turret protruding from the Mule's hull almost felt like flying. A grin spread across his face as the Mule accelerated forward, pressing him against the turret seat.

"*I hate you so much right now,*" Masako sent through the shuttle's IR.

"Should've beat me on the last VR range. I dropped anchor and got the rail cannon shot off a full half-second before you did," Roland said.

"*My own fault for teaching you to anchor in sandstone rather than shale,*" she said with a huff. "*How's the view? Not much to see in the cargo bay but the other thirty candidates from Knox and Gideon's smiling face.*"

"Spectacular." Gossamer clouds stretched across the Martian atmosphere. Looping over the equator, a swarm of construction ships worked on a partially built orbital ring, and prebuilt segments loitered near the busy end of the ring.

"You should see the Ibarra ring," Roland said. "I remember when they started work on it a few years ago. Only another ten years before it's fully operational."

"*Why is the Terran High Command putting so many resources into defending Mars and not Earth?*" Cha'ril asked from the upper turret. "*Ninety percent of the system's population is on—*"

"Better to have Mars as the target of an invasion than Earth," Gideon cut in. "Mars is the lynchpin to the system's defenses. It is the anvil the Xaros broke against during the last invasion. The planet is easier to defend with its lack of atmosphere—fighting in vac suits isn't easy for most species—and Mars' dead core keeps earthquakes from interfering with the macro-cannons. Anyone comes for Earth, they'll be hammered by Mars. Enemy comes for Mars, the rest of the system's defenses will make them pay for every second they're in system."

"In theory, right, sir?" Roland asked.

"Do you see any Vishrakath or Naroosha ships anywhere?"

"No…"

Roland saw a long shadow cast across the Martian

surface and followed it back to a wide shield volcano. A cloud bank ran up one slope, dissipating to nothing before it reached the caldera.

Olympus Mons rose twenty-one miles over the surrounding plains, two and a half times taller than Mount Everest on Earth. The long-dead volcano was almost round, reminding Roland of the shields Spartans once carried into battle. The entire mountain could have fit snugly into France, if such a thing as countries still existed back on Earth.

Roland looked down at his new home and touched the nubs on the back of his skull. Soon. Soon they'd receive their plugs and finally become armor.

Wisps of flame and superheated air ran along the Mule's reentry shield as it descended into the atmosphere.

****

With a whine, the Mule's ramp descended and Roland and the other candidates marched into the hangar bay, falling into formation in front of Gideon, whose face had softened for the first time since Roland had met him. If he wasn't careful, the candidate would almost guess that the scarred man was happy to be here.

He looked up at the massive metal door in the roof and ran a hand across the emergency hood in a pouch on his thigh. The Mars ground uniforms that they all wore incorporated an environmental layer and small air tanks that would protect them for up to two hours beyond the pressurized confines of Olympus.

The cadre had forbidden them from eating or sleeping during the three-day trip from Earth until they could don their emergency hoods and gloves and pressurize their suits in less than ten seconds.

Roland hoped the safety measures were just a precaution, and that exposure to the deadly thin Martian atmosphere was an exceedingly rare hazard for anyone stationed here.

A dozen other Mules and a few of the larger Destrier transports took up most of the hangar. Personnel in armor corps gray serviced the ships and loaded cargo onto drone carts for delivery through twenty-foot-tall and overly wide sally ports around the hangar.

A suit of armor—a patch with a blue, red and yellow triangle on its breast—walked over to the formation and stopped near Gideon, red dust clinging to the armor's legs and hands.

"Dragoon," came from the armor's speaker, "good

to see you again. Brought us new bean heads?" The armor thumped a fist to its breastplate, letting off a clang that stung Roland's ears.

Gideon returned the salute.

"Not bean heads yet, Captain Rapp. I'm taking them to surgery now," Gideon said.

"Ha!" The armor's helm looked over the candidates. "See you all on the high ground."

"Surgery?" Masako asked quietly from her spot in the line next to Roland. "So soon?"

"Can't get much further without the plugs," Roland said. "It'll be all right. This is what we've been training for, right?"

"Platoon!" Gideon called out. "By file, follow me to the tram."

Masako didn't say anything else as they went single file to a platform on the far side of the hangar. By the time they loaded up into a tram pod and traveled deeper into the mountain, she'd lost much of the color in her face.

****

Roland pinched the paper-thin smock he wore and pulled it away from his legs. It wafted cold air over his bare body as it fell. The small exam room had no clock, and he hadn't bothered to keep track of how long he'd been waiting. Medical readouts of his nervous system clicked through a succession of images.

There was a knock on the door and Dr. Eeks came in, wearing surgical scrubs, and a face mask dangling from her neck. Tongea and an officer with a cross for his branch insignia came in behind her.

"Candidate Shaw," the doctor said, "all your readouts are in the green. Bend over slightly and let me get those nubs out for you. Tongea you know; Chaplain Krohe you don't."

Roland leaned forward and lowered his chin to his chest. He felt Eeks' touch against his neck and his skin went numb after a slight hiss of air.

"There's an issue we need to go over," Tongea said.

Roland felt a chill of fear in his chest. Did the cadre know he went to Bailey's bar? Wouldn't they have cut him before sending him to Mars if they knew?

"Do you know what redlining is?" Tongea asked.

"It's something that happened to that Iron Heart, Elias. I've heard it mentioned, never explained."

"Apropos that he brings up Elias," Eeks murmured. Roland felt a tug on his neck.

"Once you receive your plugs," Tongea said, "your nervous system is at risk of overloading while in your armor. You can push the suit to do more than your body is capable of, but the feedback from armor can be more than your brain can handle. Similar to a fighter pilot blacking out if they pull too many gravities in a maneuver, or like crashing if you're driving a car too fast when you make a sudden turn."

"I can wreck myself if I'm not careful," Roland said as he felt another tug at his neck.

"The armor has a number of safeguards to stop you from redlining, but they can be broken if the situation calls for it," Tongea said. "Breaking the restraints won't redline you immediately, but you'll be dangerously close to it."

"And what situations call for this, sir?" Roland asked.

"Elias, who you mentioned, redlined after a data spike from firing two gauss cannons. He did it to save his ship, the *Breitenfeld*, during the Battle for Ceres. Others have fallen while trying to compensate for battle damage. The Naroosha used a nerve-shock limpet mine that...neutralized...two lances before we found a countermeasure. Most redlines happened in the early days of the Corps."

"We've improved our screening procedures." Eeks tugged at Roland's neck again and he heard small pieces of metal fall into a tray. "Your risk factor is in a lower tier compared to others."

"So on the battlefield I've got to worry about being shot at and my brain exploding?" Roland asked.

"The former is much more likely." Eeks spritzed the back of Roland's neck and slapped him on the shoulder. "Done."

He sat up and put a hand to the back of his neck. The flesh where his nubs used to be was soft.

"What happens when I redline?" he asked.

"Your synaptic links are scrambled," Eeks said, snapping off her surgical gloves, "resulting in a coma bordering on locked-in syndrome as you're unable to do much in the way of cognition. Some cases are worse than others."

"But Elias…didn't he recover from it?"

"Barely," Eeks said. "Bringing him out of his redline damaged his brain stem. His womb took over those brain functions to keep him alive. He never came out of his armor again."

Roland rubbed his palms down his legs. The thought of spending the rest of his life inside a womb…

"But how?" Roland asked. "Why not do it for the others who've redlined."

"It was a miracle," Tongea said solemnly.

"It was not," Eeks snapped at him. "The human neural system does not work on faith. She joined Elias' neural connection and managed to coax his consciousness back to the fore. That her body was already compromised is probably the only reason she survived the experience."

"Who're you talking about?" Roland asked.

"We've never replicated the…event because there is too much risk to all parties involved," Eeks said. "No matter how often you armor jockeys ask to do it. So…bottom line for you, Mr. Shaw, you redline—there's no coming back. Understand?"

"Yes, ma'am."

"The next thing you must know," Tongea said, "is that there are some side effects to the procedure. Minor numbness and tingling in the limbs when out of the suit. Epilepsy is uncommon, but possible. Batten's Disease is a risk—but small—and we monitor for it."

"What's—"

"Degenerative neurological condition. Terminal if not treated," Eeks said.

"Is all this good news why you brought the

chaplain?" Roland shifted back on the exam table.

"Many candidates take solace in a moment of prayer before surgery," Krohe said.

Roland touched the back of his head.

"Chief, would you mind turning around for me?" he asked Tongea. The cadre member twisted to his side and let Roland see his plugs. "You ever have any regrets?"

Tongea faced Roland.

"The only regrets I have in life are the things I did not do, not the actions I took." Tongea held up his off-colored hand. "In the Corps I make a difference. I have no doubts as to my purpose. I am armor."

"Then let's do this," Roland said.

"Here comes the fun part," Eeks said, pressing a hypo to his neck. "Everything's going to be awesome in a few minutes."

"Are you one for faith, my boy?" Krohe asked.

"Not really, but…" Roland's hands began to tremble. "Is this normal?"

"It's normal to be scared," Krohe said. "I can pray with you, for you, stay…leave. Up to you."

Roland looked at the cross on Krohe's uniform, then to the Templar symbol on Tongea's shoulder.

"Chief, I heard you praying once. Would you and

the chaplain...do that one for me?"

Tongea raised an eyebrow, then looked at Krohe.

"She wouldn't mind," the chaplain said. He put a hand on the back of Roland's neck and bowed his head forward. Tongea put his hand over Roland's neck and the three men formed a small huddle.

"*Sancti spiritus adsit nobis gratia,*" Krohe and Tongea said together, "*Kallen, ferrum corde...*"

CHAPTER 15

Roland snapped awake. He saw an oil-stained floor and reached out to steady himself against whatever ladder or walkway he was on before he fell. His arms and legs didn't move. He tried to look around, but his head would only move a few degrees in any direction. He blinked, but his vision remained unsteady.

"Synaptic pathways nominal." He heard Eeks in his ears but didn't see her. *"Bit of a feedback loop through the shunts, compensating."*

A suit of armor stepped into view, its helm looking him right in the eyes.

"Shaw, you hear me?" Gideon asked.

"Yes, sir." Roland struggled to lift his right arm, then a metal appendage with a double-barreled gauss cannon attached to the forearm came up.

"*He's green across the board, but don't push it,*" Eeks said.

"Shaw," Gideon said, as the cadre's armor tapped him on the chest. He felt the touch, but the point of contact was beyond his body.

"You are armor. Walk."

Roland took a step forward and the stomp of metal on metal filled the room. He looked down at his armor's legs and watched them stride forward. His balance shifted and Gideon caught him before he could fall over.

"Easy. Takes a little getting used to," Gideon said.

"*Equilibrium adjusted, change logged with his womb,*" Eeks said.

"Synch rate?"

"*Thirty-seven percent and climbing fast,*" she said.

Gideon released him and stepped back.

"This…is a little different." Roland's words came from his armor's speakers.

"You're doing just fine," Gideon said, his helm motioning toward an air lock, "but you need to walk a bit. Get your synch rating up through some locomotion. Doors." He said the last word loudly.

Red warning lights snapped on next to the air lock as the door cracked open in the middle, the barren red world of Mars opening before them.

Roland reached for an emergency hood at his hip and banged his hands against the servo rings that served as his armor's waist.

"What do you need that for?" Gideon asked. "What're you breathing?"

"I…" Roland felt a slight sensation of moisture within the armor. "I'm in the womb. I don't need air."

"You're not a crunchy anymore, Shaw. You need to forget your old limitations and become your armor. You're next to useless in combat without at least a sixty percent synch rating. Still a long way to go before you've earned your spurs. Follow me."

Gideon marched through the thin force field separating the outside from the hangar, leaving wide footprints in the rust-colored dust.

Roland walked forward, feeling the floor through the armor's feet, the force field sending a slight tingle over his body as he passed through. The bite of Mars' air hit him like a cold shower and he came to a stop, kicking up rocks and dust.

"Get it?" Gideon asked.

"*He's a little sensitive. Let me dial him back,*" Eeks said.

The chill faded away. Roland took in the pink sky, the thin clouds over the short horizon, and turned back to the hangar door. A solid rock cliff extended as far as he could see to either side and miles into the sky.

"Whoa..." Roland sank slightly as vertigo overcame him.

"Quite the sight," Gideon said. "Mars' volcanoes are the only ones in the solar system with escarpments like this. We've managed to hollow out a few hundred square miles. Still have to add aegis shielding and more rail cannon batteries along the slopes. It'll take another twenty years before the initial concept is complete. Work continues after that."

"Always improve your fighting position," Roland said.

"Correct. How do you feel right now?"

"I can *feel* the armor...and myself in the womb. It's...weird."

"The neural shunt feeds the suit's sensor information to you in a way your brain can process it. You'll learn to dissociate from your body and that will help with your synch rate. The hardest part is compensating for battle damage. Take a shaped charge through your shoulder servos, the suit will feed you a pain response, but nowhere near as bad as taking the hit to your true body."

"How long will it take to get used to this?"

"Six months in the suit to be fully combat-rated. But before that…catch." Gideon tossed a rock into the air. Roland's hand opened and the stone landed in his palm.

"Good. Your armor does most of the calculations. Your mind provides the impulse; the armor does the work.

Roland's fingers closed on the rock and crushed it into jagged fragments.

"You mean to do that?" Gideon asked.

"Yes, sir. Curious how strong I am."

"Your womb is limiting most of what you're capable of, for now. More will come in phases." Gideon kicked a loose rock and rocketed it toward Roland's helm. Roland's hand snapped up faster than his flesh-and-blood limbs could ever manage and caught the projectile.

"Not bad, Shaw. How far can you throw it?"

Roland brought his arm back and his torso twisted to the side. He hurled the rock into the air. It sailed up…and he lost track of it as it shrank away.

"By the time you're ready for combat," Gideon said, "you'll be able to rip through a starship. Shoot the enemy with both cannons at the same time and call in an airstrike while you're ending any crunchy alien that gets within reach. You will become the mailed fist of humanity's might. But for now, you need to learn to walk. Come."

Roland walked beside Gideon, watching his footfalls over the uneven terrain. The cadre motioned toward a ravine in the distance.

"Why did the Armor Corps build our base on Mars?" Gideon asked.

"The Corps was assigned here during the second Xaros invasion," Roland said. "The cannons, the real big ones, the defenses weren't ready when the Xaros showed up. Armor was split up to defend the emplacements from the drones."

"Half the Corps fell in battle," Gideon said. "Far fewer than we lost taking the Crucible and the battle against the Toth. Most of the dead were new Dotari recruits. They learn fast, are just as capable in the armor as we are, but they had no combat experience. Carius, the old Corps commander, declared Olympus hallowed ground for the sacrifice paid that day."

"You were there?"

"I was. Still hadn't earned my place in a lance back then, but I had a high enough synch rating to fight. Battles against total annihilation demand every gun in the fight, no matter what a bean head I still was."

Gideon stopped at the edge of the ravine. Roland looked over the edge and into the fissure almost a hundred yards deep.

"We call them wadis," Gideon said. "Old armor term from when the American tanks practiced in the California desert. Now that you've got walking down, it's time to learn to fall."

He grabbed Roland by the shoulder and shoved him into the ravine.

Roland's arms pinwheeled as he tipped end over end. He let off an undignified yell until he careened off the other wadi wall and went spinning. When he hit the wall again, he managed to grab a handhold. The rock snapped away, barely slowing his fall. He slammed his fingers into the rock, remembering when the Toth android had dragged him through the Australian mud and how helpless he'd felt.

He tore furrows through the wall until he finally came to a stop. He looked up for Gideon, but he wasn't there.

"Shaw," Gideon said from behind him.

Roland tried to turn around, but his grip was absolute.

"Turn your head, not your body," Gideon said.

266

Roland's vision panned around until his helm had rotated 180 degrees. Gideon stood a few yards away.

"Are you floating?" Roland asked. He kicked his heels in the air.

"Look down."

Roland found himself a few feet off the ground. He pried his fingers loose and thumped into deep sand.

Roland touched his armor and helm where they'd bounced off the rock during his fall, and wiped dust away.

"You're armor. You think a little fall in this gravity will hurt you?" Gideon asked.

"This whole day's been full of surprises. What's next? Tongea jumps out and shoots me with a gauss rifle to see if I flinch?"

Gideon twisted a heel in the dust, and Roland felt like the older soldier was staring daggers at him.

"Sorry, sir."

"Onward." Gideon walked through the wadi that widened and deepened as they went into a narrow canyon. Scorch marks appeared on the upper edge of the walls as they turned a corner. Roland sidestepped around broken hunks of rock almost as large as his armor.

"What happened here?" he asked.

"Admiral Garret and Marc Ibarra played off the

battle against the Xaros as an impossible victory," Gideon said. "But I was there. The only reason we won was because the Iron Hearts finished off the Xaros General back on Earth. The drones reverted to their base programming and became easier to predict, to beat. Mars held...barely."

Gideon hesitated a few steps from a narrow passage through the canyon. Shadows dominated the other side.

"You go first," Gideon said.

Roland rolled his shoulders back and forth, feeling the extended range of motion his armor enjoyed over his true body. The thought of how useless it was to limber up mechanical parts before a potential fight struck him.

He sidestepped through the gap and found a suit of armor lying in the sand, its head and shoulder propped against the rock wall, its arms bent at the elbows and helm turned up, like it was frozen in rigor mortis. Four enormous claw marks scarred one side of the breastplate, the marks deepening to a full breach of the armor. The armored womb that should've been inside was missing. Small eddies of sand whirled around the armor, its legs already buried beneath a tide of red dust. The ripped remnants of a fleur-de-lis patch on the breastplate were faded and sand worn.

Roland's stomach heaved. His true hand pressed against his womb and his armor recoiled.

"No no no...what's happening?" Roland stumbled backwards and landed hard. One leg cocked to the sky, his metal arms flopping like a fish out of water.

"Override, code gamma," Gideon said. Roland's armor froze. "I am armor, Shaw. Say it."

"I am armor." The feel of cold sand and rocks beneath his back intensified.

"Your synch rate dropped below ten percent when you saw the wreck. Your mind imagined the damage to your true body and it created a dissonance between you and the armor. Be the armor. Now get up."

Roland's limbs returned to his control. He rolled over and got to his feet, his legs wide like a newborn deer standing for the first time.

"What happened to him?" Roland asked.

"The Xaros General ambushed us. It took out one of our Dotari recruits, Han'va, first," Gideon said. "Captain Dorral landed a few shots...but bullets weren't enough to kill that thing. I hit it with a quadrium round, managed to disrupt the General's matrix enough to get him to back off."

"What were you even doing down here?"

"Trying to help," Gideon said, looking up.

Wedged between the canyon walls, the scorched,

battered remains of a frigate hung suspended a few dozen yards over the ground. Armor panels hung from the hull and Roland could see into the ship through ugly rents along the hull.

"The *Nashville*," Gideon said. "Lost most of her engine power over Noachia and burned into orbit. Her skipper managed a decent landing, all things considered, but she hit with enough force to send her bulldozing through the dirt and into this canyon."

"Any survivors?"

"Eighty-three. The captain wasn't one of them."

"Why didn't you bring the armor back to Olympus? What happened to Han'va?"

"Han'va's with the Dotari brigade on their world. Lost his legs and eyes to exposure, but he's still armor. The suit is a total loss. The captain decided to keep it here, let it remind bean heads like you what it means to fight. Dorral was a good lance commander. We are less without him. Now," Gideon said, pointing to the sky, "we climb."

****

Roland watched the as the sun set beyond the rim of a distant crater, the dying glow of the Martian twilight

270

filtering through dust particles high in the sky. A faint gust of wind swept over the small mesa where he and Gideon stood.

"Nothing like home," the cadre said, "not that we'll be here long."

"Is there another war? Thought the rest of the galaxy would've got the message after the Cygnus campaign."

"Armor can go where the crunchies can't. Deep space. High-pressure atmosphere. Irradiated area. There's a whole tour of the solar system waiting for you. Fighting on Mars isn't a challenge."

"When will I join a lance? How does that work?"

Gideon motioned toward a plume of kicked-up dust emanating from behind a nearby hill.

"When you're fully certified, the lance commanders will decide where you go. Some are more particular than others. Not everyone goes into a lance. Some are better suited for specialist loadouts and fall directly under the squadron commanders…who's that coming around the hill?"

Watching as a pair of armor strode into view, Roland said, "It's Masako and Tongea."

"How do you know?"

"By the way they walk."

"Very good, bean head."

A column of light erupted over the horizon, tapering away to nothing as it stabbed through the upper reaches of the atmosphere. Roland backpedaled, waiting for a reaction from Gideon.

A faint thunderclap came through Roland's microphones.

"Macro-cannon," Gideon said. "Rail guns too large for the navy's ships. There are hundreds built into the surface across the planet. Each one can put a munition through a goal post on Pluto. Calibration shot, by the look of the contrails. Never forget that Mars is a fortress, and armor guards the battlements. Let's get you back to the bays. Eeks will need a look at you."

****

The skin around Roland's plugs was raw, his nerve endings protesting every time his fingertips brushed past the implant. He swept his hand over his bald head. After his last shearing at Knox, his hair had finally regrown to the point where he could comb it, and it was taken all away while he slept.

He splashed water across his face and left the restroom.

"How'd it go?" asked an also-bald Aignar in the hallway.

"It happened." Roland shrugged and tapped the plug.

"You keep playing with it and you'll get a cone around your neck." Aignar twisted around and gave Roland a look at his new implant. "I've had worse surgeries. At least the plugs are inorganic. My body's immune system won't try to murder it like a new vat-organ." He pinched his fingers together with a snap.

"Hello, boys!" Masako said. She still had much of her hair, but it was cut into an inverted bob, high enough in the back to leave her plugs exposed. Cha'ril was with her...and looked no different.

"Cha'ril, what happened?" Roland asked.

"My surgery was successful. Why?" She looked down at her uniform for a discrepancy.

"Why did the rest of us get a barracks-special haircut and you're the same?" Aignar asked.

"My quills are not 'hair.' They help regulate my body temperature and are full of blood vessels. Cutting them off would kill me. Just because your species is constantly shedding does not mean the rest of the galaxy does the same."

"And here I thought getting plugs would mellow her out," Roland said.

"There's a formal function in the mess hall," Cha'ril said, tapping her gauntlet, "six minutes from now."

Roland fell back and walked beside Masako.

"I saw you out there with Gideon," she said.

"He's a bit different in the armor. How was your walk?"

"I had some trouble with terrain." A tic pulled at one side of her face and she rubbed her fingertips against the spot and smiled at Roland. "Eeks gave me a good workover and cleared me. Sounds like you had an easier...ahh..." She turned her head to the side and sucked air through her teeth.

"You OK? Should we get you back to Eeks?"

"Just some nerve endings figuring out their new place in the world. It's nothing. Like my new 'do?" She fluffed the tips of the angled hair coming down the side of her head. "I look like something out of those old anime comics."

"It suits you." Roland touched his forearm screen, tempted to call in a medical bot to look her over, but whatever pain had vexed her was gone. Roland's stomach rumbled.

"Me too," Masako said. "Haven't had a bite to eat since we landed."

Long tables covered with red linen ran down the length of the mess hall. A small stage at the far end had the Armor Corps, Terran Union and Dotari flags on either side. Almost two dozen candidates were already there, heads shaved and boasting fresh plugs. The clash of plates and steam came from an adjacent kitchen.

"What's all this?" Aignar asked.

"Big day for us," Roland said, "maybe it's a party."

"Or there's a bunch of Denevian spider wolves under the tables and we have to fight them off with our cutlery," Masako said. "Don't give me that look, Cha'ril. Who knows what the cadre are up to this time."

A master sergeant in the armor auxiliary uniform— gray in contrast with the Mars-red of the candidates' uniforms—and a chest full of ribbons stepped onto the stage.

"Candidates! Be seated."

Roland sat between Cha'ril and Masako. He tapped a foot beneath the table, searching for a false panel.

"No spiders," he whispered to Masako.

"Maybe ninjas will fall out of the ceiling. Stay alert," she said.

Silence fell as a colonel walked onto the stage. His uniform was bare but for a Templar cross on his shoulder and an armor badge on his chest. Roland gripped his chair, waiting for the command to rise to attention that should have come when any superior officer entered the room.

"Stay seated," the officer said. "I am Colonel Martel. You're all still recovering from your surgery and normal decorum is suspended for the near future. Congratulations on your First Walk. You reached this point through commitment and fortitude. I'm proud to have you all in my Regiment."

The colonel looked to one side, and a half-dozen officers entered the room and formed a line beside Martel. Four had the Templar Cross; two—one being Gideon—had other lance patches and wore their medals and ribbons.

Masako's hand began shaking atop her lap. She grasped it firmly and squeezed her eyes shut.

Roland gave her shoulder a nudge, but she shook her head quickly and pushed his touch away.

"These men and women are lance commanders. They will take part in the next and final phase of your training. In all likelihood, you will be assigned to one of them once assessment is complete," Martel said.

A trio of service robots rolled out of the kitchen, each holding ten trays in its segmented arms. Each human candidate got a plate of identical food and a drink bottle filled with blue liquid. The Dotari received a bowl full of steaming nuts.

"Eat, please," Martel said, waving a hand. "You've been without solid food longer than you realize. Let me introduce the first lance leader, Lieutenant Silva." He stepped away from the podium and Silva took his place.

Suddenly, Masako hissed and turned her face to Roland, her lips pulled back in pain. A hand slammed onto the edge of her plate, flipping it over and tossing food across the table. She looked at Roland for a second, then her eyes rolled back into her head. She fell backwards, limbs thrashing in a seizure.

Roland caught her, knocking over his chair as he set her to the ground. He grabbed her by the wrists and tried to stop her out-of-control movements. She kicked her chair over as the seizure grew stronger.

"Medic. Medic!" Roland cried.

Blood trickled out of her mouth as her jaw snapped open. He jammed the side of his hand into her mouth and took the bite, trying to stop her from severing her own tongue.

Colonel Martel pushed through the ring of candidates and knelt beside Masako. He took a hypo from off the small of his back and tapped it against her neck twice. Masako's convulsions faded, but her limbs and face kept twitching.

"Back to your quarters!" Martel called out. "All of you. Now."

Masako whimpered and curled into a ball. Roland pried his hand out of her mouth, ignoring the pain from the torn skin.

"Masako? Can you hear me?" He gave her shoulder a gentle shake.

"Shaw," Martel said, looking him straight in the eye, his word laced with the authority of command. "Return to your quarters. The medics are on the way. Go."

Hands grabbed Roland by the shoulder and pulled him up, then Gideon moved Roland through the cordon of lance commanders. Martel stayed at Masako's side, one hand cradling her head.

Roland's world shrank down to Masako, her body jerking as if it were receiving shocks every few seconds, her face slack and eyes unfocused.

"We've got this," Gideon said, putting a hand to

Roland's chest and nudging him backwards.

Roland, his mind and body numb, turned away.

CHAPTER 16

The barracks room Roland and Aignar shared was little different from their quarters back at Fort Knox, but this room had a holo screen in place of a window. Random Martian landscapes cycled through the projection, the light levels in tune with the world just outside Olympus.

Roland paced up and down the room, rubbing the patch of spray-skin on his hand. Aignar dug a screwdriver into his left forearm, his fist closing with each twist of the tool.

"What happened to her?" Roland asked. "None of the cadre seemed that shocked. Did they know it was coming?"

"All a bunch of veterans. I'm sure they've seen everything by now, and I doubt the Corps promotes any panickers to lance commander." Aignar's fingers clicked up and down at random and through a range of motion that his flesh and blood hands couldn't have matched without breaking bones and tearing tendons.

"Wait…are you OK? Not you too…" Roland slapped a palm against his plug.

"Settle down. This one's been on the fritz since we left Earth." He bashed the back of his hand against his table, and the fingers opened and closed with their usual stiffness.

"How can you sit there and be…calm! She's your friend, too, and all you've done since they kicked us out is sit there." Roland jammed his hands to his hips.

"What should I do?" Aignar asked. "Write my congressman? Go to the med facility and press my face against the glass as the docs work on her?"

"You could…could…*act* like you care." Roland sat on his bunk and leaned forward, elbows on his knees, hands laced behind his head. "It's not fair. She was better than all of us. Why did it have to happen to her?"

"War isn't fair, either," Tongea said from the open doorway. He waved the candidates down before they could stand to attention. "Candidate Yanagi had a hemorrhagic stroke. Complications like hers are rare, but not unheard of. We identified her as a high risk early on, disclosed everything to her, but she chose to continue selection."

"Why did you let her take the risk?" Roland's hands gripped his bunk with white-knuckle intensity.

"We are armor. We are the force of decision on any battlefield. Shying away from something just because it is dangerous is not our way," Tongea said. "The Corps needs soldiers, and we will take any with the desire and ability. Yanagi is brave, and had her system taken to the plugs, she would have made a fine member of any lance. She'll have her implant removed and then we'll return her to Earth."

"What? That's it?" Roland sprang to his feet. "You're just going to toss her aside like she's nothing?"

"Roland...," Aignar said.

"Shaw, what would you do if Yanagi earned her spurs, the two of you joined the same lance, and she died in battle right next to you?" Tongea asked. "There," he continued, picking up a towel from the sink in the room and tossing it to the floor at Roland's feet, "she's dead. Vishrakath walkers are coming for you. What do you do?"

"I—" Roland flinched back as Tongea's punch stopped an inch from his nose.

"We cannot suffer because we've lost someone we care about." Tongea pulled his hand back.

"I lost squad mates on our first drop," Aignar said.

"No time to mourn during a battle. Got to buck up and drive on."

"I'm willing to die for my lance but I shouldn't care about them?" Roland asked.

"There's a time and a place," Tongea said. "You push back the pain until you can mourn. Lose your iron before then, you put the rest of your lance—and the mission—in jeopardy."

"I've no mission. No lance. I can't just sit here and do nothing." Roland flopped his hands against his sides. "Can we at least see her?"

"She's in surgery and will be in an induced coma for days to come." Tongea shook his head. "At times like these, I find comfort in my faith."

"Like any of that will make a diff—" Roland stopped as Tongea's expression lost what little compassion it had. He felt Aignar's icy glare against the back of his head. "Forgive me, gentlemen. I'm not one for faith."

"Candidate Aignar, you know the Saint?" Tongea asked.

"I do, sir."

"Come with me." Tongea opened the door for the veteran. Roland sat back down and unstrapped his boots as Aignar practically flew out of the room to be with the cadre member. Tongea turned to leave, then paused. The Maori's head tilted down, then he slowly half-turned to Roland.

"Candidate Shaw...I feel...I feel as though you should come with us," Tongea said.

"I'm not one for prayer. Like I said."

"You have nothing to lose, and everything to gain. Perhaps you will find your faith with us. Come."

Roland, his hands in the middle of undoing the second strap, sighed. The Armor Corps honored the fallen; he'd seen the statues at Memorial Square enough to know that. Honoring Masako somehow would be better than staying in the room and feeling sorry for her...and himself. He redid the straps on his boots and followed Tongea.

****

Roland and Aignar sat hip to hip in the back of a small personnel tram, Tongea in the front. The enclosed tram whipped through airless tunnels, propelled along magnetic rails. The hyper-loop railway system ran through several levels of Olympus, a warren of tunnels connecting every last weapon emplacement, habitat and hangar.

"Sir? Where are we going?" Roland asked after the tenth silent minute of travel.

"Why did we win the Ember War?" Tongea asked, not bothering to look at him.

Roland traded a frown with Aignar, who shrugged at him.

"We had technological help from the Qa'Resh and that probe of theirs that worked with Marc Ibarra," Roland said, his mind struggling between old homework assignments and pondering what the cadre was really asking. "Then there was the Dotari/Ruhaald fleet that allied with us to make the assault on the Xaros Apex and—"

"Providence," Tongea said. "There are many who believe Providence—divine intervention—saved us, and the entire galaxy. The ship present at many pivotal moments during the war, the *Breitenfeld*, do you know what her motto is?"

"*Gott mit uns*," Aignar said, his throat speaker struggling with the words. "God is with us."

"We should not have won the war," Tongea said. "The Xaros should have destroyed the surviving fleet after they scoured the Earth and the rest of the solar system of every last trace of humanity. The Battle of Ceres was a shoestring tackle. The second Xaros invasion…the assault on the Apex. Miracles. Every last one of them. Marc Ibarra had a plan, one he set into motion decades ago, but one that had many flaws to it. We should have lost. But each time the *Breitenfeld* was put against impossible odds, she and her crew prevailed."

"I'm sure Admiral Valdar would explain how every battle was won without divine intervention, sir," Roland said.

"Do you think the admiral was without faith?" Tongea asked.

"I…wouldn't know."

"He came to Mars when we built the tomb. Paid his respects to the Saint and the others. Valdar told Martel…no, that's not for you yet. Here…" Tongea reached under his seat and tossed the two candidates dark hoods. "Only the Templars know the location of the tomb."

Roland looked at the hood and suppressed a chuckle. Aignar jabbed an elbow into his arm and Roland put the hood on with a shake of his head.

He felt the tram make several turns, then slow to a stop. Cold, dry air washed over Roland as the tram door whined open. Tongea tugged the hood off Roland's head.

A rough-hewn tunnel on one side of their unmarked stop led to a brass door guarded by a pair of armor, each holding a sword taller than Roland in front of them, the tips buried between their feet.

Scenes of armor fighting Xaros drones, Toth warriors and aliens Roland didn't recognize were embossed on the brass door. The images ended with two armor beside a damaged suit lying in Martian soil.

Tongea got out of the tram and beat a fist against his chest.

"Who goes there?" one of the armor asked.

"Pilgrims," Tongea said. "We seek the Saint."

"They have not taken their oaths," the other armor said, the voice feminine.

"The circumstances are...dire," Tongea said.

"I want the Saint to help someone," Aignar said. "She's in the hospital. The Saint gave me strength once. Now Masako needs that same gift."

One of the armor looked at Roland.

"I don't...I would do anything to help her," Roland said, looking down at his feet.

There was a snap of locks disengaging, and the brass door swung open. A narrow corridor led into darkness.

Roland followed the other two through the doors, each containing a fractal silver lining pressed between armor plates. The doors slammed shut behind them.

On either side, chambers the size of an armor suit

were carved into the Martian rock, empty spaces extending down the corridor. Tongea and Aignar fell to one knee, their heads bowed in prayer.

Roland backed away and looked at an eye-level nameplate with raised letters next to the first empty chambers. The left side of the plate was smooth, shinier than the rest, and gave a brief history of a soldier named Vladislav. Inside the chamber was a set of unfinished hooked wings with broad white feathers partway down the spines. The set was large enough that it could have only been fit to a suit of armor, not a soldier on foot. The next chamber had another set of wings and a nameplate for an Adamczyk, his date of death the same as the first.

Tongea got up and ran his fingers down the smooth side of the second name plate.

"When our bodies are missing, we inter a memento mori, something to remember the fallen," Tongea said quietly. "The Hussars wished to complete their armor, but they were lost before they could finish."

Roland turned around. The other side of the tunnel chambers held white tunics and red crosses.

"These are…these are all the soldiers from Memorial Square. The ones that died fighting the Xaros Masters at the last battle," Roland said.

"That's correct." Tongea tilted his head to the darkness at the end of the tunnel.

They passed chambers that held different mementos: a small carving of an armor soldier, a cane, and a threadbare shirt with Dotari writing stitched into the hem. An electric candle activated as they neared the darkness, illuminating a life-sized statue of a woman in a wheelchair on a chest-high base, her hands folded neatly on her lap, head tilted downward slightly. Behind the statue, a damaged suit of armor stood in a chamber, a broken sword gripped in one fist. Red dust and old, dried blood marred the armor.

Aignar stopped, his breath coming faster and faster.

"This is Saint Kallen, of the Iron Hearts," Tongea said. He motioned to a pair of worn patches in front of the statue. Aignar went to his knees, his face turned up to the statue's, cyborg hands pressed together awkwardly.

"She wasn't at the last battle," Roland said, looking over the damaged armor from where he and Tongea stood behind Aignar.

"She was there…in spirit," Tongea said. "She died here on Mars. I remember the day Elias and Bodel carried her armor back to Olympus. Chaplain Krohe's tended to the souls of those remembered here…It was Elias who asked that his final deeds be witnessed so that he would be found worthy to fight at Kallen's side in the next life. The veneration of the Saint formed soon after that. We take the Templar oaths to ask for her intercession, so that if we are lost to the void like those who faced the Xaros Masters at the end, our souls may find their way back to God."

"How did she ever become armor?" Roland asked. "She wasn't in that chair when she joined?"

"She rolled up to Fort Knox the day the Armor Corps announced they would take candidates who were physically ineligible for other service. Carius told her to leave, that she had no chance of being selected. She waited outside for three days. Didn't move. Didn't take food or water. Then Elias and Bodel, back when they were just bean heads, got a weekend pass. They decided to stand beside her outside the main hall. Got her to eat something...Carius finally let her in. She'd been paralyzed as a child, but she could wear her armor through the plugs.

"She came down with Batten's Disease years later. Refused treatment. Refused to leave her armor even though it was killing her."

"She didn't leave...because of the other Iron Hearts. They'd have to fight without her and she refused to abandon them even though she knew it would kill her,"

Roland said.

"You're learning." Tongea pointed to a chamber flanking Kallen's statue. Inside, a bloodred faceplate larger than an armor's helm with thin eye slits hung from a chain bolted to the rock. The outer edges were deformed, as if gripped by a giant hand. "That is the last-known remnant of the Xaros Masters. Elias took it as a trophy after he defeated the one designated 'the General' on Takeni. Elias left nothing else behind to use as a memento mori. More of the General remained after he was killed on Phoenix, but those remains were...lost to us."

Roland went closer to the chamber with the Xaros artifact. The mask seemed to quiver ever so slightly and the smell of ozone and smoke hung in the air. This was the face of the enemy that had killed his parents, murdered billions of human beings and an unthinkable number of innocents during their march across the stars. A slight smile tugged at the corner of his mouth. Thanks to Earth, and the Armor Corps that he was almost a part of, the Xaros were gone forever. He had the privilege to stare at the bones of a dead star god and the Xaros, the nemesis of every sentient being in the galaxy, were extinct.

He felt a presence behind him. He turned, but Tongea and Aignar were where he'd left them. Roland looked across the empty chambers, at the places where the dead soldiers should have been interred in their armor, and felt a knot in his chest.

The Iron Hearts, Templar and Hussars had all given up their lives to secure that final victory over the Xaros…and Roland had gone on a single walk in his armor. The crush of sadness and insignificance weighed on his heart, a feeling he'd had during the long lonely nights in the orphanage.

I'm still nothing… he thought.

Aignar's knees ground against the floor as he got up. He wiped tears away on his upper sleeve, then jabbed at the worn spots with a stiff hand.

"You, Roland."

"I don't know if I should," he said.

"Do it for Masako," Aignar said.

Roland took a deep breath, unsure of the right way to honor this saint, or if he risked some sort of curse by parroting Aignar's faith. He knelt in the same place and felt his cheeks flush as he tried—and failed—to remember a single prayer from his youth. His shoulders sank.

Saint Kallen, I don't know Latin. I don't know how the Templar honor you. I don't even know if I really believe in any of this, but my friend Masako Yanagi is in a med bay somewhere. Her dream of becoming armor is gone and her body...it's not good. Aignar, a bunch of others, they all say you've helped them get through tough times. If you can, help Masako. Whatever...grace could ever have been used on me...give it to her.

Roland looked up and into the face of the statue. Kallen's sharp features and kind eyes stared down at him. Then, in the corner of an eye, a bloodred tear formed and ran down the side of her face.

Roland fell back and scrambled away, his heart racing in his chest as his mind frazzled, trying to comprehend what he'd just seen.

"She favors you," Tongea said.

Roland pointed at the statue, his mouth agape in shock, then he heard the sound of a drop of water striking stone. A patch of wet rock over the statue dripped onto the statue's head, just behind an ear.

"What does it mean?" Aignar asked.

"Some of the order believe it's a sign." Tongea narrowed his eyes at Roland. "Those that receive a tear are destined to die in their armor."

"That's not what I asked her for," Roland said.

Tongea pulled him to his feet, then brought him to the base of the statue.

"There are some that come here for years and never receive this gift," Tongea said. "Don't let it go."

Roland lifted a hand to the statue's chin and touched the side of his forefinger to the drop quivering against the stone. He brought the tear to his lips...the taste matched the smell of Martian soil.

"Time to leave," Tongea said.

****

Later, during the long, quiet ride back to their barracks, Aignar leaned over to Roland.

"When you put the tear to your lips, how did you know to do that?"

"I didn't...just felt right." Roland shrugged. "How you feeling?"

"I haven't been like this since my son was born," Aignar said. "I'm happy. For the first time in years. Truly happy. You?"

Their tram sped through two stops before Roland answered.

"Lost."

CHAPTER 17

Roland pressed his armor against a steep hillside and the back of an arm against the sharp edge, bending an elbow backwards. The targeting cameras integrated into his forearm cannons made a quick sweep of the small valley on the other side of the rock. A pole with a limp green flag stood in the middle of the open area. He sent a picture through an IR link to Aignar and Cha'ril, both taking cover nearby.

"Looks clear," he said.

"That's the problem," Cha'ril sent back. "Sensors in orbit detected a defending element during the last sweep."

"So who do we believe?" Aignar asked. "Our own lying eyes or some vacuum breather that's been spoofed a dozen times during the trials?"

"The blue team must have left their flag

undefended, doubled up on their assault element and hoped to overwhelm *our* defenders before we realized they were screwing with the satellite. Again," Roland said.

"But if they know we know—"

"Grab the flag and take route Echo back to our base," Roland said, cutting off Cha'ril. "Aignar on overwatch. Go in three…two…one."

Roland spun around the side of the hill and ran toward the flag pole. His armor took great leaping strides, tiny thrusters in his shoulders firing to keep his armor from rising too high over the ground. Data fed from his passive sensors and into his eyes, creating an overlay through the vision centers of his brain. He "saw" from the perspective of the optics in his helm.

He ran on, his metal limbs never tiring, the hum of adrenaline in his ears.

A target icon popped up to his right. He brought both his shoulder and forearm cannons to bear on the boulder where his sensors read a power signature. Cha'ril cut toward the other side, covering Roland as he sidestepped around the boulder.

A battery pack pulled from a gauss cannon was wedged into the side of the boulder, a piece of metal bent between the leads.

"That's how they spoofed the satellite," Roland said. "They're not here."

"Less talking, more winning." Cha'ril swung her shoulder cannon toward the flag.

"Aignar, we good?" Roland sent through the IR as he ran to the flag. He slowed, waiting for an answer.

"Aignar?"

"Must have lost line of sight, we'll pick him up on the way out," Cha'ril said.

Roland skidded to a halt in the ankle-deep sand next to the flagpole. He felt a slight tremor through his heels.

"What is that?"

An arm burst out of the sand and smashed into the back of Roland's knee. He toppled backwards, loose sand spilling over his optics. He rolled over and came face-to-face with a double-barreled gauss cannon, sand pouring down the side.

The cannon flashed and his helm went off-line. Roland lowered the vision slot on his breastplate and womb, giving him a narrow view of the outside world. A blow shook him inside his armor and another knocked him flat on his back.

Roland saw Gideon standing over him. The cadre raised his foot and his anchor spike popped out of his heel.

He rammed the spike toward Roland's vision slit.

PILOT KILL flashed across his eyes and his armor shut down. Roland had no choice but to remain very still within his dead armor.

Full function returned a few minutes later. Roland went to where Gideon and an equally dusty Lieutenant Silva stood facing Aignar and Cha'ril, the candidates' helms bowed slightly, shoulders tight.

"Pathetic," Gideon said. "Absolutely pathetic. Your tunnel vision sent you right into an ambush. Roland. Explain why you didn't pull back after you lost comms with Aignar."

"Sir, I thought it was a line-of-sight issue with the IR."

"Cha'ril, why didn't you try to reconnect?" Gideon asked.

"I was too focused on the objective, sir," she said as her head dipped lower.

"You chose an overwatch position with excellent observation and fire line," Lieutenant Silva said to Aignar. "It was also the most obvious spot for an overwatch, which is why I set my ambush there."

"Signal from the noise," Gideon said. "We've been over this. The satellite sent you data that a defending element was here. You found the battery pack we hacked. But what did you all miss?"

"You didn't ping anywhere else," Roland said. "If you were anywhere else in the exercise area, the satellite would've picked up your signature there...and here. We found your battery and assumed you were gone."

"Some decent analysis at last," Gideon said. "But figuring out your mistake five minutes after you're dead doesn't help."

"Why didn't our sensors read you?" Cha'ril said. "Even underground your power signature should've tripped our passives."

"We were dark," Gideon said. "No systems online. I waited until I felt your footsteps through the ground before powering up."

"Same," Lieutenant Silva said.

"Patience is a virtue," Gideon said. A Mule shuttle crested the horizon, heading straight for them. "There is a time to attack, and there is a time to hold back. You all made the wrong choice. Hoof it back to Gate 37-C. I'll meet you there for your next assignment."

The cadre walked away.

Roland pulled up a map, chose a route back to Olympus that followed an above-ground hyper loop connecting the fortress to a nearby spaceport and sent it to his lance mates. He concentrated on his armor's legs and the internal treads folded out of the housings on his thigh and calf armor. He rolled toward the lip of the crater, churning up a cloud of dust in his wake.

"Well...that could have gone better," Aignar said.

"Cha'ril?" Roland twisted his helm to look at her, motoring behind and to his left.

"I made a number of errors. I should have stopped you from moving on the flag. A magnetic scan would have revealed Gideon's trap."

"I think that's the closest she's ever come to an apology," Aignar said.

"Don't push it, ape," she snapped. "The Dotari staff in Olympus tell me that expressing self-criticism during an after-action review is an acceptable trait among humans. I'd prefer if you two would internalize your guilt and perform better at the next exercise without having to share with me. That's the Dotari way."

"Baby steps, Cha'ril, baby steps," Roland said. "It was my first time as assault element lead and I screwed it all up."

"At least you didn't get rail-gun sniped off a hilltop," Aignar said. "Yes, I know that happened to you,

Cha'ril. I'm externalizing your guilt for you. Baby steps."

Cha'ril swerved her treads over a rock and kicked it at Aignar. He swatted the rock into fragments and laughed.

"Come on, Cha'ril, giving you shit like that means I like you," Aignar said.

"I thought human males gave the object of their affection severed plant genitals, not…shit."

"There are different levels of affection," Roland said.

"Which level lets me kick him in the throat the minute we've decanted?"

"I can never tell if we're getting closer or drifting apart," Aignar said.

"Before you two start an impromptu live-fire exercise, any idea what's at Gate 37-C?" Roland asked. "That's to the east of the mountain. Squid territory."

"The Ruhaald are here?" Cha'ril asked.

"Squids are navy personnel. Old nickname for them," Aignar said.

"You think they'll have bots to clean us up?" Roland asked. "Or do we get to spend hours on the racks vacuuming out every speck of dust?"

"Cadre save the bots for winners," Aignar said. "Right now, that ain't us."

****

The hangar behind Gate 37-C rivaled the new Phoenix University stadium in size and volume. As a child, Roland had marveled at the immense structure the few times his orphanage had dragged him and the other children out to an American football game, the teams drawn from fleets and Marine divisions. That the Martian engineers had built something so immense within Olympus gave Roland a crushing sense of irrelevance, even while he was inside his armor.

Four *Esquiline*-class corvettes formed the corners of a square on the hangar floor, each in different stages of retrofit. Scaffolding and spider-bots surrounded each ship, removing hull plates and swapping out components. One ship was split open from stem to stern, her inner workings displayed like a vivisection.

"Which one's the *Scipio*?" Aignar asked.

"The one taking on supplies and going through pre-launch checks." Cha'ril shared a target icon that pinged on a ship on the far side of the square. The ship boasted turret-mounted rail cannon and several point defense nodes around the hull. "Logically, I doubt the cadre sent us here to reassemble a ship."

The three walked around the perimeter of the shipyard, drone-controlled supply carts slowing and veering out of their way to let them pass. If he'd been on foot, Roland would have never trusted the machine intelligences to not run him over. In his armor, his old flesh-and-blood fears felt like a child's memory of what goes bump in the night.

The *Scipio*'s crew, a mere two dozen sailors and officers, formed two lines at the foot of the ship's loading ramp. Gideon, in armor, spoke with a female commander as an armor support team rolled equipment into the ship.

"Right on time," the commander said to the candidates. "I'm Tagawa, welcome aboard my ship. Not the first time she's been worked over by the yards, but the old girl needed the attention. The *Scipio* is part of the new rapid-reaction task force forming on Ceres. Our primary weapon is you tall sons of bitches. Got just enough room to squeeze you four in, and not much else. Our trip's as much for shaking out the bugs as it is to see how cranky my crew gets hot-bunking and sharing a single shower. Embark at your leisure, but we leave in ten minutes."

Gideon tapped a fist to his chest lightly and the

commander turned her attention back to her crew.

"Follow me." Gideon led them up the ramp and into the repurposed cargo space. The ship's sole Mule transport and EVA vehicles were gone, replaced with four armor maintenance bays, coffin-like structures with scaffolding running chest-high across from where their suits would stand. Racks of armor weapons, spare parts and crates of ammo filled most of what space remained; the only gap on the floor left a round hatch uncovered.

The scaffolding folded up and shifted out of the way as they marched into the armor bay.

"Your first cemetery," Gideon said. "Welcome."

"Awful small ship to carry armor," Aignar said. "When did High Command decide this was a good idea?"

"The good-idea fairy must have done the rounds at the headquarters under Camelback Mountain," Gideon said. "Regardless, this is the next step in your training. Get in your coffins and let the techs give you the once-over. Dismount for checks at med bay, then calisthenics once we've broken orbit. For those of you who've never been on a navy ship before, just stay out of the crew's way."

Roland backed into a coffin and the apparatus scanned his armor, feeding the data to him. Tubes and power lines connected to his suit and the scaffolding unfolded back into place. A short walkway extended to the armor's waist. He cycled down his suit's power and relaxed. His armor's HUD pinged with a system update; a new suit-to-suit communication link caught his attention as he skimmed the patch notes.

Roland opened a channel and invited Aignar and Cha'ril.

"Here we go again," Aignar half-sang a soldier's marching cadence through a private IR channel, "same old stuff again." His head and shoulders came up in a window to one side of Roland's vision. The Aignar in the window wore his Ranger uniform and looked from side to side. "Figures that the techs upgrade everything right as I figure out how to use it." The veteran's mouth actually moved when he spoke, and the speaker in his neck was gone.

"Aignar...your lips are working," Roland said.

"What the devil..." Aignar touched his mouth and throat. "Odd. My freak show's still in the same spot."

A window with a blond-haired, blue-eyed woman opened.

"The ship's internal comms has a VR emulator," the woman said with Cha'ril's voice. "Dotari ships have had such a system in place for generations. Seeing who you're talking to on other vessels increased the empathy levels…there must be a rendering error—both your mouths are open."

"Cha'ril? Is that you?" Roland asked.

"Of course it's me. Do you think there's another Dotari crammed into this vessel somewhere? Aignar, honestly. If we were dismounted, I swear your mouth would catch flies. Let me check my camera settings…" She let off trills and snaps in her own language.

"What is this bovine feces?" The humanized Cha'ril prodded her hair.

"I don't know…you look kind of hot as a human," Aignar said.

"I am sending a user feedback form. Right. Now." Cha'ril's window closed.

"She mad? Oh, she's mad," Aignar said.

"If you could avoid pissing her off for five minutes, we might do better during trials," Roland said.

"We all show our love in different ways. Would you look at that? We've got ourselves our very own hell hole."

"A what?"

"The hatch. Air-assault-configured Mules have hell holes for fast rope and grav-cushioned drops. Hitting a hot landing zone through one of those is a significant emotional event when you're in Marine power armor. Can't wait to see what Gideon's got in store for us."

"Fun times," Roland said with little enthusiasm. "I'm going to drift." He closed the channel and accessed his message folder, but there was nothing there. He checked his sent folder and glanced over the many messages he'd sent to Masako. All had been read.

Roland shut down all his feeds and tried to drift away in the abyss, but his mind kept churning.

****

"Roland."

He heard the word, but wasn't sure if he was awake or dreaming inside the womb. He stretched his legs slightly and noticed a blinking cursor in the darkness. He brushed his mind across it and a still photo of Cha'ril—as a Dotari—opened up.

"I hacked the comms," she said, "and sent another user feedback form detailing the fault in their coding."

Roland brought his systems online and checked the *Scipio*'s telemetry feeds. They were in the void, on course for Ceres still a day off.

"You woke me up for this?"

"Aignar and Gideon are both adrift," she said. "I

received a message during our last data synch with Olympus…I'm unsure if I should share it with you, as human language seems to leave a great deal to interpretation, even though this English of yours seems to be four distinct languages mashed together solely to confuse new learners."

"You're going to have to share the message with me now."

"I was asked not to, but I did agree to the request. Dotari obtain confidentiality before sharing secrets. I will feign cultural ignorance if her humors are upset."

Roland felt a tinge of fear through his heart.

"You heard from Masako?"

"That your hormone levels were so elevated around each other leaves me to believe you had feelings for her, a distraction that I'm certain impacts your efficiency levels. Aignar's passion doesn't extend beyond breaking things."

"If you have something from Masako, then you'd better share it or I will plug myself into your suit and get it myself."

"I see my assumptions about you were correct. Sending."

Her picture shrank away and a video file opened up in its place.

Masako, sitting in a hospital bed, smiled meekly at the camera. Her hair was gone, replaced by a red bandana. Her face was worn, tired. She rubbed her left hand up and down her other arm.

"Hey, Cha'ril, I'm in Hawaii." Her smile broadened slightly. "The recovery center here is really impressive. Have my own team of docs and an on-call bot that will bring me real food if I ask. Couple soldiers and Marines here from Cygnus. They got hit fighting—I just lost a roll of the dice."

She picked up a scratching stick with her left hand and rubbed the edge against her right leg. Her other arm didn't move. At all.

"They took my plugs away," she continued, her smile vanishing. "Not 'no,' but 'hell no' would I ever be armor after my…episode. The docs are talking about neural grafts to make everything work the way it used to, but it takes time to get those out of the vat. If the grafts don't work, then there are nerve bridges, artificial neurons, stem-cell therapy…lots of reasons to believe I'll be 100% normal-ish when I do leave here.

"Dr. Eeks is *not* advising on my treatment." Her face wrinkled with anger. "Which is fine by me. She's not real popular around here. A detailer came by this morning, promised me any career and assignment I wanted. I'm getting a good dose of the Medical Corps right now…maybe I'll stick with it. Everyone's so bubbly and optimistic around here. After the cold shoulder we got from the cadre all the time every time, I'm a little suspicious. Maybe they're trying to butter me up before more bad news…maybe I'm just being paranoid.

"Do me a favor—don't show this to Aignar or Roland. Aignar doesn't need a reminder of his…situation. God bless him, I don't know how he survived hospitals for so long as a patient. Roland might—might make a rash decision—and I don't want him to see me like this when I'm such a mess. Keep them both focused on getting through training. I'll catch up with you all in the future. There's a whole galaxy out there for us to explore, but the military can be a small world, sometimes."

Masako reached toward the camera and turned off the video. Cha'ril appeared again.

"I have not replied," the Dotari said. "Should I tell her you saw this? I am unsure how angry she will become."

"Don't mention me," Roland said. "Masako made her decision."

Cha'ril's image flickered.

"Roland, human coupling is rather different than

310

Dotari relationship cycles. I thought you two were enamored with each other. Why have you both chosen to forgo contact?"

"If you think I'm an expert on relationships, I've got some bad news for you."

"She mentioned a 'rash decision.' Are you contemplating breaking into her hospital while in your armor and taking her to find other treatment?"

"That's not rash, Cha'ril; that's ridiculous," Roland said. "Thank you for sharing that."

"Was it helpful to you?"

Roland closed the channel. He felt the plugs in the back of his skull, the umbilical connecting him to the womb and to his armor. Of all the cadre and other armor soldiers he'd ever come across, none wore a wedding ring. Only Aignar ever mentioned children.

He'd chosen armor. Knew the level of commitment it demanded from those that became armor. With Masako gone, he realized just how much he'd given up to join the Corps. To cut off so much of adult life the day he arrived at the SEPS building in Phoenix…he realized that making that decision so close to his eighteenth birthday was terribly shortsighted.

Part of him wished he'd never met that stranger

outside Memorial Park, never heard about the heroes immortalized in stone. His mind wandered to Saint Kallen's tomb, remembered her gentle face.

She had volunteered for armor training, fought countless battles and chosen to keep fighting beside the Iron Hearts when she could have taken an easy way out. Roland felt a wave of shame come over him as he realized just how selfish his thoughts were.

He was armor. He'd given up a part of his life not for gain, but as a sacrifice. There were still younger children back at the orphanage. If he fought, and fought well, perhaps no other parents would die defending their children. Families—families that remained whole—could endure.

He gripped his arms against his chest, feeling the press against his skin.

Maybe he was just trying to justify a truly rash decision. There certainly wasn't a chaplain on a vessel the size of the *Scipio*. He longed to share these doubts with someone, but doing that with his lance mates or Gideon felt like weakness.

If only Chaplain Krohe was here…or Tongea.

He called up a music player and blasted a song through his plugs and into his cerebrum.

CHAPTER 18

Their asteroid home tumbled slowly through the void. Roland, his back pressed to the dusty surface of an ancient impact crater just big enough for his suit, tested his anchor's grip on the rock beneath his feet. The smear of the Milky Way passed through the stealth shroud lying over his armor, fixed to the asteroid with tiny hooks as the lump of slate-gray rock and dust orbited Ceres. The interplay of the passing moon, Luna, Earth and the universe writ large had been fascinating when the armor first took their positions around the sub-moon.

"Time," Roland said.

"Nineteen hours and thirty-seven minutes," Aignar answered. "Cha'ril's turn."

"You two should be alert and ready for the target, not playing these useless trivia games," the Dotari said from the other side of the rock.

"This trial—like all the others—didn't come with a duration," Roland said. "We can either discuss something or lie here, under sensor shrouds, and wonder if the *Scipio* and Gideon forgot where they left us."

"That option hadn't occurred to me, thanks, buddy," Aignar said.

"We're not to break radio silence until the target appears and is destroyed," Cha'ril said. "We've all spent longer periods in the pods—without talking to anyone, I might add. I don't know why you insist on speaking now. Unless you're doing it just to annoy me. Is that what this is, Aignar? A long, drawn-out attempt to damage my calm?"

"Sounds like I win!" Aignar said.

"Son of a...you cheated," Roland said.

"Wait...you two have some sort of wager?" Cha'ril said.

"Twenty-four hours before you snapped at one of us," Aignar said. "I had the under; Roland had the over. Guess who's paying for the first round the next time we find beer?"

"You are a dickhead." Cha'ril pronounced the insult with an Australian accent. "And a runt. No, a tunt. You are a tunt."

"I think you mean—"

"Let that one go," Aignar said.

A target icon flashed onto Roland's UI.

"Got it…reads as a Vishrakath shuttle, heading thirteen mark two-two-nine. Your fire arc, Aignar."

"Engaging," Aignar said.

Roland pulled the shroud away and rose to his feet, his rail cannon vanes lifting up from his back and tilting over his shoulder. The target continued just above the truncated horizon of the asteroid. Roland waited for Aignar's rail cannons to fire…and waited.

"Got a malfunction! Batteries read charged but there's no polarity down my vanes," Aignar said.

The target dipped below the horizon.

"Cha'ril?" Roland asked.

"Not in my line of sight," she said.

"Balls," Roland said and raised his anchor from the rock, pushing himself forward with his jet pack. Rounding the asteroid, he reacquired the target and pinged the asteroid's surface with radar, searching for another anchor point. Only one small patch of dust read as "marginal."

"Dropping anchor." He raised his right boot, and a diamond-tipped spike extended from his heel; he rammed it into the ground as the anchor screwed into the regolith.

"Are you locked?" Cha'ril asked.

"Close enough." His rail cannon vanes hummed with power as he unsnapped a shell the size of his flesh-and-blood forearm off his thigh and pressed it into the weapon's breach. His armor made minute adjustments to the cannon's direction, and a tone hummed through his mind.

The shell shot down the powerful magnetic field between the two vanes and tore off into the void, the recoil traveling down Roland's armor and into the anchor spike. The asteroid broke, shooting Roland back and tumbling end over end, a jagged boulder fixed to the anchor. Roland's view alternated between a blur of stars and the passing asteroid as his momentum eclipsed exit velocity in a split second.

A jolt rattled him within his womb and all he saw were unmoving stars.

"Got you," Cha'ril said. She had Roland by the ankle. Her own anchor was half out of the asteroid, her armor stretched open like she was about to do a basketball layup. As she tugged at Roland's armor, he bounced off a dust patch and bashed the lump of rock off his anchor, then returned the spike to its housing.

"Did I hit it?" Roland asked.

"Target destroyed," Aignar said.

"You almost went ass over quills into the void," Cha'ril said. "You're lucky I anticipated the worst possible outcome and dropped anchor where I could stop you."

"Right, thank you. I'm going to stop making bets on pissing you off."

"Speaking of taking a piss..." Cha'ril spun around and pointed at Aignar. "Explain."

"My rail cannon malfunctioned. The diagnostics—"

"*I disabled his cannon remotely,*" Gideon said over the radio. "*No fault on his part. You all should have set up secondary and tertiary engagement criteria while you were emplaced. And you should have sunk anchor points to cover multiple fields of fire. That I'm not directing the* Scipio *to recover a Flying Dutchman before Roland became another bit of space junk is a miracle...well done.*"

"Was that a compliment?" Roland sent to his fellows over an IR beam.

"Shh, don't spoil it," Aignar said.

"*There are three rocket packs six meters behind Roland, inside a locker. Conduct a High Orbit Low Opening assault on the following coordinates. Destroy all hostile targets. You have...ten minutes to complete the task. Time starts now.*"

Roland swept dust off the locker embedded in the asteroid and ripped the top off in his haste.

"Oops," he said and tossed rocket packs to Cha'ril and Aignar before slinging the last one over his head and onto the mag locks on his back that set it into the right position. Screws extended from his armor and into the jet pack, locking it tight against him.

"I have a flight plan," Aignar said. "Synch with me and launch."

Roland crouched slightly and leaped off the asteroid. His jet pack fired and he angled toward Ceres. Red circles rotated within a crater on his HUD. He maneuvered behind and to Aignar's left, Cha'ril to the right.

With their jet packs burning at full power, they'd make landfall in six minutes.

"This'll be close," Roland said.

"No target intel, crater's a dust bowl." Aignar adjusted their course to land just outside the crater rim.

As the acceleration pressed Roland's true body against his womb, he looked between his lance mates hurtling through the void. Months ago, he was a busboy. Now, he'd just blasted off an asteroid to drop onto Ceres. He hoped someone on the *Scipio* got a picture of this. His parents would have been impressed.

"Is all human military training this way?" Cha'ril asked. "Chaos after chaos?"

"This is what war's like," Aignar said. "Nothing ever goes according to plan. And anything that can go wrong, will, and at the worst possible moment. Which I just experienced. Damn that Murphy."

"Who?" Cha'ril asked.

"Ancient human philosopher."

"We need an assault plan," Roland said. Through his optics, the target area was still a barren plain of dust accumulated over the billions of years since Ceres formed into a sphere.

"Violence of action," Aignar said. "Movement."

Stepped pyramids and blocky buildings rose out of the dust. Threat icons appeared in the crater as weapon emplacements slid out of the emerging structures.

"Dive, go nap-of-the-earth." Aignar pitched down and the three made straight toward the moon's surface. Red energy beams snapped between Roland and Cha'ril just before they pulled up and skimmed the surface by a few yards. Ceres' horizon kept the weapon emplacements from drawing line of sight to the armor.

"Trident or a dangle?" Roland asked.

"Dangle," Cha'ril said. "Feed data to the other two before we strike."

"I'll take the hit," Aignar said. "Break on three…two…break!"

Roland veered to the left as Aignar popped up, his forearm cannons blazing. Images of bullet-scarred stone buildings captured by Aignar fed into Roland's armor. He marked priority targets with a flick of his eyes, then cut his jet pack.

"Missiles," Aignar called out, "got me painted. Pulling back to break line of sight."

Roland rode his momentum over the horizon and swung his feet forward, bringing him perpendicular to the surface. He slowed just enough that his feet touched down and he broke into a run as the crater came into view.

Gatling guns mounted atop the crater rim slewed toward him. Roland blew them apart with quick bursts from his forearm cannons, then vaulted over the crater rim and into a maze of buildings…that were moving. Structures the size of Destrier transports shifted on tracks embedded into the surface.

Roland used his shoulder cannon to shred a missile-targeting array. He pressed his back to a building spinning in place and took single, well-aimed shots at laser emitters within open panels.

Suddenly, the space behind him fell open, and Roland dropped to his knees as a massive gauss cannon blasted shells over his head. Roland slid to one side, stood up and slammed a hand onto the cannon. His fingers bent metal and he ripped it off its seat and threw it away. The cannon bounced off a spinning building and skipped down a street.

A pair of doors taller than him snapped open across the way, revealing a giant creature that looked like a jellyfish made of compacted crystals. Roland held his fire, spinning in place and engaging a suit of armor with floating plates and burning with light as it pointed a hand toward him, the fingers alive with fire.

Three oblong black metal objects rose out of a stepped pyramid, each the size of his body. Bent metal arms snapped up from their sides and the mock-ups of the now-extinct Xaros drones dove toward him. With a blast from his forearm cannons, he destroyed one, sidestepped a laser beam from another and stepped directly into the path of the third.

Roland swung a punch that connected with the drone's forward tip, cracking the shell and leaving an indentation of his fist that extended up to his wrist. Using the remains as a shield against the remaining drone's lasers, he ducked down as it approached. The blade in his forearm's housing snapped out. The drone flew right overhead, and he rammed his sword into its belly, ripping it in two as it passed.

Kicking the drone off his hand, he spied Cha'ril and Aignar fighting back-to-back through the spinning buildings.

A swarm of missiles erupted from a roof and angled toward the pair.

"Link rotaries," Roland said. The three suits connected and their shoulder-mounted Gatling guns opened up with a flurry of bullets that shredded through the missile barrage. Cha'ril took a single hit to her armor's thigh, but kept firing without missing a beat.

Roland joined them, and the three wrecked a pack of faux Xaros drones the second they appeared from a false panel within a building. Then the spinning structures slowed...and stopped.

The armor kept their weapons raised, scanning their sectors as gauss shells cycled into their cannons and empty ammo canisters on their backs ejected, spinning through Ceres' slight gravity.

"*Exercise complete,*" Gideon said. "*Return to the*

Scipio *for debriefing.*" An icon flashed on Roland's HUD and he saw that the ship was a few craters over.

"I haven't felt this good in a long time," Aignar said.

Roland felt adrenaline coursing through his body and unclenched his true hands within the womb.

White light flashed overhead from the Crucible. Roland zoomed in on a single ship—a destroyer—as it emerged. A gash ran down her flank, trailing atmosphere into the void like blood trailing through water. Scorch marks dotted the hull.

"We need to get back to the ship," Roland said. "Now."

****

Roland moved through the force field separating the *Scipio*'s pressurized cemetery from the near-vacuum of Ceres' surface like he was walking through water. The energy wall stripped most of the moon dust from his armor, and sound returned to his sensors once he'd stepped free of the morass.

Gideon had both hands to a control console on the upper section of the scaffolding, his armor's chest open and ready to receive him. The other coffins were open, and trios of support technicians were at each, anxious with energy like a pit crew waiting for a race car to pull in.

The damaged destroyer hung in a screen over Gideon's head, the face of a woman with a wrinkled face and gray hair on another. A hologram of Commander Tagawa stood next to him, looking at the same screens from her doppelganger position on the ship's bridge.

"If there are life signs, why aren't they answering hails?" Tagawa asked.

"I sent rescue teams from the Crucible," the old woman said. "How long until the *Scipio* can make intercept?"

"Soon as the anti-gravs warm up. Three minutes to liftoff. Maybe ten to dock with the *Ticonderoga*," Tagawa said.

Roland stepped into his coffin and extended his right arm. A technician brought a mechanical claw up from the lower level and used it to clamp down on the weapon. It came away with a snap. Armor panels on his back opened and battery packs popped free of their housings and were swapped out by the coffin's auto-loaders.

"What's going on?" Roland asked his chief technician, an older man named Henrique.

"Something in the Ash system," Henrique said. "Gideon's got a fire in him. Told us to drop your system limitations to zero. Go for full-combat configuration."

"Combat? Henrique...combat against who?"

A new twin-gauss cannon attached to his forearm, this one boasting the flamethrower attachment. A grenade launcher snapped onto his back. Ammo trackers lit up on his HUD as his techs loaded him down with every round his armor could carry.

Roland felt his world come into sharp focus. This was not a drill.

A new holo screen came to life on Gideon's command console. A sailor in full vac suit, with emergency sealant tape on his shoulder and one half of his helmet, tapped his camera. Behind him, a support beam from the ceiling had crushed the captain's chair. A flickering force field held back the raw vacuum of a hull breach.

"Crucible command, this is Commander Fallon of the *Ticonderoga*. A Vishrakath task force arrived through the Ash gate thirty minutes ago and declared a planetary interdiction. They scrambled everything coming off the surface, but we managed to get a tight beam from Doctor Lowenn on Barada." Fallon held up a data slate displaying a grainy video of a woman with long hair and thick glasses, tall jungle trees and an azure sky behind her. The video distorted and skipped as she spoke.

"—repeat we found a gamma-level artifact in the Barada ruins…pathfinder team went missing somewhere in the Shard Jungle…Vish…know, but haven't reached it yet. We need back up imme—ly!"

"Vish fired on us as we broke orbit," Fallon said. "They broke off pursuit once we got close to the gate. They're holding to the exact letter of the Hale Treaty. Bastards." A wire diagram of the Ash system came up. Two dozen alien capital ships formed a cordon between the planet Barada and the jump gate.

"Minder, have any more Vishrakath ships gone through the gate?" Gideon asked.

"No," the older woman said as she cocked her head to the side, her eyes unfocused, "they've activated a quantum distortion field near the gate. It's tricky…but I can break the pattern in another few hours to get our alert task force through."

"Then the artifact is still on Barada," Gideon said. "Can you send the *Scipio* through?"

"Wait just a second," Tagawa said. "This ship can do precisely jack and squat against that many Vish ships."

"Just the *Scipio*…I can. It'll be rough passage and a

one-way trip until I break their distortion algorithm," Minder said. Roland zoomed in on her face; she seemed rather familiar for some reason.

"This is *my* ship," Tagawa said. "What do you think she's going to accomplish?"

"Get us close to this Shard Jungle Lowenn mentioned," Gideon said, "and my lance will drop in and secure the artifact. You rendezvous with the pathfinder ships in orbit and stay out of the way."

"This is insane," Tagawa said.

"Gamma-level artifacts can change everything, Captain," Gideon said. "They're on par with the omnium-reactor technology, the Qa'Resh codex that taught us to build our own Crucible gates. If we let the Vishrakath get it, the balance of power might shift far beyond our ability to adapt. We must go."

"Message from Phoenix command," Minder said, "they're—"

"Ordering the *Scipio* to the Ash system," Tagawa waved a hand in the air. "I'll go on record saying this is a bad idea, so if we all die, know that I'll spend the entire afterlife saying 'I told you so.' Helm, take us out."

The deck rumbled as the *Scipio* lifted away from Ceres.

****

The amniosis engulfing his body felt colder as Roland watched Gideon climb into his armor. The lance leader's womb shut, and Roland opened an IR channel to Aignar and Cha'ril.

"Quick, while he's off-line during hookup, do you two think this is real?" Roland asked. "The cadre have done nothing but screw with us since the very first day."

Chat windows with the other faces came up on his HUD.

"We should behave as if it's real," Cha'ril said evenly. "Success and victory are the only acceptable outcomes in any training evolution. Now is not the time to drag our feet."

"This is a combat mission," Aignar said. "We're led by officers, not actors. There's an air to all this that I haven't felt since Cygnus."

"We've had our suits for a few weeks," Roland said. "I thought it took years to—"

"We don't have years," Gideon said, popping into the center of Roland's UI. "We have a critical situation that armor can solve. If we sit around and wait for a committee

328

to come up with a better solution, the artifact will be in Vishrakath hands. This is a time for action."

"What's the plan, sir?" Aignar asked.

"I'm working on that…none of you have made Low Orbit Low Opening drops yet…or done adverse-conditions training. Damn it."

"Sir, how 'adverse' are these conditions?" Roland asked.

Gideon pushed a data file for the Ash system to the others. Roland sifted through survey data and skimmed over conditions on the other two habitable planets, Nicto and Klaatu. Barada was once home to a sentient species that had colonized several nearby star systems using sub-light seed ships. Images of vine-covered stone temples and foliage-choked decaying cityscapes popped up on a map of Barada. From what the initial Pathfinder Corps could piece together, the entire species had died out over the course of a few hundred years. When the Xaros drone armada had come to the dead world, they'd built a Crucible and placed every last trace of the Baradans in stasis fields that held back the inexorable grind of time and the elements.

"These weather patterns are…unusual," Cha'ril said. A time-lapse photo featuring a continent formed along a mountain ridge that ran from the northern pole to the equator showed a massive hurricane assaulting the lower third of the continent. The storm's progress was glacially slow over several days. Roland zoomed in and found that the hurricane had several eyes scattered over the land mass.

"Sir, when you said 'adverse conditions,'" Roland said, "did you mean we're doing an orbital insertion through the hurricane?"

An icon labeled SHARD JUNGLE popped up...over the hurricane and some distance from one of the stable eyes.

"The key to any orbital drop is velocity control and a decent landing zone," Gideon said. "This drop will be a bit more complicated due to high winds...and lightning."

Roland heard Aignar curse softly.

"All right, you three, analysis: if the Vishrakath found the artifact in the Shard Jungle, where is it now?" Gideon asked.

"Can their aircraft operate in that hurricane?" Cha'ril asked.

"No, they may have decent warships and infantry," Aignar said, "but their in-atmo craft are all rotary wing. Can't handle high winds. Their void fighters might make it, but they'll move with all the grace of a drunk on a high wire down here."

"Can ours?" Roland asked.

"Not with all that electricity in the air," Aignar said.

"Then they're on foot or in ground vehicles," Roland said. "No roads in any of these Pathfinder Corps survey pics…thick jungles…so they're on foot?"

"Why did the Baradans preserve their buildings and not their roads?" Cha'ril asked.

"Something to collect taxes on," Aignar said.

"Focus," Gideon snapped.

"So they're on foot, in a storm…where are they heading?" Roland asked.

"The eye," Cha'ril said and pinged the nearest gap in the storm. "Conditions are stable in there. A lander can get in and back to orbit if it does a corkscrew approach—fuel-intensive and difficult, but possible."

"Then we set down in the eye and wait for them to show up," Aignar said.

"Won't the Vishrakath have the same idea?" Roland asked. "Something this important, you want extraction waiting."

A topographical map of the continent around the stable eye came up. Three wide valleys led through the Shard Jungle area to the eye.

"Which one, Roland?" Gideon asked.

"Sir..." He zoomed in on each, looking for something like a collapsed canyon or deep gorge that would block travel, but they all appeared open. "I don't know the Vishrakath that well...they were major players in the old Alliance against the Xaros. They're the head of a coalition of several other species...I don't know how they fight. Aignar, you were there on Cygnus. What do you think?"

"I spent a week ducking Vish bullets and murder-bots. Didn't give much thought to their high strategy while I was killing them."

"Sir...I don't know," Roland said.

"Vishrakath commanders are cautious," Gideon said, "content to trade space for time and welcome battles of attrition when they have the greater numbers. They control the orbitals...we need to know where the Pathfinder team was lost. The Vish will use the closest route to the eye."

"Now hear this, now hear this," boomed through the ship's loudspeakers. "Prepare for contested wormhole jump."

"Roland, why didn't you choose a route?" Gideon asked.

Roland's heart sank at the question. "Because I

didn't have the best answer, sir. I could guess, but I didn't want to take that kind of a chance with the lance."

"Well done, Roland," Gideon said, and the candidate's ears perked up. "Excellent analysis from all of you."

"I hope we survive this to tell the others we got a pat on the back," Aignar said.

"Stow it, candidate. None of you have earned your spurs yet," Gideon said.

"Yes, sir. Sorry, sir."

Roland felt a chill through his body. All the color around him faded to white.

"If I fall," Gideon said, "get the artifact. Nothing else matters."

Roland's entire universe fell into a white abyss as they passed through the wormhole.

CHAPTER 19

The *Scipio* broke through the white plain at the center of the Barada Crucible and arced toward the planet below like an arrow fired from a bow.

On the bridge, Captain Tagawa gripped her command chair, her jaw set as she watched a holo projection of the entire planet, their projected course, and the location of the Vishrakath ships arrayed over a small continent near the southern pole.

"Get me an IR line to Dr. Lowenn," Tagawa said. "Helm, keep us on course to swing around the planet and overfly the research station. Engage secondary heading on my mark."

"Got Lowenn," said the communication's petty officer, "we'll have line of sight to her for the next…five minutes."

"Open channel." Tagawa swiped a finger over her gauntlet and brought Gideon into the call.

"*Scipio*, this is Lowenn at Magellan Base…where's the rest of the fleet? Did the *Ticonderoga* not tell you how critical this is?"

"Vish set off a disruption field that's holding back transit of anything larger than my ship, Doctor," Tagawa said. "My girl may be small, but she's fierce."

"Where did your pathfinder team last make contact?" Gideon asked.

Lowenn tapped a keypad off screen and coordinates flowed across her image.

"The Vishrakath are all over the Shard Jungle, Captain Tagawa. What does Phoenix think you can accomplish?"

"I'm carrying four suits of armor, the Iron Dragoons," Tagawa said.

"Four?" Lowenn leaned toward the camera. "Just…*four*?"

"We are all," Gideon said.

Lowenn shook her head quickly, then her feed grayed out to static as the *Scipio* flew beyond Magellan Base's horizon.

"I have faith in you," Tagawa said. She plotted the

location Lowenn had sent her and double-tapped a spot along the ship's projected path. "Here?"

"It'll have to do," Gideon said.

"Hold on down there. We let you go too fast, you'll turn into a flaming lump of good intentions and poor planning all the way down. Scope is clear of any Vishrakath ships this side of the planet. Small favors."

"Does she know we can hear that?" Cha'ril asked.

"Shh! Shut up," Aignar hissed.

"We'll signal for extraction when we have the artifact," Gideon said.

"God's speed," Tagawa said and closed the channel. "Helm, set for insertion. Keep the aft thrusters primed just in case the Vish take offense to our little maneuver."

****

Roland stepped out of his coffin and rolled his armor's shoulders forward. He gave his rotary cannon a quick spin and cycled bolts into his forearm cannon. Intellectually, he knew he was the most heavily armed and armored weapon system humanity had ever produced. Inside his armored womb, anxiety and fear beat in tune with his heart.

Gideon marched up to the closed hell hole and slammed a sabaton to the deck. It mag-locked to the plating.

"Brace," their lance leader said. "Be generous with your thrusters on the way down. Your armor has the path."

Roland widened his stance slightly and locked his feet to the deck.

Gideon sent a live feed from his optics to the three candidates, who formed a ring around the hell hole with their leader, and Roland saw his armor. Tall. Strong. The suit bore none of the raging emotions that urged him to step away from the hell hole and back into his coffin.

"I am armor," Gideon intoned. His helm looked across the other three.

"I am armor," he said again.

"I am armor," Roland, Aignar and Cha'ril repeated the words.

"I am fury."

Roland felt a sense of calm come over him as he said the words in time with his fellows.

The hell hole slid open and a smear of gray clouds ripped across the sky below. The *Scipio* lurched forward as her thrusters cut her forward velocity. Amber lights blinked around the edge of the hell hole.

"I will not fail," Gideon said as he unlocked his boots and stepped into the hole just as the lights turned green. Aignar crossed himself and followed. Cha'ril punched Roland in the shoulder and dove down.

"I am armor." Roland hopped forward and fell.

The *Scipio* drifted overhead, his and the ship's velocity a near match. The hell hole closed and the corvette rocketed forward on burning thrusters. Barada stretched out around him, the atmosphere breaking into blue bands on the horizon, the system's star casting long shadows behind massive thunderheads, breaking apart the gray monotony of the massive hurricane's cloud cover.

The sight was nothing like he, an orphan child once lost in the shuffle of Earth's largest city, had ever imagined.

He leaned forward and angled his head toward the planet. His HUD projected rings ahead of him, setting a path to the landing zone Gideon had chosen, close to the last-known location of the pathfinder team that had the artifact. Icons for the other three armor soldiers pulsed.

To the south, an eye in the hurricane seemed to taunt him with the promise of clear skies and an easy descent. Light glinted off a lake formed into a perfect circle.

Wind rustled against his armor as the atmosphere

thickened. He, with all the aerodynamic qualities of a brick, kept his focus on the course. Although he drifted dangerously close to the edge of the rings, he resisted the urge to fire the thrusters on his jet pack. A blast of anti-grav particles or a stray heat plume would be a nice fat clue to the Vishrakath that something was amiss over the Shard Jungle.

"Hitting the cloud layer," Gideon said, "will lose IR in a few seconds. Rem—beacon."

Gideon's icon blinked rapidly, then vanished from Roland's HUD.

"Anyone else wish we were back on that rock?" Aignar asked. "Just orbiting Ceres...no big deal."

"I find your lack of focus worrisome," Cha'ril said.

"I'm just a leaf on the wind right now," Aignar said. "A big metal leaf. With guns."

"If you're trying to upset me again, it's working," she said.

"Clouds. See you kids on the ground." Aignar's icon blinked out.

"Is this how humans always approach combat? With...levity?"

"I wouldn't know. I don't find anything funny about this. At all."

"Curious."

Roland watched as the hurricane swallowed her.

As the gray pulled closer, he took one last glance at the sky above and a slap of wind sent him rolling over and toward the opposite side of the course. Rain lashed across his optics as the clouds darkened further. He tapped his thrusters, leveling out.

"Okay...I've got this."

A fork of lightning slashed through the sky just in front of him, his optics going dull as they compensated for the deluge of light. A clap of thunder slapped him aside with enough force to shake him inside his womb.

He steered back into the center of his flight path, then the whole thing angled sharply to the right. Roland swung toward the ever more distant rings and activated the thrusters in the flat of his sabatons and up and down his legs. His HUD pulsed red, urging him back on course. He'd almost reached the outer edge of the ring when his thrusters cut out.

Tiny strands of electricity slithered up his legs.

His armor was rated against lightning strikes, but Roland did not want to test the engineer's promises in the middle of a combat drop.

ALTITUDE. ALTITUDE flashed on his HUD and

rang in his ears. He fired his jet pack as he descended through the gray void. Columns of flame ripped from the pack, the heat strong enough that he felt the effects through the womb and damage icons flashed on his ankles.

The clouds parted, and Roland found himself falling straight toward a cliff face. He angled away and managed to soften the collision against the rock wall. His feet and hands ripped furrows down the rain-swept rocks, sending a cascade of shards and pebbles down the mountain.

The jet pack snapped off and he came to a halt, gripping the side of the mountain for dear life. His jet pack pinged—overheated and nearly out of fuel. Sheets of rain fell from the sky. Deep-gray columns dotted the horizon, torrential downpours from the roiling storms all around him.

"Not great." Roland looked down and into a chasm that ended in darkness. A cracked slope ran from the opposite side of the chasm to the edge of a jungle. His jet pack came back online.

"Stay up here, exposed and asking to be shot," he said, "or…" He pushed off the cliff face with a burst of force from his legs and arms, sailed backwards and kicked his feet out toward the slope. He fired his jet pack and shot forward. Everything but his knees cleared the edge of the cliff. The impact knocked a boulder loose and sent it crashing down the chasm, the impacts matching the sound of thunder overhead.

Roland got up, his lower legs stiff as the armor retuned the actuators to compensate for the landing. He felt an ache in his own calves and ankles as his nervous system sent commands to the armor that the armor couldn't carry out perfectly.

He lifted a sabaton off the ground and the ankle snapped into place with a jolt of pain, but the ache subsided.

Roland dropped the spent jet pack to the ground and kicked it into the chasm. He wouldn't leave anything behind for the Vishrakath to find. His weapon systems came online and Roland looked around.

The storm filled the air with the impact of rain on stone, with rolling thunder and the rustle of trees against each other in the driving wind. His first alien world, and it was miserable.

"Roland, over here," Cha'ril's voice came over the IR, tinny and distorted. A marker pinged at the edge of the jungle and he ran toward it, taking great loping strides down the slope.

He found the rest of his lance just inside the tree

line, none looking worse for wear.

"Well, you managed to walk away from that landing," Aignar said as rainwater poured down a tree and onto his shoulder. He angled his forearm cannon away from the deluge.

"It was either incredibly skillful or lucky," Cha'ril said. "Given your experience level, I will assign it to the latter."

"I have the pathfinder team," Gideon said. "Three kilometers to the south. Wedge formation. Follow me." The lance leader started moving, his feet splashing in the inches-deep runoff from the slope.

"Did you use a radar ping to triangulate our location?" Roland asked as he took his spot to Gideon's right.

"Pathfinders seed mountains, any terrain feature they can, with IR beacons, passive system. Vish wouldn't be able to find them unless they know the exact frequency to ping. The beacon knows exactly where it is from GPS. Shoot it with an IR beam and it'll send back your location," Gideon said. "You all would have learned about this next week during your training."

Roland stepped over a fallen tree, the roots exposed at the base and washed clean, reaching through the air like the ends of a nervous system.

"Are we weapons-free?" Aignar asked.

"Negative. Shooting the artifact with gauss shells is not how we accomplish our mission. Be judicious with your targets and your aim," Gideon said.

The jungle thinned, giving way to groves of blue-barked tree trunks with no branches. Gideon slowed to a stop a little more than arm's distance from one of the strange trees and reached a hand toward it. A thorn of hardened sap stabbed out of the tree and cracked against the palm of his hand. The misshapen spike tried to recede into the bark several times before it pulled back inside.

"Good to know," Gideon said.

"Shard Jungle," Roland added.

"There…" Gideon ran around the shard trees and pointed to a pile of stones along an overflowing stream. His lance formed a triangle around him, scanning the surrounding jungle as Gideon flicked a stone the size of a man's head off the heap.

A nearby tree bore scars from bullet strikes. Roland flicked his rotary cannon from side to side, then switched to his thermal optics, and saw little else in the rainy gloom.

"Found them." Gideon lifted a stone with both hands. Six dead Terran soldiers, all soaked to the bone, lay in a pile of limbs and equipment. Gideon pressed his hands between two corpses and lifted one out onto the ground. The man looked to be in his early twenties, his pale eyes staring, uncaring, into the sky. A sensor wand snapped out beneath Gideon's left wrist and he ran it up and down the body.

"There's no physical trauma," Gideon said.

"That's not how Vish kill us," Aignar said. "I've seen it in person."

"Cha'ril, Roland," Gideon said, pointing into the jungle, "they set off an emergency buoy from another hundred yards or so that direction. Go see what's there."

"Sir," Roland said and pressed forward, Cha'ril at his side. A thick stand of tall reeds blocked their view of where Gideon had told them to go. Roland put the fore of one boot against the base of the reeds and pressed the thick wall of vegetation down, something a soldier on foot could never have managed. A reptilian creature scurried away, squealing in fright. A robot pack carrier lay against a tree, raised wheels spinning in the rain.

"Found their packer," Roland said. Fragments of bark on surrounding trees had been ripped away, thick rivulets of sap bleeding down the sides.

"Why were they firing so high?" Cha'ril motioned

to the damage high over their helms. "The Vishrakath should not have had air support here."

"They're like ants, aren't they? Maybe they climbed up, set an ambush."

"Foolish. An ambush from a fixed location with no cover? Excellent way to get killed," she said. "Dotari are trained to charge into a close ambush. As are Terrans."

Roland nudged the packer off the tree. Rucksacks were hastily strapped to the sides and the large cargo bed was empty.

"Sir, have six packs here," Roland said.

"Six bodies," Gideon sent back.

"Cargo bed is clear, must have been carrying something big." Roland caught a glimmer of reflected light next to a root and zoomed in with his helm's optics. "Got an empty emergency float. One of them must have sent up the balloon when they were under attack."

"A what?" Cha'ril asked.

"Beacon with limited text capability," Roland said. "Knows its location when released, helium balloon will take it over any terrain—to include this crap of a hurricane—and broadcast a message to any satellite or ground station in line of sight. That must be how Lowenn knew they were in danger, and that they had a gamma-level

346

artifact."

"I'm beginning to doubt the Vishrakath killed them," Cha'ril said. "No bullet wounds. They had the time to type out a distress signal with key information while under attack? Something isn't right."

"*Poison*," Gideon said. "*Some residue on their faces and hands. My bio sensors are on fire.*"

"*Not Vishrakath*," Aignar said. "*But how we found the bodies…is. Came across a few mass graves on Cygnus. All like this. Piles on top of their gear, the stones.*"

A rattle of snapping bones sounded in a copse of swaying trees and tall ferns. Roland switched to his thermals, and a bright patch of warmth shone out from behind the foliage.

"Cha'ril, check your—" The bright patch burst out of the bushes. His optics washed out as something splattered against his helm. He switched to the secondary cameras on his chest and caught sight of a blue and gray striped animal the size of a car just before it slammed into him. The impact staggered him back a step.

The creature's wide, needle-tooth mouth clamped down on his left forearm and shook it from side to side hard enough to force a groan from the servos. Roland hauled his arm into the air, and hooked claws the size of scimitars ripped at his chest and legs. Roland struck the creature at the base of its neck, snapping the spine with a crack. It went limp, jaws still embedded in his armor.

Two pairs of black eyes on limp stalks lolled to the back of its flat head. The jaws slackened and it fell to the ground in a heap. Green slime sloughed off his arm. He lifted a hand to his marred optics, and a finger snapped open. Nitrogen mist sprayed out and froze the muck solid in an instant. He slapped the side of his head and the ice fell away.

"Nice of you to help," Roland said.

Two more of the beasts lay at Cha'ril's feet, her blade unsheathed from the housing and dripping black blood. She pried open the jaws of one with the flat of her blade, then pressed a digit to the side of its mouth. Green fluid spurted from a gland.

"Rather toxic," she said. "Think we've found our killers."

"Seemed intent on eating me…but the whole team is back there," Roland said.

"Either of you see a stasis chest over there?" Gideon asked.

"No, sir," Roland said.

The lance leader walked over and nudged one of the

dead creatures with his foot.

"Good that you didn't use your gauss weapons—might have alerted the Vish that we're here," he said.

"Yes, sir. That was our plan," Roland said as he brushed dried venom off his arm.

"Found this." Roland held up a small device between his fingertips. "Tracker unit for a stasis chest. Things cost almost as much as a starship, can't have them getting lost."

"The Vish were here," Aignar said. "They must have taken the chest."

"What's the range on the tracker?"

"Higher we go, better chance we'll have." Gideon's forearm snapped open and he dropped the tracker into a small chamber. "We need a mountaintop."

CHAPTER 20

The four climbed a steep slope, trudging through driving rain and gusts of wind that would have knocked an unarmed human flying, until Gideon stopped at a flat summit. Roland stayed ready to keep going; this wouldn't have been the first false stop up this cloud-covered mountain.

The lieutenant held up the arm with the tracker inside, and waited.

Roland opened a private IR channel to Aignar.

"What do we do when we find the Vishrakath?" Roland asked. "If the wildlife killed the pathfinders, then we're not exactly at war with the Vish, are we?"

"We kill them," Aignar said. "All of them. Vish consider anything but their leadership caste expendable— they extend that same courtesy to us."

"And if we come across one of their leaders?"

Aignar shifted his perch against a cliff face. His arm blade snapped out, then retracted just as quickly.

"Low-frequency radio pulse in three…" Gideon opened a data connection with the other armor and the tracker in his arm pinged. A split second later, the stasis case responded and an icon in a wide, dashed circle appeared on Roland's UI. The case sent another pulse and the circle shrank. He waited for the next pulse, but received only silence.

"The Vish broke the case?" Cha'ril asked.

"Or they're jamming it," Gideon said. "Either way, we know where it is…they're close to the eye."

"Here…" Roland zoomed in on his map and found the remains of a road through a swamp leading toward an eye. "They have to cross through this area to get to the eye. Ambush."

"Not a lot of cover to hide behind in a swamp," Aignar said.

"Shame on you, human," Cha'ril said. "Did you learn nothing on Mars?"

****

Gray light wavered through the open viewport on Roland's breastplate. What little sunlight made it through the raging hurricane diffused to a hazy memory of daylight by the time it passed through the two yards of swamp water over Roland. His armor was powered down completely; not even his womb's life-support systems were active. He could survive for days on his hyper-oxygenated amniosis.

They'd been in place along the road for hours. The interlocking hexagons had eroded over the years, leaving gaps between the bricks. The shoulders had fallen into the swamp, forming a lumpy bed beneath the water for Roland to lie on.

I wonder who the Baradans were, he thought. *Did they know future races would fight over the scraps of their empire as they were dying out? Did they extinguish themselves in the face of a Xaros invasion, maybe hoping something would outlast the drones, give them some kind of immortality? But hoping someone remembers you doesn't strike me as the best plan.*

He shook his head, swishing the amniosis across his face and churning the liquid through his womb.

Too much thinking for a combat mission.

As an electric blue eel with long, fin-tipped arms crawled across his view port, a wide eye with a horizontal iris looked into his armor.

Who's the more alien here?

When a sharp thump passed through his armor from the ground beneath his back, Roland brought his armor online. He felt two more thumps and burst out of the water, mud and weeds running down his armor.

A pair of Vishrakath hover tanks and a dozen soldiers were on the road. The lead tank's turret wavered between Roland on one bank of the collapsing road and Gideon on the other. Cha'ril and Aignar were on Gideon's side, flanking the Vishrakath and forming a textbook L-shaped ambush.

The armor aimed their cannons at the road just short of the surprised Vishrakath. Roland felt the shock of their sudden appearance melt away as the aliens pulled close to their tanks, weapons ready but not trained on the armor.

We could have crushed them in an instant, Roland thought. *But this is what Gideon wants.*

A hatch flipped open on the lead tank, and a Vishrakath with a golden-embossed bandolier rose up, letting off a brief flurry of clicks from its mandibles.

"Move," his suit translated.

"You have something of ours," Gideon said, sidestepping directly into the path of the Vishrakath leader's tank. "Give it to us and you're free to go."

"We have salvage, recovered from this extinct culture and ours by the Hale Treaty," the tank commander said. "Do you want the subsection read to you?"

"Paragraph nine, clause 'c' of the recovery and exploitation section gives full possession of any items to the living culture that possesses it," Gideon said. A blue line rippled down the Vishrakath's pale flesh.

"It was not in human possession when we found it. Your people were dead. Not our doing. We drove off the animals, paid respect to their remains."

"That is the only reason you and the rest of your kind aren't dead right now," Gideon said, the rotary weapon on his shoulder spinning back and forth.

Roland and the other armor cycled bolts into their gauss cannons.

"Give us the artifact," Gideon said. "This is my last courtesy to you."

The water around Roland's knees rippled. He activated a camera on his back and saw a pair of Vishrakath walkers coming through the rain, their limbs pulled tight to their bases, floating on an anti-grav field. Their legs stabbed into the road and the water lapping over the edges. Massive cannon arms unfolded and came to bear on Roland

354

and Gideon.

Roland turned toward the new threat. As armor, he never thought he'd be outgunned by anything short of a starship, and the two Vishrakath walkers did not seem as intimidated as the alien foot soldiers.

Gideon stayed rooted in place.

"I'm done conversing with you abominations," the tank commander said. "You will move or...wait...that mark...You were on Cygnus."

One of the walkers moved forward, and power cables running up from the base of the cannon arms to the walker's midsection came alive with a hum.

"We lost that world because of you," the tank commander said.

"Roland," Gideon sent over a tight IR beam, "on my mark you—"

The lead tank fired a bolt of plasma that caught Roland in the side and tore through his armor, kicking him forward and onto his knees. As he tried to get up, his armor felt sluggish, the sound of plasma blasts and gauss cannons erupting around him.

His ribs burned in pain, suffering along with his armor.

Unfurling the shield on his left arm, he got one foot

up in front of him. The nearest walker leveled a massive cannon at him.

Roland felt the impact on his shield like the slap of a god's hand against his chest, and the sharp tingle of pain across his limbs as the impact ripped him across the decaying road and into the water.

He drifted, his armor and body refusing to heed his mind's commands. A single point of light opened in the distance and cold fear replaced the pain in his body.

Is this...am I...

The light grew brighter. He tried to pull away, but there was no escape.

"Roland," a woman said. "You have to get up."

Out of the blinding light, a figure in a wheelchair morphed into being, her face hidden behind a veil of gossamer stars. She looked into his eyes and her head tilted to the side.

"Fight."

The world snapped back. Roland's UI flashed damage reports, but it was still functioning. He lay half in, half out of the water. Both walkers were between him and his lance battling between the two hover tanks.

Rolling onto his hands and knees, Roland tilted to one side and saw that his left arm ended in a mangle of twisted metal just below the elbow. He steadied himself against the ground and sent out a radar pulse.

Lurching to his feet, he raised his anchor foot up and slammed it into the middle of the road. He went to one knee and brought his rail gun off his back and over his shoulder. Slapping a round into the breach, he angled his gun toward the nearest walker.

"I am armor." Roland unleashed the rail gun and the thunderclap of the round accelerating off the vanes echoed across the valley. The hypervelocity bullet split the top of the walker like an ax.

Roland pulled his anchor and charged the remaining walker, aiming his gauss cannons at the missile pods on the back of the Vishrakath machine and pounding the armored compartment until a single bullet pierced through. The explosive cores of the micro-missiles erupted with a ripple, shaking the walker back and forth like the needle of a seismograph during an earthquake.

The walker charged power to a cannon aimed at a burning tank where Cha'ril and Aignar had taken cover.

Roland sprinted forward and unsheathed the blade in his right arm. He chopped down and severed the walker's rear leg, tilting it backwards and angling the cannon blast into the hurricane above.

The walker recovered and swung a cannon at him like a club. Roland ducked forward, then leaped up. His remaining hand crushed the edge of an armor plate. He kicked off the side of the walker and rammed his anchor into its side.

Roland reared back and rammed his blade into the walker. The alien machine jerked and slapped a cannon at him. Roland knocked the blow aside and plunged his sword home again, twisting it to the side and roaring as he ripped it up and into the crew compartment. His blade slid free, covered in alien blood.

The walker trembled, then settled to the ground, cannons digging into the loose bricks.

Roland pulled his anchor free and dropped down, stumbling against the walker's leg but raising his gauss cannons.

"Everyone...OK?" he called out. Dead Vishrakath littered the ground. Both tanks were smashed, the rear tank's turret blown away and lying on its side in the swamp.

"Over here," Gideon said.

Roland found the three standing around the Vishrakath commander, its legs broken and body torn open, bleeding into an expanding pool.

"I showed...your kind mercy," it said.

"And that is why I will end your suffering," Gideon said, and crushed the alien's head with his foot.

"Find the case," he said to the other armor. "Roland..." —he looked over the damaged armor— "status."

"My womb is banged up, but the seals are good." He touched the hole through the right side of his armor, then a massive dent on his helm. "I can still" —he turned around, as if he'd find the apparition behind him— "fight."

"Got it." Cha'ril held up a cube from a compartment on the back of a wrecked tank.

"Bring it here," Gideon said. He pointed to Aignar, then to Roland.

Aignar grabbed him by the shoulders and ran a scan laser down Roland's battered breastplate.

"You took one hell of a hit," he said. "Thought we'd lost you."

"Aignar...I saw her. I saw the Saint."

Aignar froze for a moment, then put a hand to the back of Roland's helm.

"I believe you...but keep this between us for now. OK?"

Roland's helm bobbed up and down.

"Aignar?" Gideon asked as he mag-locked the stasis case onto Cha'ril's back.

"His womb isn't compromised. Synch rating is low, but the damage report he gave is sound," Aignar answered.

"Can you transform?" Gideon asked Roland.

Roland shifted his treads out of the leg housings and settled back on his hips. His left leg caught on the way down, servos whining against each other. Aignar bashed a fist against Roland's leg and it fell into place.

"Well done, Dragoons," Gideon said, "but we're not done yet."

****

As they approached the eye, the wind and rain slackened. Sunlight glared down the sharply defined cloud walls, and stratified bands flowed around the eye.

The armor slowed down and shifted out of their travel configuration. In the distance, buildings covered in vines stood within the sunlight.

"Is it me, or does this seem unnatural?" Aignar asked.

"Everyone always complains about the weather," Roland said. "Looks like the Baradans decided to do something about it."

"If there's a force field," Cha'ril said, "can we get through?"

"Those Vishrakath tanks had to have come from here," Gideon said, taking a tube off his back and touching one end to a port on his arm. He dropped it into his grenade launcher and it spat into the air with a *thunk*. A balloon popped out of the tube and it shot up and disappeared within the clouds.

"Extraction will be here soon," the lieutenant said. He cycled rounds into his gauss cannon and ran forward.

Roland kept up, his gait awkward with half an arm missing and a slight limp in his left leg. He flexed his left hand within the womb and got a stinging rebuke from his armor.

"Stop, or you'll redline," Gideon said. "If you upset the resonance between your suit and your plugs, it could form a feedback loop that'll fry your brain."

"Sorry, sir," Roland said.

"Watch your sector," Gideon said.

They crossed the city's threshold, a deep dam directing water from the hurricane around the city and to the ocean on the other end of the eye. A stone bridge with a pair of tall statues on the near end extended over the gap. Moss covered the statues, both bulky humanoid shapes with wide heads and spindly arms. They almost looked like frogs to Roland.

Gideon radar-pulsed the bridge, then raised a hand.

"It'll hold, but one at a time," he said and ran across.

Roland went next and took cover next to a vine-choked building, columns of stacked amphibian-looking heads on each corner. He glanced around the roof to the crystal-clear azure skies above, the calm in sharp contrast to the passing storm. Dark pinpricks appeared above the calm, growing larger as they descended.

"Here come the birds," Roland said.

"You're right," Gideon said, "but they're not ours."

A zoomed-in video feed came up on Roland's UI. Domed ships on clusters of thrusters crossed beneath the upper edge of the hurricane. Pairs of Vishrakath fighters trailed the larger landing ships.

"Are they here because they heard us call for an exit," Aignar asked, "or to pick up the other team?"

"Doesn't matter." Gideon raised his cannon arm. "Three of us will engage with rail cannons. Roland on overwatch. Let's find their landing zone. It'll be the easiest place to shoot them down…and probably where our flyboys will want to land."

They ran through the city, the buildings rising in height as they neared the center. The vines stopped growing after the third story. Every building corner had the same set of statues, all flat-headed and double-eyed, frog-like humanoids holding spheres in their over-long fingers.

The road opened into a small square surrounded by squat buildings. What might have been a grassy patch was now overrun with reeds and loops of tiny bell-shaped flowers.

"Got line of sight on the aircraft," Cha'ril said.

"Drop anchor, single salvo," Gideon said.

As Roland tore through the undergrowth that seemed to clutch at him, his acoustics isolated a sound behind the vine-choked buildings. He ducked down and looked through a window ringed with broken glass. Through an open back door, a dozen Vishrakath soldiers pushed their way in. More—many more—were behind them.

Roland dropped down and spun his rotary cannon to life.

There was a single, high-pitched sound from the lead alien before Roland's weapon tore him, and the three soldiers behind him, into bloody chunks. Roland fired his gauss cannon into the building, the heavy shells penetrating the back walls, turning the ancient structure into shrapnel that pulverized the Vishrakath infantry massing behind the building.

Roland activated his grenade launcher, lobbing shells high over the road leading to the square and the opposite side of the buildings.

The front of the structure collapsed, kicking up a cloud of dust. Scattered Vishrakath soldiers filled the road, all of them now with a clear shot at the armor.

Roland's mortar rounds burst in the air over the aliens' heads, showering them with a spray of shrapnel. In the confusion of the bombardment and snap shots from his rotary and gauss cannons, the Vishrakath infantry broke and ran.

A massive thunderclap broke behind him, the blast of three rail guns firing at once pushing him forward and into the fallen building.

Overhead, two of the alien landers were expanding fireballs. The third wobbled in the sky and flew into the hurricane where wind yanked it aside and into the gray morass. Flashes of explosions followed moments later.

"Who missed?" Roland asked.

"I want crap from you, I'll squeeze your head," Aignar said.

"Fast movers coming in," Gideon said, pointing to an avenue between the tallest buildings.

Roland stomped through the destroyed building and caught a movement next to where the walls still stood. A Vishrakath soldier lay on its back, chest heaving, two of its four legs bent at painful angles, one arm reaching for a plasma rifle leaned against the wall next to it. Roland snapped his rotary cannon toward the Vishrakath.

"Your choice," Roland said.

The alien knocked the weapon away.

Roland ran down the narrow street, keeping his rotary cannon aimed at the wounded soldier until it was out of sight.

A shadow fell over the armor as they ran down the street, the shimmer of a lake at the far end. The whine of jet engines echoed down the Baradan-made canyon.

"Six o'clock," Cha'ril said.

"Phalanx," Gideon said and they spread out into a line. Four Vishrakath fighters dove between the buildings and charged straight for the armor. A line of energy bolts cut through the air and stitched down the road, blasting up hexagon tiles. Roland and the rest threw up a storm of bullets into the fighter's flight path and two of the fighters exploded instantly. The third turned aside and crashed into a skyscraper, bouncing from building to building before shattering against the road.

The fourth pulled up and banked out of sight.

"Other side," Aignar said.

Amber icons flashed on Roland's UI.

"Low on ammo," he said.

"Same," Cha'ril added.

As a stack of enemy fighters formed over the lake and sped toward them, the uppermost burst apart. The next two flipped over and spiraled down, trailing smoke. The survivor pulled up out of the narrow attack path and exploded just as it cleared the buildings.

A pair of Eagle fighters slashed through the air high overhead.

"Thought we were the cavalry," Gideon said. "Hurry."

"*Iron Dragoons, this is Skull Leader off the* Matterhorn. *We see your handiwork but not you. How copy?*" came over the radio.

"Skull Leader, this is Dragoon actual. Package secured. Need to evac it before more Vish show up," Gideon said.

"*Can do better than that. Destrier spiraling down now. Think Admiral Stolzoff and the rest of 3rd Fleet convinced the Vish to play nice*," the pilot said.

The armor came out and onto the edge of an opal-blue lake. A Terran transport ship, flanked by Eagle fighters, angled toward them.

Roland looked at the case locked onto Cha'ril's back, unsure exactly what was in there and if it was worth all the death and destruction. He spun his rotary cannon down and felt an enormous weight come over his shoulders. He stumbled to the side, and Aignar caught him before he went into the lake.

"You all right?"

"Roland, your synch rating's bottoming out." Gideon rapped knuckles against his breastplate. "Who are you?"

"Shaw, Roland—"

Gideon punched Roland's chest hard enough to send a ripple through his amniosis.

"Who. Are. You?"

Roland pulled himself up and pushed Aignar away.

"Armor. I am armor."

"I am fury," Aignar said.

"We did not fail." Cha'ril touched Roland's shoulder and gave him a gentle shake as the transport closed in on them.

CHAPTER 21

Roland tugged at the collar of his dress uniform. Wearing actual clothes after so long in the womb felt more and more unusual as time went on. He double-checked his scant ribbons and looked at Aignar's chest full of color and at Cha'ril, whose dress uniform was a bright white tunic, long skirt and sandals with a sash over her chest.

The three stood before a metal double door built into the cold Martian rock beneath Olympus.

"Roland, you first," Aignar said.

"Why don't you—"

"Because you're the hero of the day, kid." Aignar punched him in the shoulder. "Next time, don't come back from the dead and save my ass."

"That's not what happened. Saving your ass, yes, not the other part."

"Thank you for my ass." Cha'ril punched him on

the other shoulder. "Idioms! What fun."

"I wonder if the Terran exchange armor on Dotari have to put up with this," Roland muttered.

One of the doors opened slightly, and the three snapped to attention. It swung open and Lieutenant Silva, in his dress uniform, motioned Roland forward, leaving the other two outside.

Behind the door, a wide red carpet led to a raised platform. Pairs of armor faced each other over the carpet, shoulder to shoulder, all the way to the end. Roland walked beside Silva, and the armor beat a fist to their chests as they passed, tolling like a bell.

Colonel Martel and Gideon stood on the platform, and an adjutant held a silver plate next to him. Armor soldiers formed ranks behind the platform.

Silva held a hand against Roland's chest. Tongea stepped from behind a suit of armor and blocked Roland's path.

"This one is unworthy," the Maori said. "I do not know his deeds."

"I am Candidate—"

Tongea backhanded him across the face. Roland tasted blood and felt his anger rise. Tongea brushed a thumb tip across his tall stack of ribbons.

"I fought the Vishrakath on Barada. Killed their walkers and their soldiers. My lance commander witnessed my deeds." Roland glanced at Gideon.

"No man can do this," Tongea said. "Who are you?"

"Can—" Roland stopped himself as Tongea raised his hand to strike again.

"If you do not know who you are, then tell us why you fight," Tongea said.

"To belong," Roland said, lowering his head. "To stand beside heroes and be found worthy."

Tongea stepped aside.

Roland walked to Colonel Martel. He picked up a sword from the table and planted the point between his feet.

"A petitioner," Martel said to Gideon. "Will you have him?"

"Who is he?" Gideon asked.

"I am…armor," Roland said.

"I've seen this one's iron. I will have him in my lance," Gideon said.

"Kneel," Martel ordered.

Roland went down on one knee.

"Armor, you have been found worthy in deed, honor and dedication to the Corps. Will you swear to uphold the highest traditions of our Corps, the laws of our worlds and give your life for the innocent?"

"I do," Roland said. He felt a caress down the back of his neck and over his plugs, and the face he had seen on Barada came to his mind.

Martel lifted the sword and touched it to Roland's shoulders, then he pulled the sword away and punched Roland in the face. Roland swayed to the side, his ears ringing.

"That is so you do not forget your vow," Martel said. "Rise...an Iron Dragoon."

He stood, and the armor soldiers broke into applause. Martel pressed a metal pin into his left hand. The Armor Corps insignia glinted up at Roland.

"Well done, son. Well done," Martel said.

Tongea took him by the elbow and led him away from the stage. The Maori gave Roland a quick pat on the cheek.

"Sir," Roland said quietly, "a moment."

"I have to challenge the others," Tongea said.

"I need to speak to you...about her, about Saint Kallen," Roland said. He looked away, almost ashamed at the swell of emotions in his chest.

"I'll take you to her," Tongea said. "Later."

Roland nodded, his eyes lingering over the Templar cross on the older man's chest, then falling to the Armor Corps badge in his hand. He squeezed his hand around the piece of metal and felt the edges bite into his flesh.

CHAPTER 22

Minder, as she preferred to be called, walked around the open stasis cube with her hands clasped behind her back. She kept her normal shape, that of a straight-backed but elderly woman, while fractal patterns played across her shell.

A golden lattice made of solid light sat in the cube, tiny white motes moving along the lines randomly.

As the last-known Xaros drone moved her hand over the lattice, her fingers grew longer, playing in the hue over the artifact. After days of examination, she had come to two inescapable conclusions, both of which filled her with dread.

She flicked a hand toward a sensor on the ceiling of her laboratory deep in the Crucible, and two holograms filled the room.

President Garret sat at his desk, staring at a slate. He

did a double take once he saw Minder. The other hologram was scrambled, the outline breaking up again and again.

"Well?" Garret stood up and tossed his slate aside. "Did we find the fountain of youth or some old collection of alien poetry?"

"It's a Qa'Resh codex," Minder said. "No doubt about that. I doubt the Baradans managed to translate any of it, certainly don't see any sign of that in their ruins."

"You're stalling." Words from the scrambled hologram came through with an altered pitch, artificial.

"Accessing Qa'Resh technology is difficult…but this is a log from a Qa'Resh starship. The final entry is of a crash, rescue efforts. We know how resilient their technology is. I believe it's still out there. It'll take time to find it."

"A Qa'Resh ship…," the broken hologram said. "They were on par with the Xaros before they vanished from the galaxy. Finding that ship would change the galaxy forever."

"If it's a race, we're behind. Way behind." Minder shook her head. "Someone accessed this before me. I see her fingerprints in the quantum lattice. It can only be her. She must have left it behind to taunt us."

Garret cursed and knocked a data slate off his desk.

"Not what we need right now," he said. "The Vishrakath and their allies are two seconds away from declaring war on us. Are you sure? Absolutely sure?"

"Yes," Minder said. "The Ibarras found this device before we did. If they find that ship before we do..."

"We don't owe them anymore," the broken hologram said. "It is time to destroy them before they turn the rest of the galaxy against us."

"Agreed." Garret sank back into his chair. "Minder?"

"Do it," she said.

THE END

Roland's story continues in **The Ibarra Sanction**, coming Summer 2017!

FROM THE AUTHOR

Richard Fox is the author of The Ember War Saga, and several other military history, thriller and space opera novels.

He lives in fabulous Las Vegas with his incredible wife and two boys, amazing children bent on anarchy.

He graduated from the United States Military Academy (West Point) much to his surprise and spent ten years on active duty in the United States Army. He deployed on two combat tours to Iraq and received the Combat Action Badge, Bronze Star and Presidential Unit Citation.

Sign up for his mailing list over at www.richardfoxauthor.com to stay up to date on new releases and get exclusive Ember War short stories. You can contact him at Richard@richardfoxauthor.com

The Ember War Saga:

1.)   The Ember War
2.)   The Ruins of Anthalas
3.)   Blood of Heroes
4.)   Earth Defiant
5.)   The Gardens of Nibiru
6.)   Battle of the Void
7.)   The Siege of Earth
8.)   The Crucible
9.)   The Xaros Reckoning

50426482R00211

Made in the USA
San Bernardino, CA
22 June 2017